WINDS OF CHANGE

OTHER BOOKS AND AUDIO BOOKS
BY JEAN HOLBROOK MATHEWS

Desert Rain

Run for Your Life

Safe Haven

Precious Cargo

The Assignment

Escape to Zion

The Light Above

a novel

WINDS OF CHANGE

Jean Holbrook Mathews

Covenant Communications, Inc.

Published by Covenant Communications, Inc.
American Fork, Utah

Printed in the United States of America
First Printing: May 2017

23 22 21 20 19 18 17   10 9 8 7 6 5 4 3 2 1

ISBN 978-152440-057-6

PREFACE

THIS BOOK IS FILLED WITH history, but it isn't a history book. It was written to share the story of Matthew McCune; his wife, Sarah; and their children—the four sons who lived to adulthood and the three sons and one tiny daughter who died in India. Matthew's journal and that of his oldest son, Henry, who was called Harry after the British tradition, form the framework for this story.

After the departure of the McCune family from India, Matthew's journals ended. He was a faithful journal keeper, so we can be sure later journals existed but have been lost, so of necessity, events following the family's departure for America are reconstructed from Harry's brief written record made near the end of his life and the journals kept by other members of the Hofheins/McCune wagon company. I have also attempted to reconstruct what the letters between Matthew, Sarah, and Harry might have said, drawing on Matthew's India and Burma journals. Spelling of places is the same as in Matthew's journals.

Where there are gaps in the records, I have attempted to reconstruct events as they *may* have happened from other historical accounts. I have taken the liberty of placing Harry in the Utah Militia, often referred to as the Nauvoo Legion by the Saints, under Captain Lot Smith during the "Utah War" since he mentioned so very little of his experiences during that time in his end-of-life remembrances.

This book is not only meant to entertain and inform but also to offer respectful insight into the lives of the McCune family and other pioneers. Matthew was of Scottish descent but born on the Isle of Man, and in every way, he was British, at times, rigidly so—the kind of man who would refuse to use contractions in his speech. He worked as a weaver while a boy in Paisley, Scotland, but upon reaching adulthood, he relocated to London, where he married, enlisted, and was posted to India. Matthew lived in five countries on three continents in a day and age when few individuals traveled more than fifty miles from home. The courage of pioneers like him and his family is reflected in their willingness to leave comfort behind and face the unknown for their testimonies of the truth of the restored gospel.

This story is part of the heritage of every one of Matthew's descendents, as well as those of us who are descended from other pioneers of courage, no matter the century in which they were born.

Jean Holbrook Mathews

FOREWORD

FROM THE SIXTEENTH THROUGH THE nineteenth centuries, "the sun never set on the British Empire." Tens of thousands of British citizens lived in British colonies around the world as part of an empire that covered nearly a quarter of the globe, spreading the English language, culture, manners, and legal system. It was a time when every British citizen was sure that God was an Englishman.

British influence gradually waned, but the lessening of that influence often came at the cost of much bloodshed. In the mid-nineteenth century, a revolt referred to as the "Wind of Madness" blew across India. Though that revolt did not terminate British power, it laid the groundwork for India's national independence several decades later.

To fully understand the history of India, one must understand the influence and power of the British East India Company, which was established by Royal Charter in 1600 in response to the petition of a consortium of wealthy merchants and aristocrats seeking the privilege of trading on the Indian subcontinent with the support of the British government. At that time, India was fast becoming the crossroads of Asian trade in cotton, silk, indigo dye, salt, saltpeter, tea, and opium.

The British government had minimal control over the East India Company during its existence, its influence resting solely in the commander in chief appointed by Parliament. With limited communications and the great distances involved, the very earliest that news regarding India could reach London was three months, usually much longer.

The numerous ruling potentates of India and its many diverse languages, tribes, and cultures kept the country too fractionalized to withstand the gradually increasing power of the East India Company, which in time came to rule large areas of the subcontinent with its own private armies and administrators.

The three armies of the East India Company (Bengal, Bombay, and Madras) were originally formed to defend against raids on its factories, warehouses, and shipping facilities, which raids were often initiated by competing European companies, especially Portuguese and French. The three large armies were comprised mainly of sepoys (native Indian troops) led by predominantly British officers.

The East India Company offered employment and security and drew vast numbers of British, European, and even American citizens to enlist, even when it meant they and their families would serve in countries far distant from home.

When war between the English and the Burmese broke out in 1852, the military men of the Bengal and Madras armies of the East India Company were transferred to Rangoon, including Matthew McCune.

In early 1857, while British military forces were spread between India and Burma, a handful of sepoys rose in revolt, the first warning sign of the coming mutiny in the Bengal army. They were motivated by an escalating resentment based upon several factors: the aggressive proselytizing by Methodist, Baptist, and Catholic missionaries attempting to convert them to Christianity, which was perceived as an attempt to destroy their ancient religious caste system; frustration at the lack of opportunity for natives to rise in rank in the company armies; the differential in pay between the British regiments and the indigenous sepoy troops, as well as poor food, unpopular postings, and increasing "modernization," which was viewed as a threat to custom and culture. Trains, telegraphs, and printed books were all looked upon with great suspicion.

The simmering pot of resentment boiled over in May of 1857 in the Meerut Cantonment when thirty-one Europeans, including women and children, were murdered. The rebelling sepoys then rode to Delhi, where they killed the British officers of the Fifty-Fourth Bengal Native Infantry. The sepoys of that regiment then joined the mutinous troops, and like monsoon floodwaters, the mutiny spread across the central part of the subcontinent.

The apparent catalyst of the revolt was the introduction, in January, of a mandatory method for loading cartridges into the new Enfield rifles manufactured in England to the sepoy regiments. The cartridges were individually wrapped with a twist of greased paper at the top, which each man was to bite off and spit out before ramming the charge, the cartridge, and the rest of the greased paper down into the muzzle of the rifle. The greased paper was intended to oil the bore of the gun. A rumor began to circulate and quickly gained credence that the grease was made from the fat of cattle and pigs—forbidden substances for both the Hindu and Muslim sepoys, who considered this another affront to their religions.

The pattern was set, and thereafter individuals carrying a grudge against the British joined the rebellious troops. Upon entering a city, the rebels would release the prisoners from the local jail, plunder the treasury, destroy the legislative court and all its records, and gut the houses of the Christians, killing the inhabitants of both sexes and of all ages.

The British reacted violently to this uprising. Native villages were burned, terrified civilians killed, and men were hung whether rich or poor, civilian or sepoy, innocent or guilty. By June of 1858, the British had suppressed the revolt. Sporadic outbreaks thereafter were quickly stamped out.

On November 1, 1858, Queen Victoria officially announced that the Crown had assumed authority for the country and that the East India Company was officially dissolved.

This book relates a small portion of the experiences of the families of Matthew McCune and Patrick Meik, both officers in the Bengal army during the prelude to the revolt. Though much of the story is based on the experiences of the McCune family as recounted in the personal journals of Matthew McCune and his son Henry, much of it has been reconstructed based upon other historical records and family accounts. Any inaccuracies and errors are the sole responsibility of the author.

CHAPTER ONE

July 1852
Calcutta

SARAH MCCUNE WAITED IN THE darkness on the flagstone veranda of the large bungalow, oblivious to the very rare sight of the stars of the Milky Way spread across the night sky like a filmy, spangled belt. The gold quarter moon lay on its back like an empty bowl. The heavy rains of the monsoon season had paused for a few hours, briefly leaving behind a sweeping vista of the night sky.

A gentle but firm nature had shaped Sarah's cheerful and warm smile, but this night her dark eyes reflected an unusual anxiety. She often sought solitude in the well-planned and manicured flower garden that surround her on three sides, but at that moment, she was not even aware of the fragrance of the jasmine that hung in the night air or of the neatly trimmed orange and lemon trees that rose like dark sentinels in each corner of the walled yard where ferns seemed to explode like silent fireworks.

Where is Matthew? He has never been late like this without getting word to me. Sarah knew her husband to be a man whose world was structured by schedules and the unflinching acceptance of duty.

The sound of slippers on the flagstones made her start, and she turned to see Sonja, her personal servant, moving toward her. Sonja dropped her head respectfully and put her hands together. "Memsahib, Endira has asked that I tell you that she has given the little lads their baths and they are hoping you will hear their prayers before they are tucked into bed."

"Yes, yes, of course. I'll go up immediately." She rose and started across the flagstones to the external spiral staircase. The black wrought-iron railing was cold and wet. At the top she paused and turned with her hand on the balustrade, looking over the wall more than a hundred feet away where the muddy road ran beside it. Customarily built for privacy and safety, the ten-foot wall surrounding Fort William was topped with broken glass and sharp rocks and divided the world of the British from the noisy, native world of Calcutta.

She watched for another minute, hoping for a glimpse of the familiar tanga that would bring Matthew home. Not seeing the small carriage, she turned resignedly and entered the drawing room, where a table was set for the two of them. As she passed through the room, the chimes of the grandfather clock told her it was nine.

After she had listened to the three youngest boys' prayers, they climbed into bed and she kissed each one on the forehead. She watched while Endira arranged the mosquito netting that hung from the ceiling around each bed before she returned to waiting, this time on the balcony.

***

Sarah and Matthew's twelve-year-old son, who had been christened Henry but was called Harry, stood at his bedroom window, feeling the damp night air as it circulated through the carved wooden privacy shutters. He shared his mother's concern for his father's unusually late arrival and watched as Sonja slipped down the circular staircase.

He threw on his sleeveless vest to mitigate the cool dampness of the night air. His personal servant, Gupta, patiently squatted near the bedroom door, waiting for his young master to signal that he wished to prepare for bed.

He stood and asked quietly, "Young sahib, may I be of service?"

"No, Gupta, I need to speak with Mother."

"Does she watch for Sahib McCune? He is late this night."

"Yes. I don't remember him ever being late without sending word to us." The boy turned away from the window. "Do you think the war with Burma has delayed him?"

"Yes, young sahib, a war with Burma will require many supplies and many ships to carry the men, weapons, and animals needed to fight the battles."

Gupta was fourteen years older than his charge, and his manner reflected the nearly parental view that came with being the boy's personal servant for many years.

Harry moved out onto the balcony just as his mother returned to her vigil. He stepped up next to her at the railing.

"Mother, are you worried about Father?" She turned to look at him before she put her arm around his shoulders and affectionately pulled him to her. They stood side by side and quietly looked out into the night.

"Yes, Harry, I must admit I'm worried."

"What's going to happen to our family now that Britain and the king of Burma are at war?"

"I don't know. I just don't know . . ." Her voice caught.

She continued to hold him against her, the two shadowy figures side by side. In another year, he would be taller than her by an inch or two.

He made no attempt to pull away. In the past, her public yet quiet displays of affection had often embarrassed him, but as he stood there in the darkness, his thoughts strayed to the night two years earlier when his mother had been distracted enough throughout the entire day that even as a ten-year-old he had noticed.

That night he had climbed out of bed and stood in the darkened hall behind the open sitting-room door and listened to his parents as they talked. He'd heard his normally composed mother stifle a sob.

"Matthew, it was eight years ago today that we buried Alfred and William. I've been unable to put it out of my mind." She paused as if to give Harry's father the opportunity to respond. When he didn't, she continued, "I wanted to lie down next to them and die. I think I would have if Harry hadn't needed me. It was such a heavy burden of grief after losing Alexander and Grace that I wondered if God was going to take everything I loved."

Matthew cleared his throat. "It was a difficult time." His voice was subdued but firm. "But as you said, we still had Harry."

"I thank God we still had Harry."

Harry suddenly felt like he was intruding on a conversation he had no right to hear. He turned there in the shadows and, in bare feet—normally a forbidden thing in a country where scorpions and tarantulas abounded—moved quietly down the hallway and climbed back into bed. That night as he drifted off to sleep, he had a vision, a dream—or perhaps it was a memory—of his parents' worried and strained faces bending down over him as his mother stroked his hair. From that time forward, he began to better understand why his mother so often pulled him close.

The sound of the tanga's wheels splashing through the puddles on the muddy road brought him back to the present. He heard his mother whisper, "Father has finally arrived. He will expect you to be in bed. I want to speak privately with him." She kissed him on the cheek. "Off you go, my lad."

He moved to the exterior door of his bedroom and stepped inside as the sound of his father's firm tread reached the top of the staircase. Their voices carried easily on the night air.

"Matthew, I've been worried. What has kept you?"

"It has been a very long day, my dear." His voice was weary.

Harry's parents' steps faded as they moved farther from the staircase and toward the door of the drawing room on the other side of the house. "We had to get eight ships loaded and headed down the river to the bay before the ebb tide weakened." The last words Harry caught were ". . . early tomorrow" and ". . . another long day."

Sergeant Matthew McCune was a slim, midsized man, and darkly handsome with quick, exacting movements. He had a long, aristocratic nose with deep-set, piercing gray eyes and wore the neatly trimmed black beard and moustache worn by all British officers in the East India Company.

His responsibilities as the magazine sergeant in the artillery division of the Bengal army included the oversight of the large warehouses that supported the military community at Fort William. Heavy as his responsibilities were, he was normally home by five in the afternoon in time for a late tea, but it was now after nine.

Disappointed that he would have to wait until morning to ask his father the questions in his mind, he knew he might as well retire. Gupta assisted him out of his clothing, and after Harry lay down, the servant released the mosquito netting tied to the four posts of the bed and tucked it in under the mattress. Putting his palms together with the fingertips under his chin, Gupta bowed from the shoulders. "May you sleep well, young sahib."

"May you sleep well, Gupta." He paused for a moment before he added, "I'd like to be awakened an hour earlier in the morning. I want to speak to Father before he leaves."

"Yes, Sahib Harry."

The servant quietly lay down on the mat in the corner of the room, where sleep surrounded him much sooner than it did his young charge.

***

When Matthew and Sarah stepped into the dining room, he wearily pulled off the white cap and unbuttoned the red wool coat that made up the distinctive uniform of the Bengal army. Before his second arm was drawn from its sleeve, Deleep appeared and lifted the coat from his shoulders.

In a disapproving voice, Matthew stated, "Deleep, two buttons on this coat came off today." He took two round brass buttons from a pocket and dropped them in his servant's outstretched hand.

"Many apologies, sahib. I will see that they are sewn on before you must wear it again." He bent and picked up the pair of soft leather slippers with curled toes from their place near the grandfather clock. His master sat down and lifted one foot so Deleep could pull the muddy boots from his feet and replace them with the slippers.

As a house servant, Deleep wore a dhoti, a wide white strip of cotton wrapped like a long skirt around the waist. Above it he wore a muslin shirt and a white turban, the white signaling his being in mourning for his long-dead father. Taking the jacket and cap with him, the manservant disappeared from the room.

Sarah took Matthew's arm and walked with him to the head of the table, where he took his seat. Deleep's wife, Leela, appeared with a tray loaded with bread, curried chicken, and rice. She wore an indigo cotton sari wrapped around her hips over a petticoat of the same color with a tight half blouse that exposed her midriff. Her thick black hair was pulled into a neat bun at the nape of her neck, and in the middle of her forehead, she wore the traditional tilak, the red dot of good luck.

As Leela moved toward the doorway, Sarah smiled and spoke. "Leela, the meal looks excellent."

The servant nodded and whispered, "Namaste, memsahib."

Sarah turned to her husband as he loaded his plate and expressed a gentle but pointed disapproval. "Matthew, why didn't you send a messenger to tell us you would be late? When you sent no word of your expected delay, I became very worried."

"I couldn't spare a man to carry a message to you. There may be many evenings that will require long hours as we provision the ships that sail for Rangoon. You must not worry. The situation cannot be helped."

Their conversation went on into the night.

***

The following morning the entire house was awakened when Matthew's voice roared through it at six, an hour before the usual rising time for the children. "In this house there is a place for everything, and everything should be in its place so that one can find it in the dark! Why aren't the buttons sewn on my coat?"

Harry let Gupta help him as he quickly dressed, and then he hurried to the drawing room where the servants scurried about trying to pacify Matthew. Deleep was holding the red uniform coat while Endira was trying to thread a needle with shaking hands.

Sarah entered the room with her hair falling loose around her face and tying the belt of a robe around her waist. She would bring peace to the situation. Harry was relieved when his mother took charge.

"Dira, be seated—there on the settee," she gently urged the servant, then, turning to her husband, she said, "Matthew, it won't take but a moment to get the buttons sewn on the coat. I'm sure Endira meant to get to the task last evening but simply forgot about it because little Edward was fussy and feverish all night. With a little patience, the matter will be remedied shortly."

Harry could see that it was not a good time to speak to his father. When the buttons were securely on the coat, Deleep helped his master on with it.

"This will not happen again." The ire in Matthew's voice had moderated, but it was clear he was stating a fact, not making a request.

"No, sahib, it will not," a chagrined Deleep responded.

Matthew gave Sarah a perfunctory kiss on the forehead and immediately left the house with a rapid step.

Sonja had followed her mistress into the sitting room. "Memsahib, please return to your bedroom where I will help you dress."

But Sarah was not listening. She was looking at Endira. "It was such a small task, Endira. Why did you not get the buttons sewn on the uniform?"

The servant was near tears. "Memsahib, Edward did not sleep well, so I allowed him to play on a blanket at my feet, but when I sat down to sew the buttons on the coat, they fell to the floor and rolled near him. Before I could reach them, the lad had put them into his mouth." She looked thoroughly humiliated. "I did not get them quickly enough." After she swallowed her nervousness, she brightened and somewhat apologetically added, "I knew they would appear in his nappies . . . but they didn't come until early this morning. I only had time to wash and polish them before Sahib McCune wanted his coat. A thousand pardons, memsahib."

Sarah wanted very much to laugh. "I see. Well, don't let the sahib find out where they were before they were put back on the coat. He would not be happy." She pressed her lips together to hide her smile.

"Yes, memsahib. It will never happen again. Am I excused, memsahib?"

"Yes, Endira." The servant put her hands together and bowed as she slipped backward out of the room.

Sarah turned to Sonja. "I will dress and have you do my hair now."

"Yes, memsahib." Sonja followed her mistress, who was careful to hide the smile still attempting to betray her.

***

Harry spent the day in his normal activities, beginning with his studies with Mrs. Senior, the children's tutor. He requested that the hour spent on geography be concentrated upon Burma. He completed his geometry lessons by measuring the height of every tree in the garden by its shadow and ended with an hour of Shakespeare's *Julius Caesar*.

His father had ordered the works of Shakespeare, Milton, Spenser, and other English authors from England not long after the family had moved from the military cantonment at Dum Dum to Calcutta eight years before. He insisted that no education was complete without a thorough knowledge of Shakespeare and the other great English writers. Harry did not completely agree, but he applied himself accordingly.

When he sought out his mother, he asked the question that had kept him awake the previous night. "Mother, will the war with Burma require that Father leave us?"

"Your father said he would explain everything this evening at supper, Harry." That was all he could get from her, but throughout the day, he noted that she seemed preoccupied.

The seven o'clock evening meal was postponed in the hope that Matthew would soon arrive. But by eight, Sarah ordered that the three younger children be fed and put to bed over vocal objections from five-year-old George and three-year-old Alfred William, who wanted to see their father.

The wind brought the rain again. While it beat upon the house, his mother waited in the sitting room, struggling to focus on the needlepoint in her hands.

"Mother, may I eat dinner with you when Father gets home?"

"Yes, Harry. I believe you are old enough to hear what he will have to say."

It was after nine o'clock when the rain diminished and she heard the sound of the tanga's wheels and the horse's hooves. Jai halted the carriage, and Matthew stepped down onto the veranda before the horses were urged toward the carriage house.

Sarah hurried down the stairs to greet him. "Matthew, I'm so glad you are finally home."

His step was a bit slower than usual as they climbed the stairs. After Deleep had taken his uniform jacket, the three of them took their seats at the table in the drawing room.

Harry had many questions but remained quiet, waiting for his father to speak.

After the servants had laid out the food and left them alone, Matthew remained silent, seeming preoccupied.

Sarah finally asked, "Matthew, will you be this late every evening now that we are at war with Burma?"

He looked up from the rice he had spooned onto his plate. "Yes, I expect to be this late most evenings for the foreseeable future. I am sorry I missed saying good night to the younger lads, but it couldn't be helped."

"What is it you have to tell us, Matthew?" Sarah asked patiently.

Matthew leaned back with his elbows on the arms of the heavy carved-mahogany chair and put the tips of his fingers together. "The military action in Burma is going to affect all of us here in Calcutta. Those of us in the company's service had expected that the regular British troops would be handling military efforts there, but as of today, all in the Bengal army have been ordered to enter the action."

Sarah's fork paused midair.

"There's no easy way to tell you, my dear. I've been ordered into the field. I leave for Rangoon in a fortnight."

Harry heard his mother's quick intake of breath. "Matthew, in seventeen years of marriage and your service here in India, we've never been separated." Her voice was tight with nervousness.

"They need my expertise in training the troops in the use of the cannons and Congreve rockets." He looked apologetically at Harry's mother. "I know this will be hard for all of us, but I can't refuse, Sarah. It is my duty."

"But, Father, how long will you be gone?"

"There is no way of knowing, Harry. I will trust Providence to make that decision." When Sarah remained silent, he added, "There will be some compensation in my being ordered into the conflict. I fully expect that at some point I will be promoted to full subconductor of ordnance. Before I leave, I will arrange for the largest part of my pay to come to you and the children. With the help of Harry and the servants, especially Jai and Deleep, you and the children will get along, and if we're lucky, the Burmese will seek a quick end to the hostilities."

Sarah struggled to maintain her composure. After a few minutes of silence, she put down her fork and pushed her plate away.

Matthew finished his meal. Rising, he held out his hand. "Let's go down to the veranda, my dear. The rain has paused. We can talk there. Harry, you're excused."

Harry respectfully stood as his parents left the table. When they had exited the room, he sat down hard, as if his legs had given out. After a few minutes, he made his way quietly to the balcony outside his room, just above the veranda.

***

Harry watched his father wipe the dampness from the cushions with his handkerchief before he and Sarah sat. They were quiet for a minute or two before she asked, "Will we be able to join you at some point?"

"I don't know," Matthew said, then added firmly, "We will hope for it."

"Do you know if Patrick Meik will be going? Mary Anne is so frail. She is with child again. How could he be asked to leave her alone with that large family?"

"Yes, Patrick will be going as well. I hope you and Harry will watch out for her. Harry may be the only male member of the Church remaining here after the army leaves for Burma."

She exhaled loudly enough for Harry to hear it. "Twelve-year-old Harry will have to grow up quickly."

After a few more quiet minutes, the wind began to pick up and a few drops of rain began to dot the flagstones. His father stood and offered Sarah his hand. "I believe we need to go back inside. The wind and rain are returning."

They climbed the stairs slowly, as if regret weighed heavily in their steps. Harry turned and quietly entered his bedroom. He was a young version of his father, with the same broad forehead and thick black hair. At twelve, he considered himself nearly a man, but his father's news settled on his heart with a heaviness that reminded him of his youth and inexperience. *Am I ready to be the man of the house?*

That night, as Matthew slept from exhaustion, the rain returned with the driving wind and swept over and around the house.

CHAPTER TWO

HARRY ROSE UNUSUALLY EARLY THE next morning, concluding that any more time in bed would accomplish nothing. He was silent while Gupta assisted him in dressing. As he tied his silk neck scarf, he asked, "Gupta, have you seen Father this morning?"

"Sahib McCune left for the warehouses an hour ago. I heard him tell Sonja that your mother still sleeps and no one is to wake her."

"Then please bring the small tanga around. I want to ride down to the landing at the river and see what all the activity is about."

"Sahib Harry, will Memsahib not be upset if we go to the wharf? The monsoon rains have raised the river. It may be unsafe."

"We won't stay long. If we are back before she rises, she won't know, so she won't worry about it. I want to see what is going on there that keeps Father from early morning until late evening."

The man put his palms together and bowed his obeisance to the boy before disappearing down the stairs to bring the small carriage.

When it had halted at the veranda, Harry climbed in and Gupta slapped the rump of the horse with the reins and turned it down the road toward the closest gate in the wall around the fort.

In normal times, the wharf and landing were dangerous places where men of questionable morals mingled with men from various countries fleeing crimes and offering their services as ordinary seamen on the ships anchored there. He was not worried about his safety this day because he felt sure there would be a sizable military presence there.

Outside the walls of the fort, the day was in full motion. The air was damp and thick with the smell of wood smoke from fires used for cooking breakfast rice.

The long, normally dusty Strand Road was muddy from weeks of rain. It passed the fort, the customhouse, and other governmental offices, taking the small carriage past the Coolie Bazaar. The citizens of Calcutta went about their business despite the rain. The tanga moved past black-leafed mango trees and lacy acacias growing spontaneously along the roadside. A large multitrunked banyan tree hosted a flock of birds, while a holy man, a sadhu, sat cross-legged and naked to the waist under its branches in the rain, his feet on his thighs, his palms turned upward, his eyes open and staring. His body was smeared with ashes, his hair uncut and matted. A begging bowl sat nearby.

As was his custom, Harry tossed him a coin, taking some satisfaction in the fact that he managed to hit the bowl this time.

Though he had spent his life in India, Harry never ceased to be amazed at the contrast between the orderly, comfortable life behind the walls that surrounded the fort and the chaos out here. They made their way past the churning crush of people shouting, pushing, and elbowing their way through the streets. At the crossroads, the market teemed with donkeys, humpbacked oxen, heavily laden camels, wandering cattle, naked children, merchants, and women who carried their wares on their heads.

The city had grown up around Fort William, which was located nearly fifty miles up the River Hooghly from the Bay of Bengal, and was now one of the great trading centers of the world. The river's source was the Ganges, and, like the Thames in London, it was fully navigable for miles by sailing ships of any size because of its breath and depth.

During the dry season, it was a half-mile wide, but during the monsoons, it was at least twice as large, rising and flooding over the ancient paths on either side, forcing the carriages to drive through water up to their wheel hubs.

The long rollers of the flood tide mingled with the brown surge and wash of the brackish river and helped lift and carry the ships to the wharves of Calcutta, where they delivered their cargo. There they awaited the ebb tide while they were loaded with cotton, silk, indigo dye, salt, saltpeter, and tea meant for England, Europe, and the United States before making their way down the sometimes poorly marked channel to the bay.

Within a few minutes, a row of enormous stone lions came into view. With the recent rains, they now stood in water almost to their sculpted knees. Beyond them Harry could see a rocking thicket of masts a quarter mile farther up the river at the wharf.

"Look, Gupta, it looks like a forest." Harry stood in the carriage as it moved slowly through the water on the road. He studied the sight. "There's a navy ship of the line with three masts and at least . . ." he paused to count, "at least a hundred guns. It must be more than two hundred feet long." He continued to study the scene. "There are two more ships like it and a half dozen brigs and five—no—six brigantines. Gupta, much of the British navy must be anchored here. Look! There are four barques, and there, beyond the big ships, is a two-masted schooner. I've never seen the wharf so busy."

He paid little attention to the far end of the wharf where personal watercraft were anchored, nearly hidden by the naval vessels, as he took in the cluster of heavily loaded barges, water taxis for those needing to get to the opposite shore of the great river, and a large Chinese junk with fully battened sails. Beyond the larger ships, scattered like chicks around a hen, were the small brown-sailed skiffs of ancient design used by the fishermen.

A graceful marble monument of Greek and gothic style dominated the area near the wharf. It had been built in 1841 as a tribute to the Englishman James Princep, who had been a special friend to India. It sat near the stairs that led down into the river where the natives often bathed or did their laundry, but the monsoon rains had raised the water level so high that it covered the stairs and inundated the monument halfway up each column.

Today a crush of human bodies covered the wharf, which sat just barely above the high-water level. It had been rebuilt high enough after the last typhoon to make it possible for business to be conducted even during the monsoon season.

Well behind the port office were the export and import warehouses of the Bengal army, which his father and Patrick Meik supervised. The overflowing river lapped at several of them.

From where he stood in the carriage, Harry counted nearly fifty polkee bearers, human beasts of burden who carried heavy loads on bent backs and shoulders and labored to load the ships' cargoes.

Above the milieu, crewmen yelled orders. Passengers stood about, waiting to board the rowboats that would take them to a clipper ship. Mixed among the crowd, company officers in red coats directed the loading of cannons, foodstuffs, and other supplies into the longboats, which then carried all cargo out to the ships anchored near the main channel.

Wharfage fees in Calcutta for loading and unloading were charged by the hour, but today, the vast majority of the ships on the river were British navy and thus would pay no fees. The port commissioner stood near the port office building in his blue-and-white uniform, arms folded across his chest and an impassive look on his face.

Harry whispered, "I've never seen *anything* like this."

Gupta had halted the carriage on the side of the road near the great stone lions. "Sahib Harry, do you want me to take you closer to the wharf?"

"No, Gupta, this is close enough." He pulled off his shoes and rolled up his pant legs. Climbing down and crossing nearer to the river's edge, he turned his attention away from the shipping activity and leaned against one of the great lion sculptures that looked unseeingly out over the wide expanse of water.

He stooped and picked up one of the flat stones that had been piled below the head of each sculpture as a tribute by passing natives during the dry season. He turned it over in his hand before he threw it with all his strength out into the river, as if the ferocity of his throw could ease the concerns that burdened him. It skipped four times over the nearly placid expanse before disappearing into its muddy depths, leaving behind a series of rings that expanded, then quickly dissipated. He threw another and another.

His concentration was so intent that he hadn't heard the arrival of a second tanga. The voice of his friend James Meik startled him. "Four skips. Good, but I can do better."

Fourteen-year-old James stood in the water near Harry and stooped to pick up a stone. In one smooth motion, he threw it in a sweeping underhand cast that made the stone skip six times before it sank.

"What do you think of that, Harry?"

Harry grinned at his friend and said with a slight mocking tone, "I bow to a superior lad. What brings you here?"

"You weren't at home, but Deleep admitted he had seen Gupta get the tanga and drive you toward the gate. I decided to follow my instincts and see if you were as curious as I am about what's going on down here at the wharf. What's happening in your world?"

Harry was silent as he picked up and threw another stone. It skipped three times. He said in disgust, "I can do better." But he didn't try. He turned to James and spoke quietly. "I heard my parents talking last night. Father told Mother he would be going to Rangoon to fight the Burmese soon. I'm sure it upset her as she wasn't up and dressed when he left for the warehouses this morning. Mother is *always* up and dressed before any of the rest of us." He stooped and picked up another rock. "He told her that I was going to have to be the man of the house while he was gone." He let the rock fly.

James dropped the stone he had picked up as if there was suddenly no more pleasure in the rock-skipping competition. "My father will be going to Burma as well. Annie and I were called into the sitting room last evening when he got home. After he gave us the news, Mother went straight to bed and hasn't gotten up yet. Annie is afraid the strain of his leaving will make her sick again. She has never really been well since we lost my little brother to cholera a few months ago, and she is"—he cleared his throat—"in a family way again."

"How is Annie taking the news?"

"She's upset, but she's determined not to let Mother see it. She is being so cheerful it is almost irritating. You know how sisters can be."

No, he didn't know how sisters could be. His parents had lost their only little girl a year before Harry was born. Aloud, he said, "Annie is a fine girl. She'll look after your mother while your father is gone."

James studied the water for a long minute. "The ebb tide has started. The ships will soon be moving toward the bay." His voice briefly had the detached quality of someone commenting on the weather until he returned to the subject that concerned them both. "Father said every man in the Bengal army will be going to Rangoon, and it's rumored that many of the Madras troops will go as well."

"A few weeks ago after Sabbath meeting, Annie told me that you were thinking about joining the naval cadets as soon as you turned fourteen. Now that we're at war with Burma, will you still join them?"

"I already have. I enlisted two weeks ago and report for training next week. If I had known Father was going to be posted to Rangoon, I wouldn't have signed up, but since I have, my father feels I should serve. To resign now would look like cowardice. I know my brother George is only ten, but he's a responsible lad. He will have to be the man of the family for a while."

"You think he's up to it?" Harry's voice was skeptical.

"He'll be fine. It's Jamal that Mother really counts on when Father is gone, anyway."

"Jamal won't be going with your father?"

"I'm sure Father will leave him to run the house. Mother couldn't do without him."

They were both quiet for a minute before Harry cleared his throat, trying to hide the emotions tightening his chest. The more they talked, the more real his father's leaving became for him. He suddenly wanted to get away from the conversation.

"I didn't tell Mother where I was going when I left the house. She'll be worried. I need to be getting back." He looked at his clothing and added, "I'll need to change my clothes before she sees me."

James suddenly pointed. "Look, there's a frigate headed for the bay." A steamer tug pulled at the bowline of the great, three-masted ship like a man trying to pull an ox mired in mud. "Look how low she rides in the water. I suppose she's headed for Rangoon."

"I'm sure she is," Harry whispered, mostly to himself.

Without saying anything more, the two boys returned to the tangas that stood side by side in a foot of water where their drivers had been talking to one another while they watched their young masters.

As the boys climbed into their individual carriages and sat, they watched as another heavily loaded ship was pulled into the current of the wide river. The Meik carriage moved down the flooded road while Harry sat for a few more minutes watching another of the great ships head for the bay.

"Gupta, I want to go to the bazaar so I can get something nice for Mother. She's very worried by the news that Father will soon be going to Rangoon."

Harry had pulled on his shoes and rolled his pant legs down by the time they reached the bazaar. He climbed out and pushed through the crowd with Gupta following in his wake, making his way past the long rows of great jars or casks heaped with a rainbow of spices. A new aroma came at him with each step—curry, paprika, saffron, cinnamon, pungent mushrooms, bitter roots, dried chili peppers, even Chinese tea.

They finally reached the seller of silk, where Harry fingered the fabric of a sky-blue scarf as soft and light as the breath of a baby with a border of woven gold-and-silver thread.

"Gupta, do I have enough money to buy this for Mother?"

"Yes, Sahib Harry."

"Then please pay the man for me. This will please her."

Gupta reached into the purse that was held by a leather belt at his waist and pulled out two rupees to pay the silk merchant.

CHAPTER THREE

GUPTA HELPED HARRY CHANGE HIS pants and muddy shoes when they arrived home before Harry joined his mother, who was just sitting down for breakfast. She loved the scarf. She rose and stood before the mirror that hung near the grandfather clock and draped it around her neck.

"I hope you're not angry with me for going off so early this morning without telling you where I was going."

"I saw you leave in the small tanga with Gupta. As long as you're with him, I don't worry . . . at least not too much." She turned toward him. "Are you so grown up that you can't give your mother an embrace? I would like to give you a hug for your thoughtfulness." She hugged him tightly for several seconds before releasing him.

"Mother, will Father be coming home late again tonight?"

"Probably. You have my permission to eat with us when he comes home, regardless of the hour, if you would like."

"Thank you. I'd like that."

"Mrs. Senior arrived a half hour ago. She was disappointed when she learned you weren't here. Right now she's in the study working with Georgie on his sums, but it would be better if you didn't keep her waiting any longer."

"I'll apologize for my tardiness. I should have been watching the time." As he started toward the study, he spoke over his shoulder to Gupta. "After Mrs. Senior leaves today, I would like to work on improving my penmanship in Hindustani. You'll help me?"

"Yes, Sahib Harry." His personal servant—and friend—followed him to the schoolroom.

***

The three littlest brothers, George, Alfred William—so named to differentiate him from two of his deceased brothers—and baby Edward James had been fed, bathed, and readied for bed well before Matthew arrived home that evening. George pouted when he learned that he couldn't see his father before saying his prayers. Alfred William, whom Harry had nicknamed A. W., demanded a story. Edward, who was not yet a year old, was nearly asleep before he was changed into his nightclothes.

When Matthew arrived, Sarah noted that his step was slower than usual and that exhaustion had carved deep lines in his face.

"Matthew, you look exhausted this evening—more so than usual."

"I spent the day supervising the loading of ordnance and artillery. It's heavy work, and the rain made the task more difficult."

"Father, I rode down to the wharf this morning. It was much busier than I had ever seen it."

"Yes, son, war makes great demands."

"Will you be involved in the fighting? Will you face the enemy?" These were questions he had to ask. He couldn't quite grasp the thought of his father at the battlefront.

"I am charged with instructing the troops in the use of artillery. What else I may be ordered to do I can only guess."

"But why do we have to fight the Burmese?"

His father laid down his fork. "I don't profess to fully grasp the source of the friction between our government and the Burmese king. This is the second time our country has fought them in the last forty years. All I know is that I must follow orders." Matthew folded his napkin and laid it next to his plate. He leaned back in weariness.

"How long will you be gone?" Harry's food was forgotten.

"Until the fighting is over, I expect." At the look of concern in Sarah's eyes, he added, "The fighting is unlikely to spread beyond western Burma, and perhaps the conflict will be short. That will be largely up to their king."

"Are the chances great that you will be put on the battle line?"

"Possibly, but you're not to worry, Harry. The Lord may have a purpose in sending me to Burma. We must hold that thought."

Harry took a deep breath and expressed the idea that had taken root in his mind since his talk with James Meik. "Father, when I turn fourteen, I would like to enlist in the naval cadet program."

Sarah looked at him in concern. "Harry, you have never mentioned this before. What makes you think you should join the cadets?"

"I think if Father can participate in the war with the Burmese, then I should be prepared to do my part. Father, will you support my decision?"

"You are looking a long way into the future, my lad, but we are, after all, a British military family, and it is only to be expected that my sons will follow in my steps and enlist in the military. Four years as a naval cadet would give you insight into the choice of which military branch you would prefer when you are eighteen—the navy or the army, as I have chosen. I wholeheartedly support your decision."

"Thank you, Father." He leaned back with a pleased expression.

Sarah sat without moving for a few moments. *Matthew leaving and Harry planning on enlisting in the naval cadets . . .* She felt as though her world were beginning to spin out of control, like a leaf blown on a gust of wind. She took a deep breath and sat up straighter.

After the meal, when his son had asked to be excused, Matthew spoke. "The rain has paused. Let's go down to the veranda, my dear. It will be cooler there." Matthew rose and put out his hand, which she took, tightly holding on to it as if it would stabilize her world.

There, they sat without speaking for a few minutes. Matthew closed his eyes and stretched out his legs. Sarah was silent as she struggled with her churning thoughts.

Matthew was the first to break the silence. "You are very quiet tonight. What are you thinking?"

Their voices floated up to Harry, where he sat in his room.

Her voice was firm. "Matthew, we have never discussed the possibility of having Harry join the naval cadet program. I wish we could have discussed the matter before you gave him your blessing."

Matthew opened his eyes and sat up. "Sarah, surely you realize that it is a natural choice for him. In all likelihood, he will eventually enter a military career. As a British military family, there are few other options. I have no title, so he is not eligible for an appointment to a government post. There are certainly few, if any, alternative careers for a young man in his position here in India." He leaned back and closed his eyes again as if the discussion of the matter were closed.

She continued to sit silently for another minute. He finally sat up and looked at her in the darkness. "Something else is on your mind. What is it?"

She stared out into the darkness for a while, then finally spoke. "I've wondered all day that . . . had you chosen another career, something that might have kept us in London when we married, how different things might have been." She paused. "Before you enlisted at Westminster, you were apprenticed as a baker. We would have lived in a simpler manner—but perhaps we wouldn't have had to bury four of our children." Her voice was quiet but firm. "And you certainly would not be facing orders to go into battle in Burma. I must admit I am a bit frightened, Matthew. I'm as frightened as I was the evening you told me you had determined to enlist."

He looked at her in surprise. "You never told me that my enlistment had frightened you."

"I didn't speak of my fears at the time. I so wanted to be a dutiful wife, but the thought of leaving England to sail so far away to live our lives in India—Oh, Matthew, for the next several mornings after you left so early for the bakery, I laid abed and wept." She dabbed at her brown eyes with her handkerchief. "I was determined to be a good military wife—but I was terrified of that long voyage to Calcutta. In my mind's eye, I could see the ship going down in a storm and no one ever knowing what had happened to us." She paused and looked up into his face. "What made you decide to make such a change in our lives? We weren't doing so badly there in London."

"There was an old soldier with a wooden leg who came into the bakery for hot cross buns almost every day. We fell to talking one morning while the bread baked, and I asked him how he had lost his leg. He explained that he had taken the king's shilling and enlisted in the East India Army thirty-five years earlier. He and his bride had been posted to Calcutta. His army pay had given them a comfortable, even luxurious life with servants and a twelve-room bungalow rented from the company at a modest price. They and their three boys had hardly a care for the twenty-five years they lived there, but one day when he was directing fifty sepoys in cutting trees in the jungle for the building of a bridge, one of the trees fell on him and crushed his leg. The doctor fitted him with a wooden stump, and he was pensioned out. His brothers in England were dead, so he and his wife returned to London to look after his elderly mother. The second winter after their return, his wife died of pneumonia from the cold, wet climate. So it was just him and his mother after that."

"You never told me about him. What happened to his sons?"

"One remained in India, where he had enlisted, and the other two sailed for America. He lost touch with them."

"How very sad."

"But he said he never regretted his service in India, nor did his wife. He encouraged me to enlist and promised me that it would give us a better life than I could ever have as a baker in London." He looked down at her in the darkness. "I regret that my decision frightened you."

After a few quiet moments, she explained, "I felt that my fears were fully justified when we suffered through that terrible storm. I spent most of those weeks so sick I seldom left my berth. I know my discomfort was to be expected. Alexander was born less than three months after we arrived, but even if I hadn't been in a family way, it still would have been a difficult voyage."

"I'm sorry if I seemed to be an insensitive, callow young husband." Sarah was startled by his statement. He was not a man to easily admit weakness. "I regret that you never told me of your feelings in the matter."

"Would it have made any difference if I had?"

"Do you mean would I have chosen not to have enlisted? No, I would have made the same choice." He briefly considered that thought before continuing. "There are always reasons for what comes to us in this life. Somehow the Lord will reveal His will in this matter, and we will come through my service in Burma and be reunited."

"Oh, Matthew, I certainly hope so." She spoke in a whisper. "I'm worried for all of us—for those of us who will remain behind without your strength and for you as you face the guns of the Burmese." After a quiet moment, she returned to her earlier thoughts. "If we had stayed in London, our cottage would have been small, probably without servants, but if you were a baker, we wouldn't have gone hungry." She gave a quiet, pensive laugh.

"'Man cannot live by bread alone,'" he quietly quoted. "Neither women nor children."

She took a deep breath and made an effort to speak more matter-of-factly. "Perhaps I'm being foolish. We can't turn back time. Decisions made then can't be unmade now." She watched the clouds gather again as the rain began to spot the flagstones. "And life has been good and comfortable here—most of the time. I could have been fully content—if we hadn't lost the children." She spread her handkerchief on her lap as if to smooth the wrinkles out of it. "There are turning points in a person's life that can be identified in retrospect. That decision for you to enlist after we were married was surely one of them."

He joined her musings. "If I were to identify another turning point, I would say it was my decision to join with the Plymouth Brethren to study the Bible three years ago. More specifically, it was the evening Maurice White brought Benjamin Richie and George Barber, those two young sailors, to our meeting from that ship under repair and they told us about the new religion they had recently accepted. Our collective curiosity prompted some of us to send that letter back to England with them to the Church leaders there, asking for more information. When they sent Joseph Richards to Calcutta to baptize those of us who were converted, a great change took place in our lives."

Sarah commented, "Indeed, a great change. I enjoyed having the members meet in our home when William Willes arrived here last December and organized a branch of the Church. I actually regretted seeing Patrick build the little chapel we meet in now." She paused and looked at him. "Do the other members of the Plymouth Brethren resent those of you who have left their group to affiliate with the Mormons?"

Matthew nodded. "Yes, there have been a few who have expressed anger or disgust." He continued to speculate. "How sad that changes in our beliefs alter the way others view us."

The light rain had stopped, and the clouds had moved away from the face of the moon, freeing it from its cloudy prison. "I have sometimes wondered if, had we stayed in London, we would have ever heard the message of the gospel," he said.

Sarah abruptly changed the subject. "I'm troubled by the fact that with both you and Patrick Meik being posted to Rangoon, there will be no one with an understanding of homeopathic medicine here to treat the sick. The army doctor will be going as well. What will we do if one of the children becomes ill?"

He responded in his usual pragmatic manner. "I'll leave copious notes that will be of some use to you on how to treat fevers or chills or other ailments. I do believe there is an English physician living in the city. He could be called upon."

"Matthew, I've heard ill of him. I've been told he believes that the cure for everything is to either bleed or purge the patient. I heard that he even suggested bleeding a young man for a broken leg. Somehow I don't feel safe in the hands of such a man."

"Then I shall leave some of my books on herbs and homeopathic medicine here for you."

Sarah stared unseeingly into the darkness, and her voice dropped to a near whisper. "The death of each child broke my heart. You could not have done anything for Alexander after he was bitten by that rabid dog, but I have always wondered if you might have saved little Agnes or her brothers if you had been experienced in homeopathic medicine at the time."

"But some good came of their loss as it prompted me to begin the study of herbal medicine."

"And that has been a great blessing to many of us who have benefited," she said as she took his hand and held it tightly.

The clouds drew a veil over the moon again, and the rain returned. "It's past time for us to retire, my dear. It's been a very long day, and there are many more to come." He stood, and she followed his example.

By the time they reached the second level of the house, they could see a carriage as it halted in front. A voice firmly called, "I need Sergeant McCune."

Deleep had hurried out of the lower level servants' quarters to hold the reins of the horse of the Right Reverend Mr. Vinton, a local Baptist minister.

Matthew paused on the balcony and answered, "Pastor Vinton, what brings you out this evening? How can I be of service?"

"My wife has sent me to bring you. The army surgeon is not available, and my wife has heard you are a master of medicinal herbs. She lies ill and has been so for some days. Will you come with me?"

"Yes, just give me a moment." He turned and hurried to his study to get his bag of herbs and the ingredients for various poultices. When he returned to the stairs, he looked at Sarah. "You needn't worry. I'll be back as soon as I can."

As Matthew climbed into the pastor's carriage, Sarah whispered, "But this is just the kind of situation I do worry about if you leave us, Matthew."

Matthew returned near midnight. "It seems Mrs. Vinton had not realized that she was with child a second time. As I asked about her symptoms, she realized why she was feeling ill. It has been seven years since the birth of her first child, and she had forgotten the degree of her discomfort and inability to hold anything in her stomach. When I arrived and we talked, she realized her situation. I gave her some valerian to help her sleep this evening and left some lemon balm with instructions on how to make a tea to help her sleep in the future."

As he dropped into bed, he murmured, "Remind me in the morning to have Harry go to the bazaar and get me additional herbal supplies." He had hardly finished the sentence before he was asleep.

***

Harry joined his parents for breakfast in the morning while the younger children slept.

"Sarah, I have urged Elder Willes to send a letter to the Church leaders in England notifying them that all of the male members of the Church, with the exception of Harry, have been required to lend their efforts to the conflict with the Burmese. That will leave the remaining women and children here without any male leadership other than his own, and frankly, I expect that he will be ordered to follow the troops to Burma to oversee the Church there. I suggested that he request the leaders of the Church in England to send missionaries to Calcutta to replace the leadership that will be in Burma."

"I hope they will do so, but, Matthew, that will take months."

"There is nothing we can do in the matter, my dear."

Jai had the tanga waiting near the veranda when Matthew descended the stairs. Jai was the only male servant who wore a tall turban and the sherwani—the silk coat worn by Indian men of upper rank. It reached to his knees and was decorated with a wide band of embroidery along the front openings and stiff collar. He was, after all, the senior servant, as nearly a *major domo* to the household as was to be found in India, as well as the personal servant of a British officer, a position reflected in his dress and bearing.

Despite the rain, he sat proudly in the raised front seat with an umbrella opened above his head. He touched the rumps of the two horses with the whip, and the carriage headed for the warehouses. Matthew sat back under the fabric roof that kept the rain off during the monsoon months and the sun during the dry season.

CHAPTER FOUR

MATTHEW ARRIVED HOME AFTER EIGHT Saturday evening. When he, Sarah, and Harry sat at the long oak dining table for dinner, they could hear Alfred refusing to go to bed. He was actively resisting his nanny's attempts to put him into his nightshirt. He managed to pull away from her and rush down the hall to the drawing room, where he threw himself at his father.

"Father"—he pronounced the word "Fodder"—"where you been? Dira says I can't see you." His voice was full of reproach. He took his father's hand and pulled at him. "Come and tell me a story." When he saw his mother frown at him, he added contritely, "Please."

"Alfred, your father is very tired and hungry. Endira, please take the lad back to bed," she ordered the servant.

"No, it is all right. I haven't seen the little lads for several days. I'll tell him a story so he can go to sleep." He rose from the table and picked up the child. "What story would you like to hear, my lad?"

The child looked into his father's face with a victorious grin. "Tell me 'bout Daniel and the lions."

Matthew returned after ten minutes and smiled as he sat again at the head of the table. "I looked in on Edward. He was sleeping. I swear he has grown since I saw him last."

Sarah looked at her hands folded in her lap. "Just think of the changes that will come to them if you are gone for very long. You will hardly know them when you see them."

"You must write to me often and tell me of their growth so I don't miss all the important things in their lives," he stated matter-of-factly.

With a tight voice, she said, "We need to eat our dinner before it gets any colder."

***

As the McCunes entered the building where Sabbath services were held each Sunday, Harry's eyes immediately searched the room for Annie Meik. When he located her, he couldn't suppress a smile, despite his attempts to remain properly serious.

The group of about forty-five individuals was made up of both baptized members and those seeking more information about the new religion and its beliefs. The building had a solid floor but was roofed and sided with palm fronds, which allowed the air to circulate. Sixty could be seated on the split-log benches.

Matthew led his family to the bench at the front of the room, which gave him easy access to the rough-hewn podium that faced the congregation. As president of the Wanderer's Branch, the responsibility of conducting the meetings fell to him.

Just before Harry took his seat, he caught Annie's eye and noted the smile she sent his way.

As Matthew stood behind the podium, the conversations of those present grew quiet, and he opened the meeting. "Brothers and Sisters in the gospel of Jesus Christ, we have gathered today to strengthen one another's testimonies and increase our knowledge of the teachings of the Savior."

After an invocation offered by Matthew and a congregational hymn, the meeting proceeded with Patrick Meik preaching on the subjects of faith and repentance. Maurice White, a bachelor sergeant in the Bengal army, followed with a sermon on the necessity of baptism to enter the kingdom of God. After the final hymn and benediction, most of the men, including Matthew and Patrick, gathered to discuss the problems that would face the little congregation once the men left to fight in Burma. The wives and mothers also clustered, talking of the difficulties that would face them without their husbands and fussing over Edward, who squirmed in his mother's arms.

Harry quickly made his way to where Annie sat. He pointed to the bench next to her. "May I?"

She smiled and nodded. "Of course." She pulled her skirt closer to make more room for him. He never quite knew how to begin a conversation with the pretty girl. He just knew he wanted very much to talk to her.

He cleared his throat. "Um—you're wearing your prettiest frock today."

"Thank you, Harry. Do you really think so?"

"Yes. The blue silk is just the color of your eyes."

She blushed slightly as she modestly dropped her eyes. "I like this one too, but I think it has been nearly ruined." She lifted her hem a few inches.

"See here—and here," she pointed, "where Gergen has used an iron that was too hot and has scorched the lace. I haven't said anything to Mother because she is much too upset about the fact that her best dress was scorched in the same way, but much worse—so much worse that hers is truly ruined." She let go of the skirt, and it slid back into place. "Does your mother have problems with any of your servants?"

Harry was quiet for a moment. He had never paid much attention to his mother's relationship with the servants. "I don't know," he finally answered. "They do as they are asked, and I've seldom seen her show any displeasure with them, but then"—he smiled as his eyes found his mother across the room—"she is a kind and warm person by nature."

Annie noted the softening of Harry's expression as he watched his mother before she continued in a mildly irritated tone. "Well, Mother seems to have increasing problems, especially with Gergen. She was hired as a cook but consistently used too much curry and saffron in the rice. No matter how much Mother tried to teach her, she didn't improve. One day she served chicken burned beyond recognition. Mother had no choice but to find another position for her. Now she's doing laundry, and all we have to show for it are two ruined frocks—and Mother doesn't even know about mine yet. I haven't had the heart to tell her."

Though problems with servants had never been a matter that had ever concerned him, he followed Annie's words closely, watching the flash in her eyes. He was so smitten that anything she talked about interested him.

"Why doesn't your mother let her go?"

"Mother says that she is the main support of her aged parents. Her only brother is a sepoy posted to Meerut Cantonment. He sends them a few rupees twice a year. Mother doesn't want her to become destitute."

"That is kind of your mother. I hope that she can find something for her to do well enough to keep her. I can hardly see the scorched spot."

Annie looked into his eyes. His heart seemed to stop. "You have a kind heart too, Harry."

Her compliment made his face feel warm. "James told me he has enlisted in the cadets. Will he be leaving for his posting soon?"

"He speaks of little else. He expects to leave day after tomorrow." She folded and unfolded her handkerchief in her lap. "Are you thinking about enlisting when you are old enough?" Her voice was quiet.

"I am thinking about it, very seriously. I told my parents that I wanted to. It would—" His words were cut off by his father's voice. "Harry, George, Alfred, it's time we were leaving." In the tone was the assumption that his sons would give immediate obedience.

"Yes, Father," Harry said as he stood. "I hope we can talk again next week," he whispered to Annie as he turned to leave.

"As do I," she whispered quietly as he crossed the room to join his parents.

The group of men had separated to locate their family members. Each couple led their children to one of the tangas that waited outside on the wide, muddy path that ran in front of the little chapel.

Matthew and Sarah seated themselves on the rear seat of the large tanga, where Sarah held a fussy Edward on her lap. Harry, George, and Alfred sat facing their parents with their backs to Jai as he sat in the high driver's seat. Alfred wanted to kneel on the padded seat to watch the passing street scenes.

Harry demanded, "A. W., stop wiggling and sit down properly."

When the child made no move to obey, Matthew reaffirmed Harry's request. "Alf, do as your brother asked. Turn around and sit properly."

With his face screwed up in frustration, the child did as he was told.

Matthew turned his attention to his eldest son. "Harry, you are paying a great deal of attention to Patrick Meik's oldest daughter." It was a statement of fact not to be debated.

"Yes, Father. She is a fine young lady—much like her mother, I'm sure." He added the second comment in an attempt to shore up Annie in his father's eyes.

"It is important you understand that there is too much of life ahead to allow yourself to become distracted from your goals by an infatuation with a young lass."

Harry remained silent.

"There will be many who cross your path as you mature. It is vital that you do not allow them to distract you from what must be accomplished." When his son still did not respond, he added, "Do you understand me, Harry?"

"Of course, Father." His lips answered properly, but his heart did not agree.

***

The following week passed much as the previous had, but upon arriving home at nine on Saturday evening, as he sat down for dinner with Sarah and Harry, Matthew announced, "Tomorrow I must direct the loading of munitions and supplies, so I will not be in attendance at our Sabbath meeting. Patrick will conduct the meeting on my behalf."

Sarah's brow was wrinkled. "Matthew, I do so hate to see you work at such heavy labor on the Sabbath."

"It can't be helped. I believe the Lord understands."

Harry looked down at his plate and stifled a smile. He would be able to freely talk with Annie after the meeting.

CHAPTER FIVE

THE TWENTY-SIXTH OF JULY ARRIVED, and Matthew was ordered, along with thirty-nine other officers and more than ninety sepoys, to report at the wharf at 8:00 a.m. with his personal effects, prepared to depart for Rangoon.

As his belongings were packed, Sarah worried aloud, "Matthew, you hardly have room for your uniforms."

"I can obtain more uniforms from the quartermaster if necessary. The other items I need as they may be unavailable in Burma."

"Father, will you practice herbal medicine in Burma?"

"Yes, Harry, if I can obtain sufficient herbs and my skill is needed."

It had required both Deleep and Jai to carry Matthew's trunk once it was packed. In addition to his uniforms and boots, he had included his mortar and pestle, a favorite book on homeopathic medicine, a world atlas, his medical bag with a large supply of herbs, a Bible, and a Book of Mormon.

Among the large ships that bobbed at anchor in the great river that morning were two great brigs with reefed sails that stood out from the wharf while the trunks of the officers were loaded into the longboats and ferried out to them.

After Jai and Deleep carried Matthew's trunk from the tanga to the wharf, Deleep returned to stay with the carriage while Jai stood quietly near Matthew.

Matthew had bid Alfred William and little Edward good-bye at home, where they were left in the care of Endira to avoid exposure to the sun or rain.

The wharf was a mass of humanity, of people pushing and elbowing their way through the milieu. Officers were shouting orders, vendors were trying to sell their wares from the baskets or trays piled high on their heads, and children were hanging on to their fathers and crying. The troops and officers waiting to board the ships made a sea of red as they tried to offer comfort to their wives and children, occasionally teasing the little ones into a hesitant smile. The sight sent a chill of apprehension through Sarah. *So many families torn apart*, she thought.

Georgie had insisted that he ride on his father's shoulders. Not yet six, the child had refused to let go of his father. At ten thirty, Matthew's regiment was ordered to take formation, so he lifted the resisting boy from his shoulders and set him on his feet. Harry watched his father as he kissed his mother on the forehead, which was as much of a display of affection as Matthew's sense of public etiquette would permit.

Matthew bent and shook Georgie's hand in all seriousness. When he shook Harry's, he laid his other hand on his oldest son's shoulder. "You will have to be the man of the house now, my lad, so it is important that you do nothing to besmirch the McCune name."

"Yes, Father."

"And, Georgie, you will be a good and obedient lad for your mother—and your brother?"

"Yes, Father." He smiled suddenly and stood as tall as his little body would permit. "I will make you proud."

Matthew turned to Jai and placed his hand on his shoulder. In Hindustani, he quietly stated, "I'm leaving my family in your care. You will watch over them for me?"

"Yes, Sahib McCune. Your family is my family."

Matthew turned to Sarah and took both of her hands in his for a brief moment. Her words were locked in her throat with the tears she vowed she would not shed in front of the children. He squared his shoulders as if to give her courage before turning away and moving through the crowd to the regimented gathering of artillery officers.

She was finally able to whisper, "Go with God."

Mentally, Harry added, *And return home safely.*

After the trunks of the officers and the kit bags of the troops had been ferried to the big ships in the river, the red-coated officers were ordered to climb into the longboats.

While Sarah watched her husband's figure move toward one of the longboats, Harry noticed Patrick and Mary Anne Meik standing not far from them. Mrs. Meik was not holding up well. The three oldest Meik children had come to the wharf to see their father depart. James, excused from his training for the day, wore his new naval cadet uniform. Twelve-year-old Annie wiped her eyes with a handkerchief as her father took leave of them. When she looked in his direction, Harry raised his hand to wave at her. She smiled weakly at him before turning back to assist her mother.

Harry returned to watching as each officer in turn stepped into a longboat that held twenty in addition to the two strong men who did the rowing. When it was loaded and riding low in the water, the oars of the sailors dipped and pulled the longboats toward the three-masted frigate, the *Agabackah*. There the men boarded by climbing one of the two rope ladders that hung over the side. Thereafter the sepoys were crowded into the longboats and followed the officers onto the ship. The last to climb on board were the two sailors who would pilot the ship to the bay.

Sarah spoke quietly to her eldest son. "These will be difficult months until your father returns, but it will give you many opportunities to grow into the man he wants you to become."

"Yes, Mother."

When the last military man had climbed onto the deck, he joined the formation that faced the shore, and on command, all saluted those remaining behind. Then the rain began to fall as if the heavens were weeping on behalf of the separated families.

Those left behind could hear the captain as he gave the order to weigh anchor and a dozen sailors began the task of turning the capstan. The clanking of the heavy links in the anchor chain reached the families watching from the wharf. A steam tug dwarfed by the ship chugged to the bow, and a line was attached so the ship could be pulled out into the current of the main channel. The sailors moved up the rigging and out along the spars, where they waited for the captain's signal to unreef the sails. The wives and children remained unmoving on the wharf until the *Agabackah* had moved down the river and out of sight around a bend.

As Sarah and the two boys turned to follow Jai to the carriage, Georgie looked up at his mother and with childish simplicity asked, "Will Father come home tomorrow?"

"No, we will not see your father for many weeks. You must be a patient, good lad."

Sarah looked up and saw Mary Anne Meik holding tightly to her daughter's arm as they neared the family tanga. James assisted her into the carriage. Her white face was tear streaked.

With seven children at home, another one on the way, and no husband to lean on, I'm not surprised she's so distraught, Sarah thought. Aloud, she said, "Thank you, Jai," as he assisted her into the carriage.

"Mother, I'll be right back." Harry hurried toward the Meik carriage, where he spoke to Annie's mother. "Mrs. Meik, if I can be of assistance in any way while your husband is gone, please do not hesitate to call on me . . . or you, Annie. Please don't hesitate for any reason. With James on naval duty, you . . . you may need some help," he added a little embarrassedly.

Mary Anne smiled gratefully at him and patted him on the shoulder. "Thank you, Harry," she whispered. He hurried back to his family and climbed into the tanga without saying anything more.

On the way home, Sarah took one of each of the two boys' hands and, looking from one to the other, complimented them. "You have been good lads who put a brave face on for your father's departure. I'm proud of you both." She was speaking to herself as much as her sons.

***

After the anchor of the *Agabackah* had been lifted, the tug began to belch great clouds of steam as it pulled the heavily loaded ship into the main channel. Matthew stood at the railing near the quarterdeck where he could hear snatches of the conversation between the helmsman and Captain Bartlett.

"How's the rudder feel?" Bartlett asked the man with the large gold earring.

"The ship is so loaded she handles like a pregnant sow, sir," the helmsman responded, irritation filling his voice. "Heaven help us if we hit a storm."

Matthew was offended by the crude language of the man but recognized its accuracy.

As the massive ship passed the first channel marker, the captain called out in a voice that could be heard the length of the upper deck, "Unreef the mainsail and topgallants. Hoist the foretop; run up the fore sprit. Look smart with the jib. The wind is with us."

Matthew watched the figures on the wharf until the ship slipped around the bend in the river, his family disappearing from view. As a British soldier, he would deny the emotions being stirred up by the separation from his wife and children. He was determined to suppress the worry and sense of loss threatening to break into his consciousness, but he noticed that all the married men on the deck were as quiet as he.

Only Captain Bartlett could be heard as he continued to shout orders. Matthew watched as the crewmen moved out along the spars with the agility of circus performers. The great sails were released and slowly draped themselves around the wind with the gracefulness of birds' wings. After an hour, the little tug released the bowline, and the *Agabackah* was lifted by the fast ebb tide and hurried toward the Bay of Bengal.

In the many years he'd lived and served in India, Matthew had studied the culture as well as the language, and as had occasionally happened, his thoughts were filled with an awareness of the complexity of the national culture. *India—an ancient society covered with a thin British veneer like cake frosting spread too thin. A land of contrasts— filth and hunger coexisting alongside splendor and pageantry, violence amid religious pacifism, prejudice and fear existing side by side with scholarship and art.*

He took a deep breath. *Thank God Jai and Deleep are there to watch over my family while I can't. And Harry—Harry is a fine lad. He will be a great help to his mother.*

His attention was brought back to the present by the senior Bengal officer on board, Colonel Sir James Withering, who had mounted to the quarterdeck. There, he looked out over the men in red and called out loudly, "Officers' quarters are on the lower gun deck, enlisted troops' on the third deck. Your trunks or kit bags have been delivered to your personal quarters."

Matthew joined the stream of officers going down the narrow stairs to the gun deck. After a few minutes of searching, he finally located his trunk under a hammock attached to two cannons chained to the deck. His eyes roamed the officers' quarters. The luxury of privacy would be nonexistent.

"These are indeed utilitarian quarters," he critically commented aloud. Someone near him laughed. He turned and was pleased to see his friend Patrick Meik.

"That they are." Patrick grinned broadly and pointed at the hammocks. "Should we make the attempt?"

To test their comfort, they both climbed into the swaying nets that would serve as their sleeping arrangements for the immediate future.

All Matthew could bring himself to say was, "Most unusual. I suppose we shall grow accustomed to the situation."

Both men had much greater difficulty getting out of the hammocks than getting in, but once Matthew had put his feet on the deck again, he stooped and opened his trunk, locating his world atlas. With it held above his head, he struggled past the sepoys still descending the stairs and finally found a small space on the quarterdeck near the stern, where he hoped to study undisturbed. He was determined to keep his mind occupied and thus prevent fears or worry for his family from occupying his thoughts.

"May we join you?" Patrick asked.

Matthew looked up and noted Patrick and Maurice White watching him. "Please do. It is my intent to learn as much about Burma as I can before we arrive in Rangoon."

***

Before they reached home, Sarah was suddenly aware of the great emptiness Matthew's absence brought. As soon as she stepped out of the tanga, she hurried up the stairs and along the balcony to the baby's bedroom, where she stood quietly watching him as he slept. He was as still as a waxen doll, the warm, humid air making his dark curls stick to his forehead and cheeks.

"Is something the matter, memsahib?" Endira asked as she rose from her chair in the corner.

"No, I just needed to see him." She bent and kissed his little fist, making him stir and smile in his sleep. "You'll be walking, perhaps running, before your father comes home," she whispered.

She peeked in at Alfred, who was also napping. "Thank you, Endira. I can always be sure the children are in good hands when you are watching over them."

Endira bowed from the shoulders in recognition of the praise.

At dinner that evening, Harry, George, and Alfred were given the privilege of sitting at the large oak table in the drawing room with Sarah. From where he sat in his high child's chair, Alfred petulantly asked, "Where's Fodder?"

Sarah tried to ignore the lump in her throat and pretended not to hear him.

He demanded again, "Where's Fodder?"

"Father has gone to war, A. W.," Harry answered for her.

"Make him come home," the child insisted.

Sarah rose from the table and hurried from the room before she lost her composure. As she passed Endira, she paused. "Dira, please see that the younger children finish their supper, and have Harry help them with their prayers tonight. I'm going to lie down."

"Yes, memsahib."

When she entered the bedroom, she motioned Sonja out. "I won't need you tonight." She closed the bedroom door behind her, threw herself on the bed, and buried her face in the pillow to soak up the tears she could no longer suppress.

At bedtime, Alfred wanted his father to tell him a story, so Harry offered, but that would not satisfy the child. Harry approached his mother's bedroom. There, Sonja met him outside the door, head bowed and palms together. "Memsahib sleeps. She should not be disturbed."

"I see. Well, I'll ask Dira to tell him a story since Father is not here and Mother is resting."

When Harry returned to the child's room, the child was refusing to allow his nanny to prepare him for bed. He sat with his arms folded tightly. "I want Foddder to tell me a story."

In her frustration, Endira threatened, "Little sahib, the Thuggee will come and steal you away in the night if you are not an obedient lad. They will take you to the goddess Kali, where they will cut your heart out and eat it."

The child looked at her with narrowed eyes. "I don't believe you," he said clearly. But he had stood still long enough that in one action she had his nightshirt over his head and buttoned under his chin.

"Endira, Mother and Father would not approve of you frightening the little lads with stories of the Thuggees. You are not to say things like that in the future."

She hung her head. "Yes, Sahib Harry. I shall speak no more of the Thuggees."

Harry suspected that in the future, when sufficiently frustrated, she would forget her promise. Georgie climbed up on the foot of his brother's bed.

Endira told "The Story of Wonders" by Rajab Ali Beg Suroor, a story she obviously loved from the look of enjoyment on her face as she talked.

"A handsome youth of noble English birth and high rank saw the beautiful daughter of a Hindu shopkeeper one day in the bazaar. He looked into her eyes and at once lost his heart, never to reclaim it. Each day he came to see her, but her father would not permit them to speak."

The story continued with Endira telling of the lovesick youth's heartbreak at his unrequited love. The father promised he would kill his daughter before he permitted her to be courted by an Englishman.

Before the story had ended, both Alfred and George were both asleep, but Harry wanted to hear the end, so he let her continue.

"In the end, the young man lost his mind in the insanity of love before dying. The heartbroken young woman threw herself onto his coffin from a second-floor window as the funeral procession wound its way past her house, leaving her mortally injured. The death of both united the separated ones. All who witnessed the scene shuddered from the sadness of their choices and the hardness of the father's heart. The parents were so grief-stricken that both soon died. This is what love, the troublemaker, has done; it laid to rest, side by side in the dust, the victims of separation as well as those responsible for it. Thousands of sad people would come to look at their tomb as the years passed." When she finished, she placed her hands together with her fingers beneath her chin and bowed slightly to Harry.

He frowned a little at the morbidity of the story. He was sure his mother would not approve of the children being told such a sad tale, but he responded, "Thank you, Endira. I'm glad to have heard the story. In the future, I think Mother would prefer that you find happier stories for the little lads. I'll take Georgie to his bed now."

As he bent to scoop up the child, Georgie stirred and spoke. "Harry, I didn't get to hear the end of the story."

"You didn't really miss anything, Georgie. It was just Romeo and Juliet all over again."

After he returned to his bedroom, Harry stood at the window watching the clouds sweep across the sky, covering and then revealing the moon, and he wondered what it was like for his father on that great ship. He wondered for the hundredth time if he was sufficiently prepared for any difficulties that might enter the lives of his mother and brothers while his father was gone.

***

Sarah fell asleep fully dressed, waking about midnight. After she donned her nightdress and robe, she stepped out onto the balcony. Below her in the garden the wind stirred the blossoms and branches, and in her mind, she saw the figure of her husband leaning against the railing of the ship's deck, staring out at the night sky.

By now the ship will have reached the bay, the miles between us growing ever wider. How long shall we be separated?

With the intensity of prayer, she told him, "Return to us soon, Matthew. We need you." As she moved inside the house, the wind began to bend the branches of the trees in the garden, and she knew the rain would soon return.

CHAPTER SIX

CARRIED ON THE TURBULENT TIDE, the ship moved swiftly downriver. One of the two pilots—a bronzed, black-mustached, clear-speaking man whose job was to guide the great ship down the channel to the mouth of the river—stood at the wheel, the captain at his side. The second pilot climbed the rigging to the lookout platform two-thirds of the way up the mainmast. There, he gave the necessary hand signals to his partner at the wheel to help him keep the ship in the deepest part of the channel. If the man on the lookout platform stretched his left arm at full length, the pilot at the wheel would correct five points to port, if his right arm was held half bent, the ship was corrected two points to starboard. That process continued throughout the day.

When the mouth of the great river was reached near dusk, the rain stopped and a few stars timidly peeked though the torn shreds of clouds as a small, steam-driven pilot boat sidled up to the ship. Both pilots climbed down the side of the *Agabackah* and into it.

The clouds returned, making the night as dark as a cloud of black ink, but by midnight, the ship was in sight of the lighthouse at Diamond Harbor, where the opposite bank of the Hooghly slipped so far west that even in daylight it was out of sight. There, the wind set up a cross-sea, making the waves of saltwater curl and break into spray against the hull. The wind that had partnered with the tide to speed the ship's travel southward quickly dropped to nothing, leaving the sails slack. The captain ordered the anchor lowered and the sails reefed while he waited for a fair wind.

The air turned sullen and heavy. Before morning, a warm, hard rain hammered the decks.

***

The men rose stiffly from their hammocks at four bells. According to Matthew's pocket watch, it was six o'clock in the morning. The rain continued, and the wind pushed the hard drizzle from the northeast, which required the ship be so close-hauled it was impossible to make any progress into the bay. The breakers roared while the flood tide tried to push the ship back up the river, forcing it to remain at anchor.

After breakfast, the sepoys were required to practice assembling and disassembling their rifles. When they were dismissed, they were relegated to their area on the third deck, where it was evident from the noise and laughter that, despite the crowded quarters, they were in high spirits. Many were playing gleek, an old, swift card game that, to be played successfully, required close attention to the betting.

The officers settled near their hammocks on the gun deck. Many of them passed the time playing whist or sat around speculating about the Burmese and the battles ahead of them. Matthew, Patrick, and Maurice White found an empty corner and jointly read the Book of Mormon.

When the rain briefly ended, some of the officers made their way to the quarterdeck, where Captain Bartlett explained to those who approached him that they were anchored near Sangor Roads, a village in the large Diamond Harbor, where the mouth of the Hooghly broadened into the Bay of Bengal. "We'll be here 'til a favorable wind can push us toward Rangoon."

***

When the early sun formed a lacy pattern through the carved shutters the next morning, Sarah stirred and murmured, "Matthew, I had such a sad dream last night. I dreamed—" She turned and realized that the spot next to her was empty. *It wasn't a dream.* She slowly arose, not looking forward to the prospect of facing reality.

She determinedly wore her most cheerful smile for the children at breakfast. "Harry, what do you intend to do today after you complete your studies?"

"Mother, I think I shall start reading Father's medical books. I have made a list of herbs and other things he suggested we might need to purchase at the bazaar should anyone in the family need doctoring. And I would like to plant a physic garden, where we can grow our own herbs. At the bazaar, when I purchased herbs for Father, I noticed that some sat on shelves in the open and were exposed to the air and dust. If we grow our own, we can make sure they are fresher and of good quality."

His mother nodded her approval, noting that his enthusiasm was increasing as he talked. "I think Father would approve if we planted basil, chamomile, salvia, thyme . . ." He paused and thought a moment. "We should include St. Johns Wort, lemon balm, ginseng, garlic, and everything else he has listed in his notes."

"I think it will be a wonderful garden, Harry." She turned to the next child. "And what do you plan to do today, Georgie?"

The five-and-a-half-year-old pursed his lips and then said seriously, "I'm going to catch pigeons and train them to take messages to Father in Burma."

"What makes you think you can do that, Georgie?" his older brother asked skeptically.

"You told me about the birds you kept when Mother and Father and you lived at Fort Dum Dum. You said that when Father was transferred here to Fort William, you let them go and they followed you here and waited for you to feed them."

Sarah smiled affectionately at the boy. "Georgie, a pair of pigeons arrived here after we settled in, but we don't know if they were the same ones."

"But, Mother, they were the same ones. I recognized their markings," Harry said.

"Harry, how can you be sure?"

"I wouldn't make a mistake like that. They're the pair that live in the mulberry tree."

"So I'm going to catch some pigeons and train them to take messages to Father." Georgie's expression was determined.

His older brother tried to explain. "Georgie, the birds wouldn't know where to find Father. If Father had taken them with him, then they *might*," he stressed the word, "they might find their way back here, but they wouldn't know where to go to find Father, and right now he's on a ship."

The child looked crestfallen, his head drooping. "They could follow the ship," he said hopefully.

Seeing that a new direction in the conversation was needed, Sarah offered, "If you would like, perhaps Deleep can help you catch another pair of birds and build a pen. Then you can feed and train them."

His head rose. "That would be good. Harry, will you teach me all you know 'bout pigeons?" His enthusiasm had returned.

"When you have caught some birds, I'll teach you what I can." He felt sure there was little likelihood of that in the near future.

"I want the ones in the mulberry tree."

"They nest too high. I don't think we can catch them, and I don't think they want to be in a pen again, but you can try."

Alfred added, "Me too. Me too."

Surely if the children can be kept busy enough, they won't have time to miss their father, Sarah thought.

***

The ship lay anchored at the mouth of the River Hooghly for another ten days. The men were not allowed to disembark lest a favorable wind should arise and a rapid departure be required. The enlisted men were required to remain on the third deck for twenty-two hours each day unless they grew seasick. Only then were they permitted to go up on the main deck. The number of those claiming seasickness increased daily, perhaps more from boredom than from illness. Below decks, the space where the sepoys jostled each other for space to sit, game, or sleep grew more and more cramped. To pass the time, some resorted to singing songs in the wailing Hindustani that was their native tongue.

Matthew, Maurice White, and Patrick Meik began to meet daily for two hours on the quarterdeck, unless the rain prevented it, to read from the Book of Mormon and the Bible and discuss religious doctrine. Brother William Adams quickly joined them, as did several men not members of the Church but who were interested in the discussions.

On the fifth day, Colonel Withering approached the small group. They quickly stood at attention and saluted. It was apparent from the redness of his face that he was not pleased with their activity. "In addition to regular training time, each man present will spend two additional hours each day studying the artillery manual and learning to clean and dismantle his personal weapon until he can do it blindfolded." In response to the startled look on each man's face, he responded, "If the Church of England is suitable for the other officers of the armies of the East India Company," his voice rose, "then it is certainly entirely appropriate for you men."

Thereafter, when the men had completed their additional assignments, they went below to the second deck and found a corner where they could more unobtrusively continue their religious studies.

CHAPTER SEVEN

"Mother, the garden planting is finished. Please come and see it. Gupta and Deleep have worked hard to help me find each of the plants we thought Father would like us to plant." Sarah followed Harry down the spiral staircase from the sitting room where she had been studying one of her husband's homeopathic volumes.

As the two of them walked beside the neatly cultivated rows, she congratulated him. "It is beautifully done, Harry. I offer my appreciation to Deleep and Gupta for their help as well."

Both servants were standing back in the shadows of the balcony where they bowed their heads over hands folded together in recognition of her praise and murmured "Namaste" as thanks for her praise.

Harry took his mother's arm and pointed out the plants. "See, Mother, this row is basil, for cuts and scrapes. In Father's notes, he says it is also useful in aiding appetite. This row is salvia, which he says is good for mouth and throat inflammation. This row is thyme. He says it will aid coughs, congestion, and indigestion. This one is lemon balm. You can see from its leaf that it looks like mint. His notes say it is good for insomnia, upset stomach, insect bites, and wounds and that a tea made from it is good for anxiety." He continued pointing out each of the plants, demonstrating his newly acquired knowledge gained from his father's notes.

"I approve of your efforts, Harry. Now we are much better prepared to deal with sickness or injury in your father's absence." She pulled the boy against her with an approving smile.

***

The elements finally turned a kind eye toward the *Agabackah*, and the anchor was lifted and the sails spread. They billowed with a freshening breeze that pushed the ship out into the Bay of Bengal. As the vessel left the harbor, it heeled over a few degrees, slipping through the water and leaving a spreading wake.

Matthew stood on the quarterdeck near the helmsman and watched as the bow plunged into the long green sea, tossing spray onto the men working or sitting idly on the deck. The white sails stretched above his head while the wind sang in the rigging and the ropes strained at the blocks. The sights and sounds reminded him of the long voyage from London after his enlistment. *Then we were setting out on a new life on a new continent. This is a new life in a new place but without Sarah or the children. All our yesterdays belong to the past. We face the future separated—at least for now.*

Men that had been somewhat troubled by seasickness while the ship had rocked at anchor became prostrate with nausea and violent retching as it moved out into the open water. Sanitary conditions on board worsened, and after eleven more days at sea, the coast of Burma was a welcome sight for all—war or no war.

Once the ship was anchored in the great harbor at Rangoon, Colonel Withering climbed to the quarterdeck to address the assembled officers. "You will report for duty at headquarters, which is in the large warehouse near the wharf. There you will receive your written orders. Each of you will be responsible to secure your own housing. The Burmese here in Rangoon are peaceful and far-enough removed from their king to pay him little heed. You are required to appear at the quartermaster's office once each week to receive your pay and any changes in your written orders. Should you be ordered to a new posting, your mail will be delivered there. While you are in the field, your pay and correspondence will be held for you until you return and collect them."

***

It was mid-October and the herb garden was flourishing when Matthew's first letter arrived. It had been carried by one of the naval ships and delivered by a young naval cadet. When Jai brought it to Sarah, she stood speechless for a few seconds before she instructed him, "Gather the children. They will want to hear everything their father has written. I won't open it until they are in the sitting room with me."

The children gathered around her wingback chair, impatient for her to break the wax seal on the envelope. After spreading the letter on her lap to smooth the creases, she noted the date of September 15, 1852, in one corner.

She read:

Dearest Sarah and lads,

It is with great pleasure that I write to tell you that the ship arrived here in Rangoon on August 17, and I have been ordered into service with the ordnance park of the Burma Field Force and detached for duty with the Pegue Division of the army. I do not know when I will be ordered into the field, but I urge you to acquire another world atlas (as I took ours with me) so you may show the children where I will most likely be serving. I do not see that our efforts to subjugate this country have any moral basis other than the principle that might makes right, but I shall do my duty.

I took up my quarters in an old pongee house where a Buddhist priest lived at one time. It is near the great Shwe Dagon Pagoda, which sits on a hill in the middle of Rangoon. Other officers that initially shared my dwelling include T. Lisby, I. Hume, E. Forsyth, T. White, and I. McDonald, who were fellow passengers on the ship and belong to the same ordnance department as myself. I believe you may have met some of them there at Fort William on some occasion in the past. We shared quarters only briefly, as three of them embarked as ordered for assignment at Prome, which is more than two hundred miles north of Rangoon. In the meantime, Brother William Adams and I have moved into a smaller pongee house that better suits our needs. Because it is the rainy season here just as it is in Calcutta, we travel almost entirely by boat, which we can hire inexpensively.

The Burmese are of a cheerful, happy disposition, faithful and affectionate in their family circles, devoted in their religion, and willing to make any sacrifice in order to make a valuable offering to their gods made of gold, silver, wood, or stone. They are always glad to earn a little money if the task is not too great.

Rangoon is a city primarily of bamboo buildings, including my little pongee house, with floors lifted four feet off the ground to withstand the seasonal floods of the great Irrawaddy River. The roofs are of thatched grass and long palm leaves.

As I have been invested with the authority to plant the gospel standard here and to build up the Church wherever my duties with the army might lead me, I have located an available place where I can preach. I sent around a circular to the British portion of the army that lay near me, inviting their attendance. I obtained permission to use a portion of the Shwe Dagon Pagoda, where I promised any who attended a lecture by a Mormon elder. A number came, and I delivered a sermon telling them of the kingdom of God and of the work of the Prophet Joseph Smith. I informed them of his calling and invited them to repent and be baptized for the remission of sins. Shortly thereafter, I obtained another larger, empty pongee house and, for a time, had crowded audiences with a number of baptisms. The work is going forth.

My thoughts are always of home, but I trust that a loving God will protect you and the children while I cannot. You will find my mailing address as a postscript. Please write to me in return so that I may be confident in your well-being.

Your husband and father in the gospel of Christ,
Matthew McCune

As Sarah closed her eyes and smiled in relief, Harry asked, "Mother, if I write to him, will you include my letter with yours?"

"Of course, Harry. Your father would be pleased to receive a letter from you."

"And tell Father I can do my sums," Georgie added.

Alfred added, "Tell him I'm going to catch some pigeons so they can carry messages to him."

Smiling, she promised, "I will tell Father everything of importance to each of you, you may be assured of that."

That evening after dinner, Sarah sat at the writing desk in the study and took up the pen.

October 20, 1852

Dear Matthew,

The lads and I received with great pleasure your letter of September 15, which arrived today. Knowing that you are safe has lifted a great burden from my heart. The lads and I are very pleased to know of your activities. We pray every night for your protection and well-being.

A few weeks after you sailed for Burma, Harry read in the English newspaper that thirteen missionaries from Utah had arrived at the Sandheads to preach in India. That gave us sufficient time to prepare to meet them at the river landing as Harry was the only male representative of the Church in Calcutta at the time. We located several additional carriages to add to our own, and taking our male servants, Harry arrived in time to see the ship arriving in tow of a tug. He engaged four longboats and went on board as soon as the ship dropped anchor, and was welcomed by the elders. One of them, Chauncey W. West, embraced him and announced, "Brethren, this is the little man I saw in my vision last night."

They asked why he had brought so many servants. They all laughed heartily when he explained that they would carry the luggage of the elders. They were quite prepared to carry their own. He brought them to our home, where we gave them a hearty welcome. Each was given a room, and I appointed several servants to wait on them. They stayed for nearly a week, until they determined their various fields of service. I fear that the climate does not agree with many of them.

Your eldest son has supervised the planting of an herb garden, so we will be better prepared to deal with illness in the family should it arise. He is a continuing blessing to me.

Mary Anne Meik has been extremely anxious because of Patrick's absence, so much so that she has been nearly prostrate for several days. Harry and I brewed a tea for her from the leaves of the lemon balm in the garden, and it gave her much relief, and she reportedly slept well for the first time in many nights.

Georgie wants you to know that he is progressing in his schooling and is improving in his sums. Alfred Wm. hopes to catch some pigeons so he can send messages to you. Edward is now one year and is walking and daily grows more sure of his step. We all miss you greatly and hope this missive reaches you swiftly.

Your loving wife,
Sarah Elizabeth Caroline McCune

Harry's letter was folded with his mother's before it was posted.

Dear Father,
With the help of Jai and Deleep, the household continues to run well, even though your presence is greatly missed. I have studied your notes on herbs and illness and, using them as a guide, have overseen the planting of an herb garden so we will be better prepared should illness arise. I have planted basil, salvia, thyme, lemon balm, valerian, and many other useful herbs. Thirteen missionaries arrived from England some weeks ago. We were able to greet them and offer room and board while they determined their areas of service. Mother read your letter to us, and we are very pleased that the preaching of the gospel goes well in that foreign land. You are always in our prayers.

Respectfully,
Your loving son, Henry Frederick

***

With his mother's blessing, Harry visited the Meik family at least three times a week. "Is there anything I can do to be of help in any way?" he always asked Mary Anne Meik.

Her answer was always the same. "No, but I thank you for your concern in the matter. Jamal is of great support to me and the children at the present."

Needed or not, as long as Annie managed to find the time to leave her studies and join him for at least fifteen or twenty minutes each time he visited, he was determined to continue to offer his services. Though they spoke of fathers who were faraway and the challenges that came with that situation, the real words between them were spoken with their eyes.

***.

Matthew's next letter arrived in late January. Again, the children gathered in the sitting room to hear their mother read.

December 15, 1852

Dearest Sarah and sons,

I received your letter with the greatest pleasure. To hear that you and the lads are doing well was as refreshing as a drink of cold water after a ten-hour march in the heat. As we face the turning of the year, I have not yet been ordered into the field, so my preaching has continued. I have recently baptized eight fine men including John Charles, a bombardier in the Madras Horse Artillery and a native of Yorkshire, England. Patrick and I also baptized Alexander Graham Young, an American from the state of Pennsylvania, city of Philadelphia. He is presently a gunner in the Madras Horse Artillery. He is a young man of superior education, a man of the kind I would have wanted to see our little Agnes marry had she lived. Also baptized George M. Carter, late of the Isle of Wight, a well-educated young lieutenant of the First Madras European Fusiliers, and several others, all men I hope to see grow to become faithful leaders in the Church. There are many others who are convinced of the truth of the gospel message but have not the courage to take up the cross. It is with the Saints of Latter-days even as it was with the ancient Saints—they are every where evil spoken of.

I am learning the Burmese language and hope to master it. At present I must limit my preaching to the Europeans and others who understand English until I have overcome the language, but we hold lectures at my dwelling twice a week, Thursday and Sunday nights.

Please remember me and all the good members of the Church here in Burma in your prayers.

Your loving husband and father in the gospel of Christ,
Matthew McCune

That evening Sarah sat in the study with pen in hand to respond to her husband's letter.

January 29, 1853

Dearest Matthew,

Your letter of December 15 arrived today. The children and I eagerly await your letters, and I reread them many times. The children are doing well. Georgie reached his sixth birthday two days after Christmas. Harry is progressing well in his studies. The weather is pleasant, and the herb garden is flourishing, even though it must be watered by hand in this dry season. I am most happy to report that the cause of Mary Anne Meik's anxiety has been relieved as Patrick arrived here in Calcutta immediately after the turning of the year, having been sent home to supervise the operations of the warehouses. It is anticipated that his presence will improve her health. Her next infant is due very soon.

I have learned that the Reverends Kinkade and Vinton have followed the troops to Rangoon. It has come back to me that the Reverend Kinkade plans to preach against the Mormons there. I hope he doesn't add to your burdens.

We are well and urge you not to concern yourself with our welfare as you have many more urgent matters with which to deal. We pray that this new year will bring an end to the conflict in Burma and you will then be able to rejoin us. We each send our love.

Your loving wife,
Sarah Elizabeth Caroline McCune

Harry added a postscript with his mother's permission.

PS. Father, as you are laboring to learn the Burmese language, I have determined to apply myself to improving my penmanship in the writing of Hindustani. My geometry is very good. I am applying myself with greater energy to Greek and Latin, and I am studying Shakespeare's Henry VI. *We look forward to your return home.*

Respectfully,
Henry Frederick

***

Matthew's third letter dated February 27, 1853, arrived at the beginning of April, as the returning monsoon rains and heat were becoming oppressive.

My dearest Sarah and lads,
The turning of the year has brought many changes. On January 3, I was ordered to take charge of the ordnance and to accompany a column under General Steele, whose duty it is to go against the Burmese troops at Martaban, Billing, Sittang, Shoewaygheen, and Tonghoo, all strongholds of the enemy. We embarked at Rangoon on the ship General Goodwin *for Martaban. Elder Peter Gibson and Brother John Saunders also accompanied the force in another vessel. We arrived off Martaban on January 8 after some trouble with the steamer tug that was to tow us into port. I was immediately made busy landing the ordnance and stores. I pitched my tent by the riverside and set to getting the guns and carriages mounted and then formed a munitions park. When my tasks were completed, I sent a circular around the camp announcing the preaching by a Mormon elder at my tent every Wednesday and Sunday when not engaged with the enemy.*

I had goodly attendance for some time and baptized three on the march, but the hatred manifested toward my message is constant. Our meetings are interrupted, the tent ropes cut frequently, the throwing of stones common.

I visited the town of Moulmain and saw the white pagoda, made a few purchases—small items for each family member. On January 16, the troops marched to the village of Feouk Deoney, where Burmese troops attacked us. We returned fire with interest, hitting and killing many of them, but as it is not my intention to describe the carnage amongst the poor Burmese committed by our troops, I will say little more of the matter.

Very nearly every evening after the sun sets, we have moved camp, marching as few as seven miles and as many as fourteen. Some of the men complain of the burden of transporting the heavy cannons and other artillery when they think the officers do not hear them. As usual, when not engaged with the enemy, I and Brothers Gibson and Saunders have preached at my tent.

On January 28, we had to cross the Sittang River, fording it at low water and bringing the ammunition over on elephants. We encamped outside the stockade at Belling, a beautiful country with delightful scenery. Like all Burmese towns, the houses are built mostly of wood upon bamboo poles. I believe that these native people need only the gospel with the cultivation and knowledge that follow its reception to make them a noble people.

Our march to camp at Loungayat lay over mountains covered with jungle and so steep that the ascent required that the guns and wagons be pushed up with elephants and let down the descent with drag ropes. We would not have admitted it aloud, but that day we were all very weary.

I try to remain positive, but many of our marches are conducted in the stifling, hot, humid air, trapped beneath the foliage of the trees where the mosquitoes come in thick clouds, making it difficult to breathe and getting into our ears, noses, and mouths. The sepoys coat themselves with mud, but little helps until we are lucky enough to reach the crest of a hill high enough that the wind blows the troublesome insects away. For days thereafter, faces are lumpy and swollen, and the monkeys in the trees that seem to be immune to their bites chatter and tease us from their places in the leafy canopy overhead.

Do not worry about me. As long as I am in your prayers, I know the Lord is in control. I will send this letter back to Rangoon with the messenger who carries the military dispatches and pray that it reaches you swiftly. Give my love to the lads.

Your faithful husband and father in the gospel,
Matthew McCune

Sarah shared the letter with the children, and that evening after they were in bed, she penned her reply.

April 3, 1853

Dear Matthew,
Your letter of February 27 arrived today. Each letter weighs very little but lifts a heavy burden from my heart and offers reassurance that you are alive and well.

The missionaries Harry met at the river some months ago have found the climate more of a challenge than some were prepared to embrace. Over half of them have returned to England to seek another field of labor or are on their way back to the Salt Lake Valley. We were so hopeful that the work here was going to go forth with vigor, but we must have confidence that all will happen in accordance with the Lord's will. Harry strives to be the man of the house and sets a good example for his younger brothers. The children are growing strong and tall, but every night Georgie and Alfred Wm. ask when you will be coming home. I remind them that patience is a virtue each of us must cultivate.

We eagerly await your next letter.

Your loving wife,
Sarah Elizabeth Caroline McCune

Again, Harry added a postscript to his mother's letter.

Father,
When Alfred Wm. fell and scraped his knees, we made a poultice of basil leaves and St. John's Wort, and the injuries healed swiftly without infection. Your herbal directory has proven of great value. I hope to learn much more about the use of herbs in homeopathic medicine.

Harry

CHAPTER EIGHT

April 1853
Calcutta

WITHIN A FEW WEEKS OF the arrival of the monsoon rains, Jai approached Sarah as she and the children were finishing their breakfast.

After offering a deep bow, he spoke. "Memsahib, I have a great need to assist my family. My mother's village has been swept away by the rising waters of the monsoon. She needs me to find her another home on higher ground. I must beg your forgiveness and ask that you permit me to leave to help her."

Sarah looked at Harry. "Harry, do you believe we can do without Jai for a week?" She knew she could not refuse but wanted Harry to feel he had been part of the decision.

"I believe we can manage without Jai for a few days. We still have Deleep and Gupta to depend upon."

Sarah smiled at the man. "You may take your leave, Jai. I will depend upon Harry in your absence."

Jai smiled and bent low in gratitude. Within the hour, he was gone.

At dinner that evening, Harry seemed especially quiet. His mother noticed. "Harry, why are you so quiet?"

"I was wondering what Father would think about Jai leaving us at this time."

"I would hope he would be sympathetic, but it doesn't need to be mentioned to him. It might cause him unnecessary worry. You and I will take care of everything until he returns, won't we." It wasn't a question.

"Yes, we will, Mother."

Jai returned in two weeks. Despite his absence, Sarah did not lessen his pay for the month, knowing that much of what he earned was sent to his extremely needy mother.

***

Matthew's next letter arrived on May 30, one day before Harry's thirteenth birthday. All the children gathered to hear Sarah read it, and upon their insistence, she reread it.

April 22, 1853

My dearest Sarah and lads,

Though we have seen much fighting, it is not my intention to describe the carnage thrust upon the poor Burmese by our troops and weapons but to confine myself with the success of my efforts in spreading the gospel in this land. However, I must let you know that our friend Mr. Lisby, who was assigned to oversee the Congreve rockets, was injured some days ago and died of his wounds. Should you be able to locate his wife and children, please extend our condolences to them. I firmly believe he stands before the judgment bar of God in good condition. I pray to that effect.

The column under General Steele camped at Showaygheen on the eleventh of this month, and we have remained at that camp, but it is rumored we will take up the march again very soon. I located a pongee house for preaching and sent around a circular to announce my intention to preach Sundays and Wednesdays. While I preached on Sunday, a mob gathered with the intention of setting fire to the place, but the Lord put the hook into their jaws like a caught fish, and they went off after some time without making the attempt, and the meeting proceeded to a close without any further disturbance. It has become evident that the authorities of the army are as adverse to Mormonism as the common soldiers but are more careful in manifesting their opposition. They hit on the plan of warning me to turn out when they claimed the pongee house for the government, as they required the timber of the building. Accordingly, I moved out and took possession of another pongee house, but the authorities soon found they required it also. Consequently, I was again officially warned to turn out.

My preaching was also stopped after I had taken possession of a Buddhist image house. It was not long before the authorities determined that they needed to enclose a powder magazine and would be putting a wall through the back of the building. I turned out, and the building was unroofed sufficiently to render it uninhabitable and then left off. Opposition grows, but the work moves forward.

Harry may see his thirteenth birthday by the time you receive this letter. Tell him to continue to be an upright, obedient, and trustworthy lad. I ask that you keep me in your prayers.

Your husband and father in the gospel of Christ,
Matthew McCune

Postscript: I was glad to learn from your most recent letter that Patrick Meik was ordered back to Calcutta in early January. That will give his family comfort and will be a blessing to the Church, as I am sure that leadership there is lacking with so many men still here in Burma.

The next morning Sarah wrote a response she tried to fill with cheerful news to cover her loneliness.

May 31, 1853

Dearest Matthew,

Your letter of April 22 arrived yesterday. Today is Harry's birthday, and he was pleased to be wished a happy birthday by his father. Mrs. Senior, the children's tutor, reports that Harry, in particular, as well as George and Alfred Wm. are progressing nicely in their studies. Alfred Wm. wanted me to tell you that he can count to one hundred and is beginning to do his sums.

Some of the female members of the Church have begun meeting in our sitting room on Sunday afternoons. We may lack male leadership (Patrick being the exception), but we have determined that we will apply ourselves to the study of the scriptures. Surely the Holy Spirit will work with us in a manner similar to that in which male priesthood holders are inspired.

We pray for your well-being and miss you greatly. We all continue well and look for the day we will be reunited.

Your loving wife,
Sarah Elizabeth Caroline McCune

Harry wrote his own letter and had his mother fold it into hers.

Dear Father,

It saddens me to learn of the persecutions you are suffering at the hands of lesser men—and they are lesser, regardless of their rank. Surely the messengers of truth have suffered at the hands of evil or foolish men since time began. I and my brothers are made better by your example. Now that I am thirteen, my plan to enlist in the naval cadets grows firmer.

Your respectful and loving son,
Harry

***

Matthew's next letter arrived mid-September, just after little Edward's second birthday.

August 8, 1853

    My dearest Sarah and lads,

    It has been a year since I arrived here in Burma, and needless to say, it has been difficult to be separated from my family for that amount of time, but duty requires that we must do what must be done. It is important that our lads understand that we pay a personal price for everything we give or receive in this world. We must always be sure we are prepared to pay the price required.

    Much has happened since my last letter. It has been difficult to write while we have been in the field engaging the Burmese. We left camp at Showaygheen on April 24 and continued our nightly marches on a fairly regular basis. The evening of April 25 we marched eighteen miles. We camped in the morning at Pegue, which had been our ultimate destination from the time we left Rangoon. It is an ancient city encircled by an immense wall but amounts to little more than a few streets of huts and a few pagodas, around the largest of which the troops are encamped. A fine river runs through the town, and the country around it is beautiful, more beautiful than anything I have seen in India.

    On April 28, General Steele announced that the column would return to Rangoon, as the territory we had covered had been secured on behalf of Her Majesty, which was our goal. He determined that the wagons, etc., should go by land, while the troops should go by water, and I being the only British officer going with the wagon train should have charge of the whole. The wagons and carts had to be pushed through the mud at the banks of the Pegue River by the elephants. The bullocks had to be dragged by men and ropes over and through the mud. The escort of fifty sepoys of the Tenth Bengal Infantry accompanied me and furnished the manpower for the task.

    There is a great probability that the king of this nation will not be satisfied with our government's allotment of a large portion of his kingdom to themselves, in which case we shall have to go on to his capital of Ava, and I suppose take the other half of his dominions from him; but if so ordered in the providence of our Father, it will be to the destroying of the abodes of cruelty and slavery and the opening up of the whole country for the introduction of the more enlightened principles of the gospel of Jesus Christ and to the blessing of the honest in heart in these latter days.

    On the first of May, we marched seventeen miles, had to cross another river, and were obliged to unload all carts, having everything carried over by the men. We also had to cut a road up the very steep bank of the river, and the wagons and carts had to be pulled up with drag ropes in addition to the bullocks. Halted after getting across. The next day or, more properly, the next night, we marched another seventeen miles, the guides having led us astray the previous night. I was obliged to throw two marches into one to avoid a scanty and bad supply of water. We reached our camping ground just before 9:00 a.m. The following evening we marched eleven miles and reached Rangoon at 8:00 a.m. after having begun our march at midnight. I took up my quarters in the house I occupied with Brother Adams before leaving four months ago to the very day.

This little pongee house is not really home, nor will it ever be, but it was very good to finally get back to it. At that time I learned that I had been promoted to officiating subconductor of ordnance, which has increased my responsibilities and pay.

I have been thinking of our future and have come to the decision that we should make plans to leave Asia and make our way to New York in America and from there to the Great Salt Lake Valley. I have corresponded with Bro. Musser, and he leads me to believe that he and his family will be joining several others, hopefully including the Meik family, to eventually make the journey to Zion. I believe that our future lies with the Saints there.

Sarah paused for a moment, as still as a statue, while she tried to grasp the enormity of what her husband had just stated.

"Mother, keep reading," Georgie urged.

She swallowed and continued.

Emigrating to America will take much preparation, but I am settled on the decision. We must walk by faith in all we do. I am sure the Lord directs the winds that blow into our lives. I have little else to tell you other than my testimony is firm, and I hope yours is as well.

Your loving husband in the gospel,
Matthew McCune

Postscript: Please wish Alfred Wm. happy birthday from me. He will have had his fourth birthday by now. Tell him Father expects him to grow into a fine lad.

When Sarah finished reading, Harry looked directly at his mother and asked, "Do you want to go to America to join the Saints?"

Putting off answering him in a manner that would reveal her true feelings, she simply said, "I don't know, Harry." Her voice was a whisper. "I must give the matter much thought."

"I think it would be exciting," he responded, but he noticed that his mother's hands were clasped tightly, so much so that they were white-knuckled.

Georgie chimed in. "Me too."

He was echoed by Alfred, who added, "Me too," not really having any idea what he was agreeing to.

After the children were in bed that evening, Sarah sent Sonja downstairs to the servants' quarters. "I will prepare for bed by myself. I need some time alone—to think."

She paced in the study for an hour. *Why does he feel we should travel halfway around the world without discussing the matter with me?* She abruptly sat down at the writing desk. *I do not intend to allow him to drag my children to the other side of the world. I will not endanger them on this whim of Matthew's. I have lost four and do not intend to lose any more.* She hurriedly located a piece of stationery. Her hand shaking with the intensity of her feelings, she picked up the quill pen and began to write.

Dear Matthew,
Surely you know that I have always tried to be a good wife, even leaving my native land without complaint to sail to a foreign place when you enlisted in the Bengal army. Through the hardships of adjusting to life here in India, including the difficulties of learning Hindustani so I could train the servants, I have tried to gracefully bear the challenges of life, but now you tell me that we must leave the familiar—leave the graves of my four children—and travel halfway around the world because you have decided we must. Matthew, it is too much! It is too much! I refuse to consider . . .

She stopped and put down the pen and leaned her head on her hand. After a few moments, she closed the inkwell, and then, as if suddenly animated by frustration, tore the letter into strips and crumpled them into a ball before throwing it across the room. She rose and hurried to her bedroom, where she dropped facedown on the bed. *The letter must wait until I am much calmer.*

***

In the morning at breakfast, Harry asked, "May I put my letter in with yours, Mother, before it is posted?"

"Yes, of course, when it is written," she said curtly. He had seldom heard her use such a terse tone of voice.

He sat quietly for a few moments before he asked, "Are you troubled about Father's . . . about Father's urging that we leave India and move to America to be with the other members of the Church?"

His perceptive question made the stiffness in her body begin to ease. She gave him a little smile and nodded. "Yes, Harry, I am greatly concerned by his request. How can I face such a journey when it might cost me more of my children?" It was not a question she expected him to answer, nor would she discuss the matter further.

***

Several days passed before she felt better prepared to sit down and write a carefully worded letter. She did not dare to let Matthew know of the intensity of her feelings in the matter. To do so would be to admit that she was less than the good British wife she tried every day to be.

September 21, 1853

> *Dear Matthew,*
>
> *We have received your letter dated August 8. Your statement that we make plans to leave India and emigrate to America to join the Saints in the Great Salt Lake Valley is overwhelming. My thoughts are filled with fearful alarm at the prospect of taking the children on a long voyage across the Atlantic to face a new life in a new world. Many disasters could befall our ship. I could not face the loss of another child.*

She underlined the last sentence.

> *Please do not think me a coward or weakling for being opposed to your proposal. The prospect fills me with trepidation. So much that is unforeseeable could happen if we were to make such a journey. I am opposed to it.*

After a few moments, she continued.

> *Harry has been my greatest blessing during these months of separation. He tries consistently to be the man of the house. I think I would have been as badly off as Mary Anne without him. The children continue well, and Mary Anne grows stronger now that she has Patrick at her side. Patrick gave us a copy of printed material that was sent from the Church leaders in England. One is a booklet entitled* Divine Authenticity of the Book of Mormon *by Elder Orson Pratt. It is a scholarly work which Harry and I have been reading each evening. Patrick promised to send copies of it to you in addition to copies of the* Millennial Star *for your work there.*
>
> *I grow weary of this separation, as I'm sure you do as well. May it end soon.*
>
> *Your wife,*
> *Sarah Elizabeth Caroline McCune*

She left her letter on the sideboard in the sitting room where Deleep would see that it was posted. Harry had written his the day after his father's had arrived.

> *Dear Father,*
> *Your letter has given us much to think about. Your statement that you want us to emigrate to America so we could join the Saints in the Salt Lake Valley has . . .*

He had paused at that point for nearly a full minute as he chose his words. He finally added,

. . . troubled Mother greatly. She is afraid of losing another family member and that such a journey might cause such a loss. I do not know how to comfort her. I believe she will need to think on the matter for some time before she will be able to face such a decision. I hope there is ample time for her to consider it fully.

Respectfully,
Your loving son,
Harry

He inserted his letter inside of hers, warmed the wax with a candle flame, and resealed it. He would rather his mother not know what he had written.

***

The next letter arrived on December 27. Sarah opened it with care as the children gathered around her. She literally held her breath. *Will he tell us again that he wants us to go to America?*
She read:

November 20, 1853

My Dearest Sarah and lads,
Elders Elam Ludington and Levi Savage arrived at Rangoon on the steamer Fire Queen *on August 10, having come from Utah via England and India. They will provide official leadership to the Church members here. With them, we held our first sacramental meeting since my return from the field. A few days later, the two of them made application to Major General Steele for permission to preach to the Europeans in one of the empty barracks but were refused. They were decidedly disappointed, but I was not surprised, having experienced much hostility in my efforts to spread the gospel. In the face of continuing opposition, we have baptized six more men.*

November 21

I had insufficient time to finish this letter yesterday and I am glad as now I will share the important news I received this morning. The conflict with the Burmese has lessened, and the queen's troops aided by the Bengal and Madras armies have subdued western Burma sufficiently that we have been notified that we may bring over our families from Calcutta. Please make plans to join me here in Rangoon early in January. I suggest you turn the house over to Patrick and Mary Anne, leaving the furnishings for them as they were left for us by the previous occupants. It is a much larger residence than the one they presently rent. You will need to explain to the children that they may only take their personal belongings and that you will be forced to leave the servants behind. I know Patrick has always liked Jai and Deleep, and I am hopeful he will be willing to add them to his household. Harry will regret leaving Gupta behind. Perhaps Patrick and Mary Anne will find a good place for him with a family as large as theirs. We will be forced to hire new servants here in Rangoon, but there is an abundance of willing helpers here.

I urge you to apply for space on the first steamer scheduled to leave Calcutta for Rangoon in January and immediately send me a letter telling me of your anticipated arrival time. I will meet you at the dock with a carriage. We will have been separated for a year and a half, and I fear that the younger lads, Alfred Wm. and Edward, may not remember me, but I look forward to getting reacquainted with them and seeing how much Harry and Georgie have grown. I await your letter telling me when I will next see you and the children.

> *Your loving husband in the gospel,*
> *Matthew McCune*

When Sarah finished reading the letter, relief surged over her like a warm tide.

He made no mention of emigrating to America! The journey to Rangoon is a voyage of less than ten days. We will deal with that. When we are reunited as a family, surely he will give up this idea of traveling halfway around the world to America.

She firmly pushed her worries about Matthew's plans to emigrate from her mind.

The three youngest boys danced around the room with excitement. Edward joined in his brothers' excitement without fully understanding the reason. Harry insisted that she read the letter again. When she did, she noted the look of concern on his face.

"Harry, what has you so worried? You don't appear to be as excited as your younger brothers about seeing your father again."

"Are you sure we can't take Gupta with us, Mother?"

"I am sure the servants must be left here as we cannot expect them to leave their own extended family members. I'm sure the Burmese will expect us to hire servants from among their people who can speak their language."

The task of moving the family to a strange land in such a short time and leaving behind all that was familiar, including the well-trained servants and friends such as the Meiks, left her emotions churning, but her relief outweighed her concerns.

Sarah leaned back and closed her eyes. Harry moved closer to her and took her hand.

Though Harry was disappointed at the thought of being so far from Annie, he understood his role as his mother's support. "Mother, I know this move will require much planning. Let me help. I will tell the servants to have breakfast ready at seven in the morning so Jai can take us to the wharf, where we can make arrangements for the boat passage."

She opened her eyes and patted his hand. "You are a blessing to me, Harry, and you are the son your father wants you to be. Will you also write a brief note to Patrick and Mary Anne Meik and ask them to dinner tomorrow evening so we can discuss the matter? They are welcome to bring Annie if they would like."

"Of course, Mother. Should I mention our plans to join Father?"

She nodded, leaned back, and closed her eyes again as Harry hurried from the room. While she sat quietly, trying to think of the many things that would need to be done, Endira came into the room and swept up Edward in one arm while she took Alfred's hand. They were led off to be readied for bed, objecting at being taken away from the fun.

Georgie approached Sarah and asked, "Mother, are you happy we are going to see Father?"

"Yes, Georgie, very much. I'm just thinking of everything we need to do before we go," she whispered as she kissed him on the forehead. "Now, be a good lad and run along to bed."

Harry was gone for a half hour. Sarah had begun to wonder where he was when he returned to the sitting room short of breath. "I've written the letter and given it to Deleep to deliver to the Meiks. I've told the servants to have breakfast for you and me ready at seven, and Jai will have the tanga waiting at eight. Can I do anything else for you this evening?"

"Before you go to sleep, will you make a list of anything you can think of that must be done before we leave? I will do the same. Then we can talk about it in the morning." She rose and kissed him on the forehead. "I'm going to go to bed now. I think we will all need our sleep."

After she climbed into bed, Sarah watched the moon cast shadow patterns through the lattice shutters onto the bed coverlet. As tired as she was, sleep didn't come for a long time.

Harry retired to bed with a confusion of feelings. He had waited to see his father for a year and a half, but now he had to face the prospect of many miles between himself and Annie—and of letting go of his servant, Gupta.

CHAPTER NINE

IN THE MORNING, JAI WAS waiting when breakfast was finished, and Sarah and her eldest son rode together to the wharf, where she booked passage for herself and the four children on the steamer *Fire Queen*, which was scheduled to depart for Rangoon on January 3. She also posted a letter written earlier that morning after she added the date the steamer was scheduled to arrive in Rangoon. Harry also posted a separate letter to his father. They would both be carried by the military supply ship leaving Calcutta the following day.

In his letter, Harry wrote:

Dear Father,

Mother has moved swiftly to take the necessary actions to make it possible for us to be reunited in Rangoon as soon as possible. She looks to this voyage with less reluctance than she feels toward your request that she consider emigrating to America to join the Saints in the Salt Lake Valley. She feels that the journey would put family members in peril, whereas the move to Rangoon is briefer and less threatening in her eyes. I know she is looking forward to being reunited as a family once more, as am I. Seeing you again is all the little lads can speak of.

Your loving son,
Harry

When they returned to the house, Sarah had Harry call the servants together so she could announce that she and the children would be leaving Calcutta in six days. A somber mood filled the house. Endira and Sonja wiped away tears.

The day was spent with Sarah moving from one child's room to the next, selecting the items and clothing to be packed as soon as the steamer trunks were brought from the carriage house.

"Georgie, you must choose the things you most want to take with you. Any clothing or toys you have outgrown should be given to one of the servants for their family."

He was perplexed. "Why can't we take everything, Mother?"

"Georgie, there will not be enough room in the trunks."

Harry had several items he offered to Gupta, which were gratefully received. Gupta had no wife or children, but he had many nephews. Georgie followed his brother's example and offered his outgrown belongings to Deleep for his children or nephews.

Harry stepped into Alfred's room and noted that his four-year-old brother had everything he owned in the pile he called the "take-with-me" pile.

Harry picked up a shirt that was obviously too small for his brother and with disapproval in is voice stated, "A. W., Mother told us that we can't take everything with us. Some of these clothes are much too small for you. Sonja has a little boy who could wear them."

"No, they're mine," Alfred William insisted as he pulled it out of his older brother's hand.

"You don't want Mother to feel sad because you won't share, do you?"

The child stood still for a moment and then asked, "Would she really be sad if I take it with me?"

"Yes, A. W."

With some hesitation, he handed the little shirt to his brother. Seeing a softening of his brother's defiance, Harry continued, "You can give it to Sonja along with the other toys you don't play with anymore."

"I'll give it to Sonja." He was crestfallen but cooperative.

Harry ruffled his younger brother's hair. "Thanks, A. W. You're a good lad. Father will be proud of you." The boy brightened.

***

That evening, Sarah and Harry greeted Patrick, Mary Anne, and Annie at the drawing room door. The younger children had been left with their nannies. The three younger McCune children would eat in the schoolroom under the supervision of Endira.

The meal conversation was filled with questions about James's naval cadet experiences, which Harry followed closely. It wasn't until the dessert was served that, in faithful British tradition, Sarah brought up the matter that concerned them all.

"In our invitation for dinner, I believe Harry mentioned that the lads and I will be leaving to join Matthew in Rangoon in less than a week. The steamer is scheduled to leave on January 3. Matthew has suggested that I offer the house and furnishings to you. If we simply allow the company to reclaim it, it might be rented to an officer with no family, and all of these rooms would be poorly used. With a family as large as yours, it would be a blessing to you." She paused. "But I have one request. Should you choose to move into the house, you take as many of our servants as possible." She gave them a moment to consider her suggestion. "How do you feel about the matter? Do you need time to discuss it?"

Patrick cleared his throat. "We deeply appreciate your offer. We fully understand your desire to be reunited with Matthew. Your separation has been difficult, I'm sure. We will discuss which servants we could use and let you know, but we will tell you right now that we will take your offer of the house. We need a larger home, and your offer is very timely."

Mary Anne pulled a handkerchief from the soft woven bag in her lap and wiped a few tears away. "Sarah, we will miss you and your family more than you can imagine."

Patrick patted his wife's hand. "But, surely, Sarah, you will all return soon and our friendship will be renewed at that time. Hopefully, the conflict in Burma will soon be ended. Let us look forward to your return."

Harry had been listening closely. He inhaled as if to strengthen his determination. "You will find a place for Gupta, won't you? And Jai and Deleep? I know they would serve you well." He waited for Patrick's response.

The expectant look on his face prompted Patrick to respond. "Harry, I'm sure we will be able to use them—and perhaps some of the others."

"I am desperate for a good cook, so I will be glad to have Leela," Mary Anne added. "And I can assure you that we will use Endira, and perhaps Sonja. A new baby has increased the need for house help."

"You can put your mind at rest." Patrick took his wife's hand in his.

At that, Harry leaned back, relieved that his personal servant and friend would have a place with the Meik family.

After the meal, the little group moved into the sitting room, where more details were discussed. Annie managed to find a place to sit on the settee next to Harry—but not too close—hoping her seat selection had not been noticed by her mother.

She spoke quietly. "Harry, I'm going to miss you very much—and your entire family," she added hurriedly. "There are so few young people our age in our Sunday meetings," she added weakly.

"I will miss you." The words were inadequate, but he knew social rules prohibited stronger ones. "But we can write to one another. Will you promise me you'll write?" It was a small consolation.

She beamed at him. "Of course I'll write. And you'll write to me." He nodded and smiled.

By the time the evening was over, Patrick had offered to keep the horses and the two carriages for the McCunes, with the understanding that the Meik family would be free to use them until Matthew and Sarah returned.

***

The remaining days passed swiftly. Bills were paid, and one trunk was packed specifically with clothing and bedding for the voyage as the other trunks would be stored in the hold of the steamship. As his final, self-appointed task, Harry cut the herbs in the garden, safely storing them in the small fabric bags he had asked Endira to make for that purpose. The plants would grow back for the use of the Meik family, but Harry and Sarah were pleased to take the herbal harvest with them on their journey.

Early on the morning of January 3, the many trunks were loaded into the Meik's two carriages, while Sarah and the children rode in the McCune tanga driven by Jai. Patrick, Mary Anne, and Annie rode in the carriage driven by Deleep. When they arrived at the landing, the trunks were loaded on the steamer.

"Mary Anne, Patrick," Sarah's voice caught briefly. "Thank you for your friendship. We will miss you and your family very much, but I am glad the two of you are united here in Calcutta. Please write to us."

"We will, my dear, we will," Mary Anne promised.

The women embraced while Harry and Annie shyly bid each other good-bye with renewed promises to write to one another.

Sarah lifted her head and, taking a big breath, led her children to the gangway of the *Fire Queen*. She was filled with anticipation at seeing Matthew but also regret that she was leaving dear friends and familiar surroundings. Stepping on deck, she turned and waved good-bye alongside her boys.

The Meik family returned the farewells and then climbed into the McCune carriages, where Mary Anne dabbed at her eyes. The horses were then turned to take the tangas and the Meik family to their new home.

Sarah turned her attention to the uniformed officer standing by the gangway.

"I am Mrs. McCune. Can you tell me where our stateroom is located?"

"Doon the stairs over there, ma'm. Mah records show that ye and yer bairns will be in stateroom C." His Scottish burr made Sarah smile as he touched his cap and turned to speak to another passenger.

When she pushed the door to the stateroom open, she stopped and stood without moving.

"Mother, is something wrong?" Harry asked from behind her where he stood with his younger brothers in the companionway.

"No, no, of course not. Everything is fine—it's just . . . smaller and more . . . rustic than I had expected."

The room was about ten feet square, with double wooden berths on each side. A skylight in the deck above allowed light in. Alfred looked at his mother and asked plaintively, "Where's my bed? Do we have to sleep on those wooden tables?"

Harry noted the strained look on his mother's face. It was early in the day, and she was already looking tired. He responded, "Mother has brought our blankets, and we will all get to sleep in the same room while the boat goes to Rangoon. This will be fun, A. W."

The boy didn't look convinced. A knock on the open stateroom door drew their attention. Two sailors in horizontal-striped shirts nodded and touched their caps.

"This be your trunk, ma'm?" She nodded. "Where do ye fancy we put it, ma'm?"

"Over there in the corner." Sarah pointed.

After the trunk was dropped and pushed into the corner at the foot of one set of berths, they touched their caps again and disappeared.

Alfred rushed to it and tried to lift the lid. "I want my blankie."

Harry stepped over and, after a few seconds, was able to open the two locks on the big trunk. He pulled out the child's blanket and handed it to him. "Now are you happy, A. W.?"

The child held the blanket against his cheek and grinned. "Yes, Harry."

The boat began to shudder, and they heard and felt a low rumble beneath their feet. Edward began to cry and reached toward his mother.

She picked him up. "Hush, hush, Edward," his mother whispered into his ear.

Harry explained to his brothers, "That's just the engine coming awake. Let's go up on the deck and watch as the ship moves out into the river." Managing an excited expression for their benefit, he added, "We're on our way to see Father."

Sarah followed the children as they hurried up the narrow companionway. As she held Edward, the five of them stood near the wheelhouse and watched the landing slip away as the large boat navigated its way into the main channel.

Harry almost found himself waving to the row of great stone lions. He would miss their familiarity.

Sarah's throat was tight. *The familiar is sliding away, and a new world awaits. What will it be like?*

CHAPTER TEN

FOR A FEW MINUTES, SARAH stood with at least a dozen other women and children, wrapped in her own thoughts as she held Edward, but rousing to her surroundings, she looked around, and a sudden panic tightened around her heart. "Harry, where are the little lads?"

He had been engrossed in watching the sights along the bank of the river as the ship passed, but the alarm in her voice grabbed his attention. "They can't have gone far, Mother. I'll find them. Just wait here so they can find you if they return."

Harry hurried away, stopping to speak to each crewman to ask if the children had been seen. Sarah stood at the railing, clinging to Edward as if to keep him from disappearing as the other children had.

Harry found George sitting in the wheelhouse in the captain's chair, watching as the captain stood near the pilot, who was directing the boat down the main channel between the markers. As he hurried in to lift his brother from the chair, the captain turned and laughed.

"Looks like you have a young seaman in the making there."

"My apologies, sir. We didn't know where he had gone. Mother will be very upset to learn he troubled you."

"No bother, laddie. He's no bother a'tall. Come back some time, and I'll show you a bit about the wheelhouse."

Harry took his brother by the hand and marched him back to Sarah. "I'll find A. W., Mother." He handed the child off to his mother and moved away again. He finally found Alfred sitting on a stool watching two large, muscled firemen soaked with perspiration as they shoveled coal into the great furnace in the bowels of the boat.

"A. W., what are you doing here?" Harry asked in complete exasperation. He was perspiring from his agitated search.

"Watchin'," the boy responded as he pointed to the big men. "The black man doesn't talk, but the other man talks to me."

"I'm so sorry that my brother has been bothering you," Harry apologized.

"But, Harry, I'm learnin' how to be a fireman on a boat." His tone was plaintive. He didn't want to be taken away.

"Ya, da boy is glad to see us work," the big blond Swede commented as he let another large shovelful of coal fly into the flames. The rhythm of the two men and their shovels was not altered by his conversation. "He has never seen da coal before, so he wanted to see how da black rocks burn in da fire."

As he lifted the boy from the stool, Harry apologized again. "I hope he won't bother you again. If he does, we are in stateroom C. Feel free to send him away."

"He be no trouble," the Swede responded as Harry pulled the reluctant child from the furnace room. When he and his unhappy little brother reached his white-faced mother, she was talking with the first officer of the boat. Harry heard him trying to soothe her feelings.

"The children be as safe on the boat as if they be in their mother's arms. Put yer mind ta rest, ma'm. We ain't never lost nobody overboard," he paused and added thoughtfully, "'cept there was that one man, but it were in a bad storm, and the gentleman 'ad been drinkin'." He brightened up and added, "If we 'it rough water, it be best if you keep the young 'uns in yer stateroom. Other times, the gun'els be high enough that they ain't likely to fall overboard."

The man tipped his hat and returned to his station when Sarah dropped to her knees and put her arms around the child. "You must never leave me like that again, Alfred. You frightened me. I thought you had fallen into the water and drowned."

The child screwed up his face in disgust at his mother's alarm. "All right, Mum, but the man told you I won't fall overboard. Don't worry 'bout me."

"A. W., don't call mother 'Mum.' You know father feels it is disrespectful." Alfred looked at his shoes at Harry's words.

Sarah interjected, "You must promise me you will always tell me where you are going while we are on the boat." The boy nodded dejectedly.

During the next ten days, George and Alfred William often forgot their mother's admonition as they investigated and explored every corner of the vessel. They watched the crew at their posts, and despite the anticipation of seeing their father once more, they began to regret the nearness of the end of the voyage.

***

The coast of Burma appeared like a low, long smudge on the eastern horizon. Passengers hurried to pack their trunks in anticipation of disembarking. It was late in the afternoon by the time the great bay at Rangoon welcomed the boat.

Sarah's heart beat so hard she could feel it pounding in her chest. *It has been such a long wait. Did he get my letter? Will he be there to meet us? Will the littlest two lads know him?* The questions tumbled about in her mind like a child's marbles spilled from a tipped jar.

As the ship neared the great wharf and the mass of humanity gathered there dissolved into individual figures, she studied each man in a red coat until her eyes found the familiar figure.

"There's your father, children. See, there he is. Wave to him," she called out excitedly.

Harry and George waved, recognizing Matthew. Alfred and Edward waved uncertainly in the general direction she had indicated but were not sure who it was they were waving at.

The passengers grew restless as they waited for the anchor to be lowered and the heavy hawsers to be tied to the pylons on the wharf. When the gangplank was lowered, the press of passengers excited to get off the boat was called to order by the captain's stentorian voice.

"Order! Please, order!" the captain bellowed. "Mothers, ye will keep yer children near at hand. Each family will be called to disembark in an orderly fashion. All trunks and other baggage will be unloaded from the hold as soon as possible."

Sarah was light-headed with anticipation. Each family was called alphabetically. When the captain reached the McCune family, Sarah took the two youngest children by the hand and instructed Harry and George, "You must stay right with me."

She had watched the other wives as they greeted their husbands. An American woman had thrown proper decorum to the wind and rushed into her husband's arms. An Irish woman had grabbed her husband and wept uncontrollably.

By the time Sarah had descended the gangplank and reached the wharf with the children in tow, Matthew had pushed through the crowd. Knowing that he would not approve of such emotional displays, she simply let go of the two younger children's hands and offered both of hers to him.

"Matthew, it is very good to see you," she said as if he had only been gone a day or two.

He took her hands and responded, "And it is good to see you—and the lads." He put one arm around her shoulders, pulling her close enough to give her a kiss on the forehead. He shook Harry's hand and stated firmly, "Harry, you are growing into a man. Your mother has told me in her letters that you have been her greatest help."

"I have tried, Father."

Matthew stooped a little and shook his second son's hand. "Georgie, you have grown so much that from now on you will be called George. You are too big to be called Georgie."

"Thank you, Father." The seven-year-old beamed.

Matthew turned to Alfred and shook his hand. "You are also growing up, Alfred William."

The five-year-old responded with pride, "Everyone calls me A. W. now." He really meant that Harry called him that, but he wanted everyone to do so.

Matthew smiled. "Then A. W. it is, or if I forget, then Alf it will be." He stooped to greet Edward at eye level, but the child tried to hide behind his mother's skirts.

Sarah took him by the shoulder and pushed him toward his father. "Edward, tell your father you are glad to see him," Sarah admonished.

The normally talkative child seemed to have been struck dumb. His father stood and lifted the two-and-a-half-year-old to his shoulders. "We'll get better acquainted now that we are all together." The child looked at his mother with wide, nervous eyes.

With Edward on his shoulders, Matthew led them through the crowd to the dusty road that ran alongside the wharf, where he had six rickshaws waiting. "We will need two of the rickshaws to carry the family, and the other four are for the trunks and baggage, which I hope are well marked."

"Yes, Matthew. There are eight large trunks, and I had Jai paint the McCune name on each so they are easily identified."

He helped his wife climb into the second of the two-wheeled carts and handed the three younger children up to her. She put Edward on her lap. There was just enough room for them on the single woven seat fixed upon two large bamboo wheels, which were bound with a metal rim and mounted on a bamboo axle. He had Harry climb into the first. "You will all wait here while I collect the trunks."

Harry stated, "Father, I can help with the trunks. I'm strong enough."

"Yes, son, but I have brought the rickshaw men for the task, and I will have to pay them whether or not I use them." He turned and looked at the boat. "It appears that the baggage and other freight is finally being unloaded." He signaled the six men standing near the waiting rickshaws to follow him. Within a half hour, they had located the trunks and the men had loaded them into the remaining four spindly looking vehicles. Matthew climbed into the first and sat next to Harry. He ordered the rickshaw driver to move out onto the road.

The man ducked between the two bars of the rickshaw and took hold of the crossbar that joined them. The muscles in his legs bulged as he leaned against the bar. The others followed, and soon, each vehicle had gained sufficient momentum to move fast enough along the dusty road to keep the man running. Sometimes an oxcart or a freight wagon would nearly block the road, but the rickshaw drivers wove their way between or around them with a deftness that stole Sarah's breath. The younger boys laughed and squealed with delight.

As they made their way through the city, Sarah couldn't help but note that the vast majority of buildings were built of bamboo and palm fronds. A few government buildings on the hillsides were built more sturdily of mud bricks or stone, and the governor's mansion was a large frame building, but the other structures sat high above the street level on bamboo stilts, apparently to survive the floodwaters brought by seasonal monsoons.

As Harry sat by his father, he stated in amazement, "Rangoon is nothing like Calcutta, is it, Father?"

"No, but I suspect that this is what Calcutta would look like if the British government had not made it the center of the Bengal Army 150 years ago."

For a mile around the bay, the town was divided into sections oriented toward the port. Near the dockside were the taverns and pubs that catered to the Europeans. Adjacent to them were the gaming houses, which were beginning to glow with the light of evening lamps. The sailmakers', ships' chandlers', and blacksmiths' shops were farther from the water. They would be closing as the daylight faded. And rising behind the port were gentle hills, where the town's quieter streets spread away from the brawling activity at the waterfront. Located in these quieter streets were the bakers, furniture workers, and goldsmiths. On the highest hill in the center of the town stood a glistening, gold-leafed, pointed pagoda that could be seen from any point in the city.

The incongruity of the building in a city of bamboo left Harry almost speechless. "Father, what is that great gold building with the spire?"

"That, Harry, is the great Shwe Dagon Pagoda I think I mentioned in one of my letters. I lived near it for some time after my arrival here."

When the first rickshaw stopped on the rutted dirt road, Matthew leaped from it and watched as the other five gradually caught up with it. Sarah wasn't sure what she had been expecting, but it wasn't what she saw.

Before them, about ten feet back from the dusty road, stood a large hut elevated on bamboo poles, very much like the vast majority of the buildings they had seen while moving through the city. Its floor was about four feet off the ground. Its roof was of a coarse, grassy thatch mixed with palm fronds, and the exterior of the structure was covered with palm fronds layered like shingles.

Sarah grabbed Edward's arm and pulled him back into her lap before he could climb out, then held him while he squirmed and she studied the building before her. It was at most thirty feet wide from side to side, making it substantially larger than most of the other similar structures they had passed. Across the front was a high porch roofed with palm fronds. To reach the porch, they would have to climb eight stairs made of notched mahogany tree trunks.

It was what was under the large hut that thrilled the three littlest brothers. They could see a pig with a litter in a large pen, a goat staked a few feet from it, and several ducks. The three youngest boys began to shout in pleasure.

"Is that our pig, Father?" George yelled.

"Oh, I hope it is, I hope it is. Father, can I ride the goat?" Alfred was standing and jumping up and down in the rickshaw, making it bounce.

Edward started to climb out again. His mother caught him by the shirttail as he yelled, "Ducks! Ducks! Mine!"

Matthew walked back to the second rickshaw to assist Sarah. He lifted Edward down. As he put out his hand to assist his wife, he said, "It took me seven weeks to build the place. Levi Savage helped me every step of the way. It is among the largest of any of those the officers are using. It is very different from what we had in Calcutta, but it has some fine advantages."

She was unable to bring herself to say anything. *Fine advantages?* At the moment she couldn't think of any. She had given up a house of forty rooms for a bamboo hut. The word *primitive* came to mind.

Harry kept his eyes on his parents as he climbed out of the first rickshaw. He noted the look of startled amazement on his mother's face. Matthew held Sarah's hand to steady her as she climbed the rough-hewn stairs. Harry followed them up the stairs and into the big hut.

As they stepped inside the doorway in the center of the front wall, Sarah looked around as if she suddenly felt she had entered a place she had not intended to go. As her eyes adjusted to the darkness, she could see that a man and a woman in traditional Burmese dress stood before them. Bago wore a wide cotton cloth tied around his waist with one end thrown over his shoulder. Both put their hands together and bowed from the waist.

Matthew made the introductions. "This is Bago, my dhobi, my personal servant. He does the laundry and is a fine tailor. This is his wife, Bundah, our cook and housekeeper. You see, my dear, we will be well taken care of."

Sarah made the effort to nod at both of them while the smaller boys surrounded them.

"Does the goat have a name?" George asked.

"Are the pigs ours? Are we going to eat them?" A. W. asked.

"Lads, do not forget your manners. Tell Bago and Bundah your names."

Each stood at attention and introduced himself.

As they did so, Sarah mentally calculated that the central room was about ten by ten feet in size. She saw Matthew's trunk in one corner. Several large pillows were scattered around. That was the extent of the furnishings. He led her to another room to the left, where she saw what appeared to be two mattresses about five feet long and perhaps four feet wide pushed together in the center of the floor. Above them was a circular canopy of mosquito netting drawn up near the center of the ceiling.

"This will be the lads' room. They can put their trunks in the corners." He bent near her ear and said in a quiet voice, "It's like an extended bivouac. They will adjust."

They will adjust, but will I? she wondered.

He took her by the elbow and walked her through the center room, where George and Alfred were still trying to become acquainted with the servants. Edward was carrying one of the big cushions around on his head like the merchandise sellers he had seen in the bazaar in Calcutta.

Matthew led her into the room at the opposite end of the hut. It also had a mattress on the floor in the center of the room, much like the arrangement in the boys' room, with a great circle of mosquito netting on a bamboo frame suspended above it.

"This is our room. There will be space here in the corners for the trunks. I have found that they serve very nicely as sitting space or even a writing desk." He had not yet noted Sarah's stunned silence and continued. "The mattresses are very comfortable. They are stuffed with the soft, white bloom of the kapok tree. The greatest advantage of this kind of bamboo construction is that the breeze moves through it freely and it tends to be cooler than the framed structures of Calcutta. The great drawback, of course, is the fact that everything you say—should you raise your voice—might be heard by anyone in the next room, or neighbors, or even passersby."

Still holding her hand, he led her back to the center room and to the rear doorway there. "See, my dear, we have a similar porch here on the rear, where you can view the placid little stream that is a tributary of the Irrawaddy River." She could see the fast-moving, burbling stream through the long branches of drooping willows and dense undergrowth. "It becomes our highway during the rainy season. It will rise and overflow, and we will travel by boat to market. When the water rises to its greatest height, we will be able to step into the boat from the lowest stair. If it rises so much that it spreads beneath the house, then we will put the animals in the field at the end of the street where the ground is higher. I have hired a man—a beesty—to tend my mount and the other animals."

He paused as if waiting for a response. When none came, he swept the room with his hand. "Note the solid wood floors, hence the extra bamboo supports for the building. I was able to purchase the Scottish pine planks from a man who was salvaging the remnants of a ship that sank in the bay last year. Most huts have split-bamboo floors, which are very strong but which are not suitable for furniture as they are uneven, but these floors are flat and will support items of furniture as we acquire them. I've been living very simply since coming here, but with a family, we will add some conveniences."

Matthew stopped talking and looked closely at his wife. "Sarah, you haven't said a word since we arrived. Is something the matter?"

She slowly turned a full circle, studying her surroundings as if still slightly stunned. Her voice was a near whisper. "Matthew, it's all so very different than I had expected—so foreign. I'm still trying to absorb everything." She paused and, with a forced smile, added, "I'm sure, given time, everything will feel more natural—more normal." But in her heart, she wondered.

"Of course, of course. Every change requires that adjustments be made. Let's have dinner. I'm sure all of us are famished, especially the lads."

"But, Matthew, there is no table—nor chairs." Sarah was still trying to deal with the lack of furnishings in the large hut.

"We'll have a picnic. We have cushions, and, if you like, we can sit on the stairs at the rear of the house, where we can enjoy the view of the stream. You'll be surprised at how many boats travel on it even in the dry season." He turned to his oldest son. "Harry, will you get your mother a cushion to sit on? We will all be eating on the back stairs after the trunks have been brought in. I'll go out and tell the rickshaw men to bring them in right now. Sarah, please instruct them as to where to put each one."

"But, Matthew, do they speak English?" she called as he hurried down the stairs to the road.

"Just point," he answered over his shoulder. When the trunks had been deposited in the hut, the rickshaws disappeared into the growing darkness. Bundah appeared with a large tray, carrying six military-style tin plates holding a dinner of rice and chicken. Despite the casualness of the meal, Sarah had to admit that the food was excellent.

Harry sat next to his father on the top step, "Father, this is very different than what I expected, but I think we will learn to like it. I have one question. Will I have to sleep on the same mattress as the three little lads? Even in their sleep they are never still. I may never get a wink of sleep."

Matthew looked thoughtful for a moment as he put another forkful of rice in his mouth. He nodded and swallowed. "I see your point, Harry. We'll get you a mattress of your own with your mosquito netting when we go into the bazaar."

Somewhat relieved, Harry answered, "Thank you, Father."

As Bundah collected the used plates and forks, Sarah rose and located one of the household trunks. Harry helped his parents carefully unpack her precious china and the bed linens in which they were wrapped.

"Is this for me?" he asked as she handed a blanket to him. "Will we need it in this heat?"

"Before morning, it can get much cooler," Matthew commented. "You'll be glad to have something over you."

She unpacked the rest of the blankets. In the next trunk, she had packed table linens, dresser scarves, silverware, serving utensils, books and school supplies that would be used by the children for their studies, and Matthew's books on homeopathic medicine.

Matthew looked at the contents of the trunk. "Sarah, I think we need to make some purchases before you unpack any more household items. We will need some shelves or bookcases."

She moved over to the trunk where her personal clothing was neatly packed, then stood with her hands on her hips. "Matthew, we have no wardrobe. Where will we put our clothing?"

"Until we can find something like that, we will just keep everything in the trunks. In the morning, we will go to the bazaar to see what we can find."

That night, as Sarah adjusted the mosquito netting around the mattress and lay back to sleep by the side of her husband for the first night in a year and a half, she asked, "Where is the kitchen, Matthew?"

"We haven't one. Bundah cooks all meals in her own hut and brings them to us across the road. When the river is high and covers the road during the rainy season, she will bring them across in a little boat."

She turned over and looked at her precious china stacked neatly against one wall. *What a strange world I have slipped into*, she thought as the sleep of exhaustion overtook her.

CHAPTER ELEVEN

January 13, 1854
Rangoon, Burma

After a breakfast of rice and white fish, Matthew announced, "Bago will supervise the three youngest lads this morning while the rest of us ride to the great bazaar near the wharf. He has hired a rickshaw for us to use. It should be here within the hour."

Harry and Sarah were quick to exchange a smile of approval. When they arrived at the bazaar, Matthew led them to a large tent where a broad variety of used, European furniture was available. With an officious, hand-wringing, turbaned merchant following in their wake, they looked over everything in the tent. Sarah selected a large round oak table with six matching chairs. Though they were somewhat battered, Matthew approved the purchase.

He commented, "I saw this table and chairs in the home of Lieutenant Colonel Lancaster before he retired and returned to England. It will serve us well. Do you see anything else you feel we need, my dear?"

"I'd like beds for us and for each of the children, but I don't see any."

"No, you're not likely to. It is customary to sleep on the floor in this country. I cannot speak for the governor, but everyone else does."

Seeing his mother's disappointment, Harry pointed across the wide tent. "I see a ladies' dressing table over there. You might find it useful, Mother."

"May we get it, Matthew?" Her husband nodded his approval.

Sarah pointed out a large, freestanding cupboard and matching wardrobe, both of which were inlaid with various tropical woods. "Matthew, do we have sufficient funds to acquire those two items? I very much need both," she said as she pointed. The cupboard and wardrobe were added to the purchases.

Harry spoke up. "Father, remember you promised that I might have my own mattress?"

"Yes, Harry, I haven't forgotten."

Once that purchase had been made and yards of mosquito netting acquired, Harry felt relieved. Surely he would sleep undisturbed in the future.

The merchant oversaw the process of having the furniture loaded into several of the hired ox carts that waited outside the great tent for such commissions. They were delivered, and Sarah watched them being carried inside the hut. *Now here is an increasing amount of civilization,* she told herself.

That evening as they lay down to sleep, Matthew mentioned rather casually, "By the way, my dear, Sabbath meeting will be here tomorrow. This is the only place large enough for the Saints to meet. There will probably be eighteen to twenty in attendance."

She sat bolt upright. "Matthew, why didn't you think to mention this to me earlier?"

"I didn't see that it was of much importance. Each person who wants to sit will bring a cushion. The ladies can sit on the trunks. All others will stand for the meeting."

He was right. It wouldn't have mattered if she had known sooner. It wasn't as if there were a lot of preparations to make. *What does one do to prepare for company when one lives in a bamboo hut?* She lay back down and tried to sleep.

***

Matthew introduced Sarah and Harry to each of the members of the small congregation as they arrived. This allowed the three youngest boys to dash below the house to play with the goat. Before the meeting began, Sarah discovered their absence and called them into the hut. She had to quickly wipe their faces with a handkerchief moistened with her tongue in an attempt to make them more presentable.

The meeting was conducted by Elder William Willes, who was the most senior leader in Asia at the time, having come from Calcutta a few months earlier. Matthew was called upon to preach extemporaneously on the subject of obedience to the Lord's commandments. She didn't remember anything said by anyone else, but she felt Matthew had done himself proud.

By the time the meeting had ended, she only remembered a few names. Sister Fitzgerald, William Willes, Elam Luddington, and, of course, Levi Savage, whom she thanked for his assistance in helping Matthew build her new home.

As they watched the members of the congregation depart, Sarah spoke. "Matthew, you gave a sterling sermon."

"Did you think it measured up to that given by Elder Willes?"

"Oh, how embarrassing. I'm afraid I don't remember anything Elder Willes said." Her tone of voice changed and became more practical. "But I must raise a different subject. I had some difficulty locating the younger boys when it was time for the meeting to begin, and when they finally came at my call, they were positively disheveled. We need someone to watch over them—a nanny or someone of that kind. I can't seem to watch all three at once. I worry they might fall into the river."

"You are right. I should have realized that we must hire someone to watch them."

It was done, and Sarah's anxiety was lessened. Bundah's brother Ravi's English was passable as he had served another British family the previous year.

Ravi's first advice in his new post as caretaker for the three littlest boys was that each be fitted with a pair of leather boots that reached to the knees so they could move around near the river and under the hut when they fed or played with the animals without concern for the snakes or scorpions that often hid there.

Harry asked, "Ravi, why do we need boots when you and the other natives wear sandals?"

The servant smiled enigmatically. "Young master, the eyes of the English do not see the snakes or scorpions as quickly as do the eyes of the Burmese."

The boots were ordered from the boot maker the next day, and Harry spent several days adding a three-foot palisade of bamboo around the base of the house to protect the animals.

***

By the first of February, Sarah felt that the family was gaining some semblance of order in their lives. A laundress was hired. At Sarah's request, while his father was on duty at the ordnance park, Harry had enclosed one end of the rear porch with bamboo so it could be used as a washing and bathing room. Matthew had acquired a large zinc tub at the bazaar, and when filled with river water, it served as both washtub and bathtub.

Matthew interviewed several individuals for the post of tutor for the children. He selected Mrs. Robinson, a recently widowed English woman who had served as a tutor to several other families of Bengal army officers. And so the children's formal studies began again.

Harry asked, "Father, will I be getting a personal servant here in Rangoon? I miss Gupta very much."

"Are you still considering enlisting in the naval cadet program when you turn fourteen? You haven't spoken of it in some time."

"Yes, my feelings remain the same."

"As that is only a few months in the future, I think it will be unnecessary to hire a personal servant for you. Since you remain determined to enlist, I will attempt to obtain a commission for you as a cadet. You must know that your mother will look upon this action with dread."

"Surely she will be proud of me."

"She has grown to depend upon your strength in the time I have been in Burma. She will miss you very much."

Harry was quiet for a few seconds before he responded. "But I still plan to proceed with my plans to enlist."

***

On the first Saturday of March, as Matthew pushed his empty breakfast dishes away, he looked at each of his sons and said in a businesslike manner, "I have something to show you boys when you have finished your breakfast. We will walk down to the pasture where we moved the animals to avoid the water of the rainy season." He smiled at Sarah and added, "I believe you will find it of interest as well, my dear."

The three smallest boys hurriedly finished their meals.

"Are each of you fully dressed—lace-up boots included?"

Edward needed help with his boots before the McCune family gathered to follow Matthew down the rutted road about six hundred feet from the hut.

"Wait here," Matthew ordered. He ducked under a rope strung across a small pasture where several animals, including the McCune's goat and pigs, grazed on a plot watched by the man Matthew had hired.

Matthew walked about a hundred feet up the gentle slope and picked up the bridal rein of a sturdy pony, which he led back to the family.

The two littlest boys began to squeal with excitement, and George yelled, "Father, is it ours? Is the pony ours?"

"Yes, lads, and her name is Honest. She will remind you every time you ride her of the importance of being honest. Each day after I come home, if you've been good boys and finished your studies, Ravi or I will help you ride her."

It was apparent that he was speaking to the littlest boys. Harry cleared his throat and spoke. "She is a beautiful pony, but I'm afraid she is much too small to carry me." Disappointment tinged his voice.

"For you, Harry, I have different plans. I will teach you to ride my personal army mount." Harry's eyes moved to the large bay grazing in the far corner. "I believe you will become a fine horseman while we are here in Rangoon."

Harry's face brightened at the compliment. "Thank you, Father. I'll do my best."

Harry's letter to Annie that evening was full of news of his future enlistment in the naval cadets and his plans to learn to ride.

***

The rainy season arrived by the end of the month, and within three weeks, the stream behind the house had become a river. As Matthew had promised, family members could step into the boat they had hired for the season from the bottom step of the rear porch. The boatman would not leave his boat at night during the week for fear of it being stolen, so for the many weeks he served the McCune's, he slept in it while it was tied to one of the support poles of the hut. On Saturday evenings he would pole it home to spend Sunday with his wife and two children.

***

Harry's fourteenth birthday at the end of May was a day of mixed emotions for Sarah. He was growing into a tall, fine young man, but he remained serious about becoming a naval cadet. The morning he planned to report to the naval dockyard to enlist, she woke with a fever and chills.

"Son, your mother is ill this morning, and she would not want to miss your enlistment, so I must ask you to put it off until she is well enough to attend the ceremony." Matthew looked grim.

"Yes, of course, Father. What has taken her so swiftly?"

"It appears to be Asiatic cholera."

The color drained from Harry's face. "Father, it was cholera that took my sister and two of my brothers. Will it take Mother?"

"We will do all in our power to see that it doesn't." Matthew was required to use all of his experience and skill with herbs to ease her pain and discomfort. He sent for Elder Willes to assist in giving her a blessing. Each night of her illness, Harry knelt in earnest prayer and pleaded for his mother's recovery. It was early July when she slowly began to regain her strength and was able to stand and walk about well enough that Harry could plan the date of his enlistment.

With pride on the part of his father and nervousness on the part of his mother, he signed his name on the enlistment contract and swore his allegiance to England and the British Navy. Sarah's emotional control was fragile. Behind her smile, tears gathered like water behind a weakened dam. *What will I do without Harry?* she wondered.

At the naval dockyard, he was assigned to H Company as an engineer apprentice and was posted on the gunboat *Diana*, a steamer that patrolled the Irrawaddy River.

***

Elder Nathan Jones, having just arrived from Calcutta, was introduced at the first Sabbath meeting in August as the newly appointed president of the East India Mission of the Church. He preached a powerful sermon on faith and obedience, and after shaking hands with each person present at the end of the meeting, he paused to quietly speak to Matthew and Sarah.

"Brother McCune, I have been prompted by the Spirit to tell you and a few other members of the Church that I believe the judgments of the Lord will be poured out upon India and Burma in the near future, and all who can should flee to Zion. I am sharing these impressions with certain people. I can't announce this kind of thing at a Sabbath meeting as there are always many nonmembers present who might report it to the governor and the leadership of the army as a treasonous statement, but I want you to give my admonition much thought and prayer."

Matthew was briefly startled into silence. Sarah's heart felt as if a cold hand had wrapped itself around it. *Here it is again, that admonition to emigrate halfway around the world, but from another source. Why must we do such a thing?*

Matthew took a deep breath before he responded. "Thank you for sharing your advice, Elder Jones. I will give it much prayer, as you have suggested."

By this time the others had left. Sarah took hold of his arm and looked up into his face. "Matthew, what does he mean—the judgments of God will be poured out?"

"I'm not sure, but we must pray earnestly about it."

That evening, Matthew wrote a letter to Patrick Meik to share the warning given him by Elder Jones and urged Patrick to give serious consideration to that warning, as Matthew intended to do.

That night, after the mosquito netting had been lowered and Matthew's regular heavy breathing told Sarah he was asleep, she lay awake. *I do not want to go, but how can I oppose Matthew—or the Lord?*

***

In October, Elder Jones proposed that Matthew be sustained as president of the Rangoon branch of the Church. Matthew selected Elders Savage and Heffernan as counselors. Feeling the weight of his new responsibilities, Matthew made the first of what would be several contributions to the Perpetual Emigration Fund of the Church to show his willingness to make plans to emigrate with his family to the Salt Lake Valley. The money was given to Elder Jones to be forwarded to Church leaders in England.

From that point on, Matthew began to speak seriously to Sarah about the probability of emigrating. She tried to suppress her fears and said little of the dangers she saw in such a journey, but in her heart, all she wanted to do was to go back to Calcutta and to the way things had been.

"Sarah, if the Lord wants us to go to the valley, we must be prepared to obey." His words were firm. She simply nodded her acquiescence. *But at what cost?* she wondered.

That evening, the sound of a rickshaw was heard in front of the house. They both turned toward the sound of steps on the stairs, and as Harry strode into the room, Sarah rose and cried out his name.

"Harry, you're home!" As she rushed to him and embraced him, she couldn't help but note that he stood nearly two inches taller than she and that his shoulders and arms were developing into a man's.

"I'm being posted to a much larger ship, the *Lord William Bentick*. I report tomorrow morning, but I was given permission to spend the night with my family." He dropped his kit bag on the floor, and his mother ushered him to a chair, where he sat tiredly. About that time, Ravi brought back the three littlest boys from their pony ride. When they saw their brother, they threw themselves at him.

"Harry, are you home to stay?" George asked breathlessly as he hung on to his brother's neck from behind the chair.

"No, just for the night. I must leave in the morning," Harry said as he eased his brother's tight hold on his neck.

"But at least we can see him tonight," Sarah stated as she pulled Alfred and Edward away from their older brother's legs. She was determined to hide her disappointment that he wasn't staying longer.

The children's conversation and questions flew around the table as Bundah served the evening meal, but Sarah simply sat quietly, watching her oldest son with an increasing sense of pride—and loss.

After the cook had gathered up the dishes, Matthew leaned back and spoke. "Harry, tell us about your responsibilities on ship."

"It's hard work, Father. I have strung lines in the rigging for sails we never use since the *Diana* is a steamer, but the sails are kept ready should anything happen to the engine—and the navigator has given me lessons in navigation." He paused as if a little embarrassed. "I have also had my regularly scheduled shift at shoveling coal into the boiler."

Alfred perked up. "You got to shovel the coal like the two big men on the boat we rode on to come to Rangoon? That is exciting!"

"It may be exciting to watch, A. W., but it is not exciting to do it. It is very hard work."

Sarah put her hand over her mouth as if to prevent the objections she felt from flowing out of her mouth. *Her Harry doing such heavy, hard work!*

The evening melted away as they talked of his responsibilities and the new challenges he would face on the *Bentick* as it sailed the Bay of Bengal. Sarah tried to hide her worry with a stiff smile.

Early the next morning, the boatman poled the heavily loaded little vessel down the fast-flowing river to the bay where the family said farewell to Harry at the wharf. He smartly saluted his parents before putting his kit bag over his shoulder and boarding the *Bentick*.

Sarah was determined not to allow any emotions to show, but she was not entirely successful. "The pain of separation increases as he grows more mature and farther from us," she said to Matthew.

"But he will eventually resign his position and go to America with us, my dear, so this separation will not be long."

For the first time since Matthew had first raised the issue of emigrating to America, Sarah felt more positive. *It will bring Harry home to us*, she thought with a relieved smile. *There is something good in these plans to go to America. Harry will rejoin us.*

CHAPTER TWELVE

November 3, 1855
Rangoon, Burma

THE MONSOON RAINS ENDED, AND Matthew sent the boatman away. After the remains of supper were cleared away, Matthew sat quietly and reread the letter he had received that day.

"Matthew, what has made you so quiet this evening?" Sarah had noted his unusual silence.

"In my hand I have a letter from Patrick Meik. In it he tells me that he has been called to serve as the president of the East India Mission in anticipation of Elder Jones's return to America. He is urging me to set aside the warning of Elder Jones and remain in service with the Bengal army until my enlistment expires. He feels that the Church needs me here and that his advice should overrule that of Elder Jones, since is it more recently given."

"What do you think, Matthew?"

"I have given the matter much thought, and I am impressed that we must not neglect the warning given us by Elder Jones."

Then the sooner Harry can rejoin us, she thought, with a mixture of hope and worry.

***

Harry's letters home had to be sufficient for Sarah. After reading them aloud to Matthew and his brothers, she carried them with her and, whenever she found a quiet moment, reread them many times. Matthew's time, when not engaged in the training of the men in the use of heavy artillery, was full of efforts to direct the Rangoon branch and to move the missionary work forward.

By the end of the month, Matthew had grown unnaturally quiet. One evening after he had retired to the mattress on the floor, Sarah said as she arranged the mosquito netting around them, "There's something on your mind, Matthew. Please share your thoughts with me. I have noticed your silence."

He had folded his hands across his chest while he stared at the ceiling. "I have been impressed that it is time to make plans to leave Rangoon and sever our ties with the East India Company."

"I see." Her words were whispered. He did not seem to recognize the multitude of emotions his words triggered.

"The foremost issue facing us is the raising of necessary funds to make the journey. I have no way of knowing if there will be any assistance from the Perpetual Emigration Fund, so I think we had better plan to fund the journey ourselves. I will write a letter to Patrick and Mary Anne tomorrow asking them to take us in when we get back to Calcutta. I am sure their door will be open to us. When we return to Calcutta, I will no longer be a member of the Bengal army, so we will need to depend upon the good graces of the Meiks as we will not qualify to rent any of the company houses."

He paused briefly before he continued. "I have also come to the conclusion that we should sell almost everything we have accumulated and so increase our funds. I will begin by selling the goats and the children's pony." He paused. "I am hopeful that one of the officers will want to buy the house."

Sarah laid back and mentally composed a list of everything that would need to be arranged before such a major move could take place. She slept little that night.

When he announced the plans to sell the pony and the goats at breakfast, the two youngest boys began to cry. "Why can't we take Honest with us to America?" Alfred asked.

"I'm afraid that would be impossible, my lad. Horses do not travel on ships very well."

"But we could take the goat and her kids. They are little and could go on the ship."

"I'm afraid not, as we wouldn't have anything to feed them on a ship,"

Edward continued to cry, and Alfred pouted, but everyone knew that when Father's mind was made up, there was no changing it. Edward cried himself to sleep that night and every night for several days after the pony and the goats were sold.

Matthew notified the men he served with at the warehouse and artillery park, as well as any other Europeans he met, that on January 28 and for a few days thereafter, he would hold an auction at his home. A list of the items that might be purchased was posted at the warehouse. He also shared the information with the Church members who attended Sabbath meetings.

When the day of the auction arrived, Sarah sat on one of the trunks in the bedroom and listened as her beloved china, dressing table, mirrors, and furniture were sold. Right up to the day of auction, she had found it difficult to believe they were going to leave everything behind to emigrate halfway around the world, but when the house was nearly empty, the realization was nearly overwhelming.

As they ate sitting on the rear steps the last day of January, Matthew handed Sarah four tickets. "Lads, I'm giving the tickets to your mother for your voyage back to Calcutta. You will be leaving in one week on the steamer *Fire Queen*, the same steamship that brought you to Rangoon two years ago. You should reach Calcutta in about ten days. There, you will live in our old home with the Meik family until your brother and I join you and we can prepare to leave for America."

That evening after the three youngest children were asleep, Matthew and Sarah sat on the top step at the rear of the hut she had never quite come to think of as home. If it were not for the nearness of their parting, she would have appreciated the night, which was radiant with stars. It was a lovely night fit to wrap herself in, but as she held Matthew's hand, it was difficult to ignore the fears filling her heart and mind. Though they talked of mundane things, her thoughts were elsewhere. *So much can happen between Rangoon and the Salt Lake Valley. How could I endure the loss of another child?*

Wanting to talk about what was really on her mind, she instead whispered, "Please make this a brief separation, Matthew."

The day before they were to leave, she began to fold and pack the children's clothing. Alfred's face was a portrait of worry. "How will Harry know where we are going?"

"Your father will keep in touch with him after we leave. He won't be left behind."

"You're sure?"

"Yes, dear. We won't be separated from Harry for very long." His face grew only a little less worried. His expression said that he was not entirely convinced.

***

February 7, 1856
Rangoon Harbor

That morning the family traveled by rickshaw to the bay, where they watched as their trunks were loaded onto the *Fire Queen*. Sarah was comforted by the welcome expressed in the letter that had arrived a week earlier in which Mary Anne had written, "This house and our hearts are big enough for all of you."

Sarah embraced her husband before he could object to the public display of affection, and repeated what she had urged the night they had sat together on the back porch. "Please, Matthew, make this a short separation."

"It will be as brief as I can make it, my dear," he responded. He shook each child's hand, then George stepped back and gave him a salute as he had seen Harry do. Then the three children, holding hands as instructed, followed their mother aboard the *Fire Queen* and stood waving as it pulled away from the wharf.

***

During the following days while Sarah tried to keep track of her three young sons on board the steamer, Matthew arranged for the sale of the house. On February 28, he received a promise of 550 rupees from Charles Garner, a conductor of ordnance and coworker, to be paid in three monthly installments. It would change hands when the entire amount had been paid.

***

Sarah's gratitude at arriving in Calcutta tearfully overflowed when the steamship reached the wharf on the Hooghly River and she saw Patrick, Mary Anne, and Annie waiting for the boat's arrival. The women both wept with joy as they embraced.

As they greeted each other, Patrick explained, "We have brought all four carriages to have room for everyone as well as the trunks. I hope four will be adequate," he added as he watched the trunks being deposited on the wharf.

Sarah was so pleased to be back in Calcutta that she couldn't have suppressed her laughter even had she tried. "We will make it work. I shall put Edward on my lap, and Alfred, too, if necessary."

As the trunks were put into the carriages, Annie stepped over to Sarah. "How is Harry doing? I haven't had a letter since before Christmas."

"I haven't either, Annie, but I'm sure he is doing well." *At least, I sincerely hope so*, she thought.

***

While Sarah and the three younger boys returned to the rhythm of life in Calcutta, Harry crewed on voyages of the *Bentick,* continuing to learn the jargon and skills of a naval cadet. Between each voyage, he was permitted to return home for one or two days where he and his father discussed the details of their plans to emigrate.

"I'll resign my post the end of May to take effect in July. Will that meet with your plans, Father?"

"Yes, Harry, and I'll do the same."

When Matthew accompanied Harry to his ship the next morning, father and son gave each other a salute. Harry was, after all, nearly a man and, like his father, in uniform.

***

July 21, 1856
Rangoon, Burma

At the last Church meeting Matthew would attend in Rangoon, he shook the hand of every man present. When he faced his friends Maurice White, Levi Savage, William Willes, and Elam Luddington, he set aside his usual reserve and gave each man a quick, one-armed embrace. "You will continue to give the Church here the leadership that will make it flourish, that I know. May we meet again someday in Zion." He then walked briskly from the meeting, focused upon a future on the other side of the world.

Matthew turned the house over to the purchaser, and father and son and their trunks were carried by boat to the bay to depart for Calcutta on the steamer *Sesostres.*

Three days into the voyage, a dark smudge of clouds on the horizon foretold a storm coming, and long, slow swells began to lift the ship and then plunge it into deep troughs that made the swells loom like gray-green mountains on every side. The dark clouds now churned on the horizon, and the wind began to shriek through the rigging. Even Harry, with his year of experience on a ship, began to look a little green, though he insisted he was just fine.

Harry noted that some of the sailors went about their duties whispering incantations. Some occasionally held three fingers in the air. They struggled to tightly reef the sails so that the ship bore only bare poles and spars for the wind to beat upon. The next day, the angry swells grew to twenty feet and were covered with foam. Many of the passengers did not avail themselves of dinner.

Though the thought of eating was not appealing to Matthew or Harry, they were both determined to prove themselves good sailors and sat at the captain's table for dinner. When he joined them, Matthew asked, "Captain, can you tell us the cause of the weather change?"

"I fear that this is the beginning of a summer typhoon. I'm sure you experienced more than one when you were living in Calcutta."

"Yes, but we had the advantage of being fifty miles up the River Hooghly rather than on the ocean, so their effect was greatly lessened."

The captain responded, "Sergeant McCune, tonight I recommend you and your son tie yourselves in your berths. The rough seas have likely only begun, and we cannot know how long this will last. I will be sending a crewman around to each passenger's cabin with some rope for that purpose."

Harry cleared his throat. Hoping that his question would distract attention from the fact that his uneasy stomach had prevented him from eating anything, he asked, "Captain, I've noted that some of the sailors have been going about whispering to themselves and even holding up three fingers. What does it mean?"

The captain laid his napkin on the table and chuckled. "Many seamen are deeply superstitious. Did you not find that on board the *Bentick*?"

"No, sir. No such behavior was tolerated on the *Bentick*."

"Well, I suspect that these superstitions will never be entirely eliminated. The crewmen believe that the three fingers represent the Godhead—Father, Son, and Holy Ghost. In actuality, the custom originated with the ancient Greeks, and the three fingers represent Neptune's trident."

"So they are ignorantly appealing to a pagan god?"

"They are not aware of it, and I like to think that the prayer goes to the god it is meant for."

That night, lightning cut the fabric of the sky like a knife blade. The thunder which followed sounded like the firing of cannons. The bow of the ship repeatedly rose and fell, shaking everything loose and making the ship creak like a creature in pain. The sea water rolled over the deck, threatening to swamp the ship. The passengers were kept below decks, and the hatch was secured for the next three days while the wind screamed through the rigging at more than sixty knots, lashing deck hands and officers with stinging pellets of icy rain. The passengers hid from nature's wrath, tied in their berths.

During a brief period of calm after the second day, Harry stated loudly, "It seems the devil himself is in this storm, Father. Do you suppose he is determined to keep us from our journey to join the Saints in the Great Salt Lake Valley?"

"If he is, then the forces on our side outweigh him."

The shrieking wind returned full force, and the ship again creaked and groaned like a living, suffering thing, heaving in the turmoil of the waves and forcing an attitude of humility upon all. The helmsman was lashed to the tiller, and a guideline was strung along the deck for a safety line lest crew members be swept overboard as the storm raged unabated. The violence of the wind and water lessened late on the fourth day, and a crewman knocked on each stateroom door. "Dinner served in one hour."

The hardiest of the passengers, including Matthew and Harry, left their cabins to acquire a meal of boiled rice, something weak stomachs could endure.

As Matthew and Harry sat at the captain's table for supper the next day, Harry admitted, when asked, that he had never experienced such a storm while serving on the *Bentick*. "Captain, how often do you and your crew face such a storm?"

"In my twenty-five years of sailing, I've been through at least a dozen such typhoons. I think we would still be caught in it if our course to Calcutta did not differ by several compass points from its track."

That night, as they rolled into their quilts on the hard berths, Matthew commented, "It is good that your mother and the younger lads were not with us during the storm. It was not an experience they would have endured well."

The balance of the voyage was filled with calmer waters, the dawn sometimes spreading bands of tangerine and rose along the smoky blue horizon, only to be swallowed up in the gray monsoon rains that returned by mid-morning and forced the crewmen to work while thoroughly soaked.

When the ship entered the wide mouth of the Hooghly River, Matthew and Harry stood at the railing watching the turbulent, rising tide carry the ship as it rippled up the wide river, its waves curling, while those that were pressed to the wide shores broke into spray.

"Well, Harry, as we did not notify your mother and brothers of the date of our arrival, we will surprise them by renting a carriage or two so we may arrive home without notice."

Harry grinned at the thought of the pleasure their arrival would cause. His smile widened as he thought of his seeing his mother—and of seeing Annie.

CHAPTER THIRTEEN

Late in the afternoon, the two carriages arrived at what was now the Meik residence. Deleep hurried to take the reins of the horse of the first. Upon recognizing his former master, he greeted him warmly. "Sahib McCune, it is a blessing to see you again. Welcome, welcome."

"It is good to be back in Calcutta among old friends, Deleep. Is the memsahib here?"

"Yes, Sahib McCune. She is with Memsahib Meik in the sitting room."

Placing his palms together, Deleep respectfully bowed from the shoulders as Matthew and Harry climbed down from the first carriage. He quickly hurried to lift the trunks from the second.

Father and son climbed the circular stairs and paused at the sitting room door. They looked at each other with a shared smile of anticipation. Matthew put his hand on the doorknob and pushed it open.

Sarah looked up from the sewing in her lap, her needle and embroidery silk suspended in the air. For a fraction of a second, she didn't recognize him without his familiar red uniform. Then her face flushed with excitement. Her sewing fell to the floor unnoticed as she rose and rushed to her husband.

As she embraced him, he gave her a kiss on the forehead. Annie shyly rose from where she had been sitting by her mother and stepped up to Harry, putting her hands out to him. As he took them, she smiled broadly. "Harry, you're back. It's good to see you."

Not sure what to say, Harry smiled and stammered, "It . . . it's good to be back."

Sarah stepped back from Matthew and turned to her son. As she put her arms around him, he released Annie's hand and returned his mother's embrace.

Finally able to speak, she whispered, "My family is united again."

The three littlest boys heard the familiar voices in the sitting room and rushed from the schoolroom in the face of Mrs. Senior's objections. When Alfred threw himself at Matthew's legs, George brought himself up short and saluted. "Welcome home, Father. You too, Harry." Harry returned the salute with a smile.

Edward hung back until his father put out both hands and motioned for him to approach. He lifted his youngest son high into the air. "You are growing very fast, my lad."

The evening meal was one of celebration, and after the dishes had been cleared away, each of the former McCune servants quietly approached Matthew and reported their pleasure at the return of Sahib McCune and young Sahib Harry.

Matthew joined his wife in the large bedroom Sarah had been using, and Harry was shown to another.

That evening when her husband was nearly asleep, Sarah quietly spoke. "Matthew, have you selected a date when we will leave for America?"

He roused enough to reply. "No, not a specific date."

"Will it be soon?"

"As soon as all can be arranged."

"Then I want to go back to Fort Dum Dum and make sure the graves of Alexander and Agnes are in good repair as soon as we can manage it."

"Yes, my dear, we will do that." With that, he was asleep.

***

Jai drove one tanga, and Deleep drove the other the ten miles to the Bhowanipore Cemetery at Dum Dum. Matthew, Sarah, and the two youngest boys rode in the first while Harry and George rode in the second.

As Jai and Deleep cut and raked the nettles and undergrowth that had begun to cover the headstones, Sarah spoke. "I am so glad that the graves of Alfred and William are in the cemetery at Fort William and have been kept in good repair. We should have come here more often to care for these."

When the task was finished, Sarah stood quietly for several minutes as the depth of her loss swept over her. When Alfred and Edward became tired and pleaded to go home, Matthew said in a forceful whisper, "Alf, you and Edward will sit quietly and allow your mother these few moments undisturbed."

Both of the smaller boys immediately sat quietly in the carriage, knowing that their father meant what he said. Finally, after wiping a tear, she turned and nodded at her husband. She was ready to go. He helped her into the tanga.

"I'm leaving a part of my heart here, Matthew," she whispered.

"Only their mortal remains are here, Sarah. Their spirits will go with us to America."

The ache in her heart was not lessened.

Jai turned the horses back toward Fort William.

By the next day, Sarah had shaken off the quiet grief that had borne down on her after they left the cemetery. She and Matthew talked after the midday meal of the necessary preparations for the voyage, as Matthew, in his orderly military fashion, made a long list.

"The children's studies will not be neglected." He listed the need to purchase picture books, school slates, pencils, puzzles, and arithmetic books. He then added soap, shoes, stockings, towels, and pocket compasses. "Very importantly, we must place orders with a tailor for the making of shirts, pantaloons, and dresses—and several large, strong twill bags for clothing."

Matthew announced that he wanted his children to learn music to enrich their education, so purchases included several finely made flutes.

"I'm sure each of you will become a very good musician," he announced to his sons.

Harry and George were willing to allow that such a thing could be, but Alfred and Edward looked at each other and wrinkled their noses. Neither had any belief that there was a musician buried in them.

On November 23, Matthew received a letter and called for Sarah to join him as he read it. "Sarah, I believe this is in relation to my application for a military pension." He unfolded the envelope and quickly read it. "My pension will be two shillings a day, but there may be a complication. It will be payable in Britain, but not America."

"Oh, Matthew, that is such a disappointment."

"Don't be too discouraged, my dear. Who knows but that the Lord will lead my path back to Britain—eventually."

***

December 1856
Calcutta

As the day for departure drew near, Harry spent increasing time with Annie Meik. On the day before the McCunes were to board the ship, he invited her to go with him in one of the tangas to the great stone lions, where they could watch the activities on the wharf.

Gupta adeptly guided the horse through the crowded streets, which were nearly blocked by the familiar clutter of life in Calcutta. Barbers worked on the sides of the rutted road hardly wide enough for two bullock carts to pass. Small shops covered with tin roofs or dun-colored sacking lined both sides. The odors of humans and animals lingered heavily in the air, but neither Annie nor Harry noticed. Their attention was focused on one another.

Before reaching their destination, Gupta halted the tanga at a crossroad while a local maharaja passed them enjoying the shade of a fringed howdah on the back of a bull elephant. He rode at the head of his caravan of smaller elephants, each carrying one of his wives. A dhoti-clad mahout carrying a long, heavy iron hook to enforce his commands walked beside the head of each animal, prepared to signal the animal to halt or kneel, as was desired.

Harry counted the animals as they passed. "He has taken his wives from the zenana to parade them before the people." He counted. "There are twelve in all. He is a rich man and wants the world to know it." Finally, Gupta cracked the whip above the horse, and the tanga began to move again.

Upon reaching the stone lions, Harry and Annie remained in the tanga, where they could see the sailing ship *Escort* being provisioned.

"That's the ship that will take you to America?" Annie asked quietly.

"Yes. It will take three months to reach New York." He turned to her. "Annie, please urge your father to follow us soon."

"He is unwilling to consider it at present. Mother and I have ceased to mention it as it upsets him."

"I'm so sorry."

"Gupta, move the carriage closer so we can watch the quartermaster working on the deck."

They watched in silence as the quartermaster plunged one hand and then the other into each barrel of pork or water to make sure none of the barrels had a false bottom. Then he used a dipper to taste the water and sniffed at the salt pork, trying to ensure that the provisions were of acceptable quality, including the hardtack biscuits. Much of the meat required to feed passengers and crew was taken aboard alive whenever possible, squawking and mooing, to be kept in pens in the darkness of the fourth deck with other supplies.

After an hour, Harry realized that he couldn't postpone the return to the Meik home any longer. "It's getting dark and will soon be dinnertime. I'm sure Father will be unhappy with us if we aren't there when everyone sits down for grace."

They said little on the ride back, but Harry held Annie's hand tightly. "I imagine America will be very different from Calcutta. I wonder if I will miss life here."

"I hope you miss some things—or *some* people." She smiled shyly at him.

"Oh, I know I will miss *some* people very much," Harry said as he cleared his throat to hide his embarrassment.

After they dismounted from the carriage, Harry turned to Annie. Taking both of her hands in his, he said quietly, "I will miss you very much. Please urge your father to bring your family to America and join us in the Salt Lake Valley." He nervously cleared his throat before he added, "Perhaps . . . we might . . . we might marry there."

Annie looked at him with eyes that glistened. "Oh, Harry. I will continue to tell him that we need to join you there, and I will write to you . . . as soon as you can send me an address where I can send my letters. We will see each other again, and perhaps . . ." She let the rest of the sentence hang in the air.

That evening, Mary Anne took Sarah aside after dinner. "Sarah, how I wish you could change Matthew's mind. Please don't go," she pleaded. "You cannot know how much I will miss you. Few sisters have the kind of bond we share."

But both knew there would be no change of plans. They embraced and shed a tear or two. "You and I both know that Matthew's mind will not be changed. I urge you to press Patrick to join us in the Salt Lake Valley as soon as possible."

***

December 10, 1856
Calcutta

On the morning they were to depart, Matthew oversaw the loading of the trunks into four carriages, two of them borrowed for the purpose, as Sarah hurried through their rooms to make sure that nothing of importance was forgotten.

Patrick, Mary Ann, and Annie rode in the carriage driven by Jamal, and the McCunes rode in the one driven by Jai. Deleep and Gupta drove two of the tangas loaded with trunks and other bags, while hired drivers drove the remaining two. They left at eight o'clock for the landing at the Princeppe Ghat.

As Matthew climbed down from the carriage, Jai turned in his driver's seat and said with sincerity and some melancholy, "May your road be smooth, brother," as he pronounced the Hindu blessing upon his master.

"And yours as well, Jai," Matthew responded.

They stood on the landing and watched the trunks as they were placed in the longboats and rowed out to the ship. Sarah and Mary Anne embraced but were determined to put on a brave front at the thought of being separated by half a world.

Matthew urged Patrick to consider emigrating soon to join the Saints in the Salt Lake Valley and again reminded him of Elder Nathan Jones's warning.

Patrick's response was a disappointment. "I think you take his words too seriously, Matthew. I plan to complete my enlistment period as I urged you to do, and then we will reconsider emigrating."

Harry and Annie stood aside and quietly renewed their promises to write to one another and to someday meet again in the valley. They parted reluctantly when Matthew called out, "Harry, it is time to board. We must not wait any longer."

Sarah held tightly to Matthew's arm as they mounted the gangplank. She couldn't help but think how after twenty-two years of residence in India and Burma they were leaving it all behind. *I pray to God we will all live to join the Saints in the Salt Lake Valley.*

As they reached the deck, the captain stepped up to shake Matthew's hand and introduce himself. "Welcome to the *Escort*. I am Captain Alfred Hussey." As the two men shook hands, a bond of respect formed between them, one that would grow stronger during the lengthy voyage.

Most of the trunks were stored in the hold. The little stateroom where the two trunks they would need during the voyage were deposited was a twelve-foot-square space with two stacked wooden berths on each side, much like the cabin on the *Fire Queen*. Its only advantage was that it was situated close to the captain's cabin, giving Matthew the opportunity to become better acquainted with Captain Hussey.

When the sea was calm, the two men enjoyed sitting in the captain's cabin discussing a variety of subjects ranging from the political policies of the nations of the world to Shakespeare. The McCune family was invited to join him for dinner twice in the first week. The two men recognized in one another self-educated men of British rectitude.

The captain's cabin was remarkably large and ornately appointed. The dining table was covered with a fine linen cloth, and English bone china settings were used for each meal. The large bed sat against one bulkhead and was covered by a brocade cover. In the evenings, a lantern hung in the corner cast a shifting light over the room. A large table was pushed against the stern bulkhead under the rear transom and was covered with maps, charts, and navigational instruments. Several harpoons were mounted on the ceiling. The three younger boys were fascinated with them.

"What are they for?" Alfred had asked upon their first visit.

"This ship was a whaler years ago. They were used for killing whales," the captain responded.

"What's a whale?"

"If we are lucky, my lad, we will see a few on this voyage."

"Thank you for your courtesy, Captain," Matthew had said. Then, turning to his sons, he'd firmly added, "My lads, the captain is a busy man. We must cease troubling him and return to our own cabin."

CHAPTER FOURTEEN

A WEEK OUT OF CALCUTTA while the ship was still in the Indian Ocean, Harry rose from the table at dinner where the family had been invited to dine in the captain's cabin, and said quietly, "I'm a bit tired this evening, and if there are no objections, I would like to retire."

"Of course, Harry," Matthew responded.

"You have a fine son there, Matthew," the captain commented as he watched Harry leave the cabin.

"Yes, he is going to make his mark in history," Matthew responded.

When Harry reached the family quarters, he rolled himself into a quilt on one of the lower berths, hoping to mitigate the clammy coldness that had taken ahold of him. He tried to sleep, but his stomach hurt almost beyond his ability to endure. He was determined not to appear weak before his father, nor did he want to worry his mother.

When the rest of the family entered the small stateroom to retire, Sarah shushed the smaller boys. "Harry is very tired. I want you to be quiet as you get ready for bed so you don't wake him."

In the morning, when her oldest son did not rise with the others, Sarah placed her hand on his forehead. Panic filled her voice. "Matthew, Harry is ill. Feel his forehead. He's very feverish." *Here it is, the possibility that I might lose another son. No. I could not live if I lost Harry.* "Matthew, do you have any herbs that might help him?"

Matthew placed his hand upon Harry's forehead. "He is burning up." He opened his bag and searched through the packets of herbs.

Recognizing that there was only one man who was the ultimate authority on the ship, George hurried to the captain's cabin and knocked on the door. "Come," Captain Hussey called out.

Timidly but determinedly, George pushed the door open. "Captain, my brother is very sick. Can you help him?"

Hussey rose from the chart table and slipped on his captain's jacket. He hurried to the McCune cabin, where he could see the alarm on Sarah's face and noted that Matthew was searching through his herbal packets in an alarmed manner.

"Bring him to my cabin. Can he walk?"

Sarah turned a white face toward Hussey. "No, he is too ill to rise. He hardly knows we are here."

Hussey disappeared for about three minutes and returned with one of the largest sailors on the ship. He pointed at Harry. "Carry him to my cabin."

The sailor picked Harry up like a child, and when he had laid him down on the captain's bed, Hussey ordered, "Now go find the ship's surgeon. Bring him here."

With a quick "Yes, sir," and a salute, the sailor disappeared up the companionway.

That evening, Captain Hussey moved into the first officer's quarters.

***

Despite the herbal teas prepared by his father and the concoctions made by the ship's surgeon, Harry steadily grew weaker and slipped in and out of consciousness. Sarah grew distraught, and though no one would have recognized it by his composed manner, Matthew was as alarmed.

The surgeon pulled Matthew aside on the seventh day and whispered, "I don't know what more we can do for him except keep him as comfortable as possible. It's typhoid fever, and frankly, I fear for his life."

Matthew tried to keep his alarm from Sarah, but she could sense his tension. "We can't lose Harry. I couldn't live through it," she whispered as they sat near his sickbed.

Harry eventually slipped into a semidelirious sleep, rousing occasionally to see one or both of his parents at his bedside, weeping quietly.

I must be very near death as I've never seen my father weep, he thought before he drifted into unconsciousness again.

On the fifteenth day of the illness, Harry was awakened by the heavy roll of the ship as it rode the becalmed waves. He could hear the slack sails flapping against the masts. It took a few moments for him to realize where he was and why he was so weak. His mother sat near him, her head bowed in silent prayer. Matthew and the three younger boys were sitting at breakfast with the captain on the far side of the cabin where they had been talking in hushed voices.

The skylight to the captain's cabin was open for fresh air, and the voice of a crewman carried inside. "Captain, there's a large shark following the ship."

The seaman's utterance roused Harry. As a naval cadet, he was acquainted with the sailors' belief that if a person was sick at sea and a shark began to follow the ship, that person was sure to die. What little strength he had melted away.

Upon hearing the crewman, Matthew leaped to his feet, toppling his chair. "Captain, what can I do?" His father knew the superstition as well.

The captain stood and pointed to the harpoons mounted on the ceiling of the cabin. "Take the biggest one."

Matthew pulled the long, heavy harpoon from its mounting and shouted with determination, "He shan't have you, Harry!"

As he rushed from the cabin and into the companionway, Captain Hussey pulled another harpoon from its mounting. Matthew reached the deck first with the captain right behind him.

He could see the cluster of sailors at the starboard gunwale, their eyes focused on something in the water. He pushed his way through the group and spotted the dorsal fin of a large shark.

"Move out of my way," he yelled. Then, with power born of parental love and determination, he took aim and threw the harpoon. The captain raised the second harpoon but held his position as Matthew's harpoon sunk deeply into the shark. A great thrashing in the water quickly turned it red and brought wild cheers from the crew. "He's got the monster. He's killed it!" the crewmen shouted.

Matthew stood unmoving as he watched the dying shark. Hussey stepped next to him and put a hand on his shoulder. "I don't know a whaler who could have done it any better."

The sailors each insisted on shaking Matthew's hand, each hoping to gain some good luck.

Sarah wiped Harry's forehead with a damp cloth and smiled for the first time in a fortnight. "You're safe, Harry. Your father has killed the shark."

Though unable to speak, Harry heard her, and from that time forward, his strength began to increase. Within a few days, he was able to sit up in bed and feed himself. When he was able to leave the bed and walk around a little, he insisted on relinquishing the captain's cabin.

Though he stood unsteadily, Harry offered his hand. "Captain Hussey, your kindness can be credited with my survival—your kindness, the harpoon my father threw, and the will of the Lord."

Within another week, he was walking about on the deck receiving congratulations from the crew and other passengers. The Indian Ocean sunsets had been unnoticed while Harry lay ill but quickly became glorious in Sarah's eyes, beginning with the first evening he was well enough to walk with her around the deck. *Harry has been spared. God has been good to us.* She noted how the gold, rose, and violet hues of the sunset blended into the cobalt blue of the night sky like delicate brushstrokes. In her heart, she thanked God for the hundredth time.

After about twenty minutes of walking that first evening, Harry began to feel fatigued. "It's good to be up and able to walk with you, Mother, but I'm feeling a little weak. I think I'll retire. At your first opportunity, please express my thanks again to Captain Hussey for his thoughtful concern while I was so ill. I can't thank him enough."

"Of course, Harry—and we will try not to disturb you when the rest of us return to the cabin."

Matthew and the captain had been discussing political events in the captain's cabin when Hussey rose to oversee the changing of the watch. As he excused himself, Matthew also left to locate Sarah. He found her on the deck. Together they stood quietly watching the stars appear singly and in groups. The mainsail above them filled with the wind, making the ship hurry like a great bird toward a new country and their new life.

"Life looks hopeful again, Matthew. Now that Harry is up and about, I find renewed belief that the future will be good to us."

"The Lord is over all, Sarah. He is over all," he responded.

***

The McCunes continued to share the evening meal with Captain Hussey at least once a week. The other days they ate with the forty other passengers in a galley where the long tables and benches were bolted to the deck. The pea-and-pork soup, boiled rice, oatmeal, and hardtack were much less appealing than the food served in the captain's cabin.

The weather steadily cooled as the ship moved nearer the Cape of Good Hope at the southern tip of Africa. A few days before reaching it, the ship halted at Port Elizabeth, where more supplies and fresh water were taken aboard. The McCunes took two hours to walk through the area surrounding the docks, where they heard a multitude of languages and dialects among people of all colors laboring to provision the many ships in the harbor.

"Father, the men seem to be speaking in outlandish tongues. What language do you suppose the white men are speaking?" Harry asked quietly as they watched the great water barrels rolled aboard the *Escort*.

"I can't say, Harry. We'll ask Captain Hussey when we go back aboard. It sounds a bit like Dutch or German to me."

"That language is Afrikaans, a language akin to the Dutch language of the original white settlers," he explained. "There is much friction between the Boers, as the descendants of the Dutch like to call themselves, and the more recent British settlers. I believe that the struggle for power between the two groups will eventually bring on a violent conflict," Captain Hussey commented when asked about it when they had returned to the ship.

After another six hours, the ship was pulled out of the harbor and into the ocean current by a large steamer tug as the captain stood near the helmsman to direct the ship's movement west-southwest toward the Atlantic.

***

After four days, the *Escort* completed its passage south of the Cape of Good Hope, and the captain directed it to the northwest. Matthew brought out the flutes purchased in India and informed his sons that it was time to learn to play them. "Lads, every good education should include music," he stated.

Harry made the first choice, selecting an ebony instrument with eight silver keys.

As he picked it up, his father stated, "That one is called a *hautboy*. It is used in military bands. You've made a fine choice, Harry."

"That seems a strange name for it, Father."

"It's some kind of French word, I'm told. You will enjoy it, I know."

George selected the twelve-keyed flutina made of boxwood. It was the smallest of the instruments, making him think it would be the easiest to learn.

The two younger brothers each selected one of the remaining flutes, their faces reflecting their lack of enthusiasm.

Matthew seemed sure the instruments could be mastered in a few minutes of trying. "Go ahead, Harry, play a scale. Show your brothers how it's done."

But his determination that his sons learn to play did not translate into immediate mastery of the instruments. Harry's flute seemed determined to interject an ear-piercing squeak into every scale at least three times.

"No, no, no," Matthew stated disgustedly. "Try it again."

Harry had only the dimmest idea of what the instrument was supposed to sound like, and he was sure he hadn't even come close, but he tried repeatedly until the crew members were moving about the ship with their hands over their ears. Even Sarah's patience wore thin.

But Matthew was unrelenting in his insistence that each son master the instrument chosen. Because the noise of more than one instrument at a time was too much for Sarah's ears, each son practiced for one hour. Harry and George practiced between breakfast and midday, and the two youngest practiced midafternoon. While they practiced, Matthew usually found other things to draw his attention, only pausing at the cabin to ask Sarah how the lads were progressing.

***

After a week Sarah pleaded, "Matthew, the other passengers and the crew do not appreciate your attempts to make musicians of your sons."

"Nonsense. Captain Hussey would have mentioned any complaints if that were the case."

So practice continued, and improvement began to show, especially for Harry and George, for which the other passengers and crew members were deeply grateful. Finally, one evening, his two oldest sons played an impromptu duet to which the captain offered his compliments. Matthew patted each on the shoulder. "I have always known there was music in my lads."

Alfred looked doubtfully at his father. Matthew returned his look and responded with confidence, "I'm just trying to bring you up as civilized lads, Alfred."

***

Harry walked the deck each morning despite the brisk breezes of the southern hemisphere. He enjoyed watching the captain as he took his readings with the sextant, which told him where the ship was in relationship to the equator.

He had been watching the helmsman and the captain confer. When they broke off speaking, he stepped forward and asked, "Captain, I've noted that the ship's course is now almost directly northward. May I ask where our next stop will be?"

The captain turned and said in pleasure, "It's young Mr. McCune. Of course you may ask. After we cross the equator, we will continue our course to the Cape Verde Islands, which lie directly west of the great hump of North Africa. There we will purchase more supplies, especially lemons and limes to stave off scurvy, and take fresh water aboard again. That will be somewhat more than halfway through our voyage. Before we reach that port, the weather will be much warmer than it is at present. You will willingly give up your coat and perhaps even be tempted to remove your shirt, as some of the crew will do."

Harry laughed, knowing he would never remove his shirt in public as the lower caste natives in India had done.

"There we will pick up the Canary Current, which will take us westward into the northeast trade winds, which will then push us toward North America.

When we reach the horse latitudes, the real temperament of the North Atlantic may show itself. The storms that occur in that area may prove unpleasant. If so, we will seek port somewhere in the Virgin Islands, but if the sea is more cooperative, we will stop for fresh water and supplies in Bermuda and then sail on to New York." The captain paused and studied Harry closely. "How is your health holding up at present?"

"I am doing tolerably well, Captain. Thank you for asking."

***

The captain was proven correct. From the Tropic of Capricorn across the equator to the Tropic of Cancer, the weather was warm and usually oppressive. As the ship neared the equator, Sarah and Matthew walked the deck in the evenings in the velvety soft night with the stars above them looking like pins holding the dark fabric of the sky in place. The luminous streak of the Milky Way crossed the heavens, stealing away any words that would have described it. Behind the ship, luminescent foam roiled and churned.

As Sarah studied the heavens, she commented, "Now that Harry is well, I am able to more fully appreciate this beautiful world, Matthew. It takes my breath."

In a matter-of-fact manner, he responded, "Yes, indeed."

She looked at him and smiled. *Well, what did I expect from him? Matthew has never been a sentimentalist.*

When the ship reached the North Atlantic, bad weather descended upon the weary travelers. The passengers willingly retired to their berths often as the ship began to pitch and roll. The ocean took on the color of polished steel, much like the blade of the saber that had been part of Matthew's dress uniform. The whitecaps increased in the churning, turbulent waves, and the wind that filled the sails was full of driving rain, making a daily walk on the deck impossible except for the hardiest of souls. Many of the passengers, including Sarah and Harry, experienced a brutal, lingering seasickness. Matthew and the three little brothers were apparently immune to it, but Sarah and a weakened Harry were not.

While the family sat in the cabin waiting for the sea to grow calmer, George asked, "Harry, was it like this on the *Bentick*?"

"What do you mean, George?"

"Were there bad storms that made the sailors seasick?"

"No, generally the Indian Ocean was much calmer than this, but I had other unpleasant experiences on both the steamships *Diana* and *Bentick*." He immediately had the attention of the entire family. "When it was discovered that I was a Mormon, I was given harsh duty. I was often ordered to shovel coal with the ordinary seamen who were much older and stronger than I. I was ordered to restring the sheets for the sails, even though neither the *Diana* nor the *Bentick* used sails. It was dangerous work. I was often called out of my bed when off duty and exhausted to some chore as simple as scrubbing the deck. I often had to settle for four hours of sleep each night."

Sarah was horrified. "Harry, why didn't you bring the matter to the attention of the captain?"

"The captain on the *Bentick* must have known. He read the assignment log each day. To complain would only have brought more disagreeable assignments."

"So you didn't mind resigning from the naval cadet program?"

"No, George, I didn't."

"But I liked your uniform, Harry," Alfred added. "Can you wear it even if you aren't in the navy anymore?"

"No, A. W. I turned it in when I left."

***

March 28, 1857
New York City

After 108 days at sea and three storms in the North Atlantic, the arrival in New York Harbor was a celebration. Alfred ran about the ship, going up and down the companionway yelling, "We're almost there! We're almost there!"

"Alf, will you stop running about and yelling? You are disturbing the other passengers." Matthew's voice was firm. "Come and help your mother pack the trunks."

After he had thrown everything in the stateroom into the open trunk, Sarah urged him to go up on deck and watch everything going on to get him out from underfoot.

The passengers gathered on the deck and cheered as the *Escort* came within sight of the harbor. They divided their attention between the crewmen who flowed up the rigging to reef the sails and the activity on the wharf. The harbor was crowded with masts and sails, more than Harry had ever expected to see in one place. There were great merchantmen loaded with freight from the orient, frigates, sloops and cutters, and even a great whaleboat, and there were barques and schooners and clipper ships. The *Escort* had to wait in open water for three hours until two steam launches could arrive to tow it to the Old Slip in New York Harbor.

The crew labored to tie the ship to the pier with its great hawsers. The anchor chain rumbled with the weight of the falling anchor, making the entire ship shudder. The passengers cheered in one great voice.

With his usual efficiency and alacrity, Matthew informed Sarah, "I will disembark and, following Captain Hussey's advice, find a rental office where I can obtain a place for us to live while we are here in New York." Before Sarah could even raise an objection, he added, "Stay on board until I return. I won't be long."

"How can you know how long you will be gone?" Sarah asked.

"Captain Hussey has told me of two rental offices not far from here on Spruce Street. I should be able to find a suitable property at one of them."

Sarah knew that when he put his mind to a task, Matthew allowed nothing to prevent his accomplishing it.

He returned in a little more than two hours. "I have rented a large house at 75 Grand Street, and four rented carriages should be at the dock within an hour or two to take us and our belongings to the house." His efficiency did not surprise Sarah. "Additionally," he announced, "I have hired a servant girl who will arrive tomorrow morning to fix breakfast and help us unpack."

When they arrived at the narrow three-story brownstone, Alfred ran through the house from the basement to the third floor. He returned to ask his mother, "Is this our new home?"

"Yes, Alfred, for the next few weeks, this will be our home."

"I want a room on the top floor. I can see a long way out of the windows up there." With that, he was off again.

Irish, redheaded Alice arrived the next morning. She had a small suitcase in her right hand and a bundle of additional belongings in a shawl in her left. "I'm yer new servant girl, Alice McGill. You be the McCune family?" She offered a quick bend of the knees to Sarah, which was meant to be a curtsey.

Sarah stepped aside and motioned her into the kitchen with a sweep of her hand. "Yes, I'm Sarah McCune." Harry appeared in the doorway to the hall and took in the scene.

Alice laughed. "As a family of micks like meself—no wonder ye be willlin' to take an Irish girl like me. Where do I put me things?"

Sarah was caught off guard by what she considered forward behavior on the part of the girl. Startled, she asked, "So you will be living here with us?"

"That be the 'greement. I git a dollar a week and room and board."

Trying to cover her surprise, Sarah turned and spoke to Harry. "Harry, will you show Alice to a room on the second floor—one with a bed?"

"Of course, Mother." He turned and led the girl up the stairs. "What do you mean by calling us a family of micks?" he asked as he led her to a bedroom furnished in a manner like the entire house. It held one narrow bed with a small bed table beside it where a coal oil lamp sat.

"Well, sure and b'golly, this will do jus' fine," she said as she put her suitcase and bundle on the bed. She opened the suitcase and pulled out a bib apron, which she donned.

"Now, I best get to fixin' breakfast."

As they returned to the kitchen, Harry asked again, "What did you mean by calling us a family of micks?"

"With all the starvin' times in Ireland, the Irish 'ave come floodin' to America, and half of us have a name startin' with *Mc*, like yours and mine."

"But I was born in India. Am I still a mick?"

"I dunno. Ye sure don't talk like one." She laughed again, this time heartily.

The breakfast was plain as Sarah had little in the house but oatmeal and a loaf of bread purchased the evening after they left the boat. As Alice cleaned up after the meal, she stated in her direct manner, "Ye have little in the hoose for meals this day."

"It's the Sabbath, and my husband doesn't approve of purchases made on the Sabbath. I'm not sure what to do."

"Well, I 'ave an answer fer that. I'll bring enough from me mum's place fer today, and ye kin pay me t'morrow. That way no money will change hands on the Sabbath. "Will that suit ye, mum?"

Sarah smiled in relief. "That would be a great help, Alice."

The girl disappeared down the street with her shawl around her shoulders and returned in two hours. As she began a midday meal of lamb stew and muffins, Matthew arrived home.

"You were up and gone very early this morning. Where did you go?" Sarah asked with a slight tone of reproach.

"I've been out and about looking for anyone who could put me in contact with someone in the Church. I finally located Elder John Taylor."

"How did you manage to find one man in all this great city?"

"I started by approaching every constable I could find—they call them policemen here in America. I asked if they knew where the Mormons met. I finally approached a police station and was told that they meet in the Brooks Assembly Hall. The sergeant at the desk called them troublemakers, but when I asked why, he had no answer." He sat down tiredly. "I arrived at the meeting place after meetings were finished. Next Sabbath, we will hire a carriage and meet with the Saints."

He looked at the stove, where Alice was stirring the stew, and stated, "You must be Alice." She bent at the knees in a little curtsey toward him. "Thank you for being so prompt this morning. When will the meal be ready? I've had a long walk, and I'm very hungry."

He started up the stairs to change his shirt. She called after him, "Everything ready in half an hour, sir."

That evening, as Alice completed drying the last of the dinner dishes, she announced to Sarah, "I begin my day at eight o'clock in the mornin', and I finish at eight o'clock in the evenin'. G'night." She removed her apron as she disappeared up the stairs.

CHAPTER FIFTEEN

April 1, 1857
New York

MATTHEW AROSE AT 6:00 A.M., as was his usual time, and after dressing, found the house quiet and nothing happening in the kitchen. Forgetting that Alice did not consider herself on duty until eight, he opened Harry's door and stuck his head in. "Harry, get up. I don't see Alice anywhere. We will need to get our own breakfast. Go down and build a fire in the stove."

Though he had never previously built a fire in a stove, it sounded like fun. Harry rose and dressed quickly. When he reached the kitchen, he located the box of kindling. His father's newspaper from the previous day was on the table. He crumpled two pages and studied the stove. He opened the large door in the front of the oven and then lifted the lid to the small firebox and scratched his head. *A good fire needs some room*, he thought.

He made his decision. He opened the oven door and quickly filled it with crumpled paper and kindling. He lit the paper with one of the matches he found in a cup near the stove.

The fire immediately burned brightly, but within less than a minute, smoke was roiling into the room. He closed the door, but the smoke made its way around its edges and the air in the kitchen quickly became thick with it. A cloud was moving up the stairs to the bedrooms.

Harry tried to fan the smoke away with the newspaper, but to no avail.

His father came running down the stairs. "Harry, whatever is the matter?" he called out.

Harry couldn't answer for coughing and sneezing.

As Alice put on her shoes, she smelled the smoke and rushed down the stairs, pushing past Matthew. When she saw what was going on, she pushed open the kitchen door and, standing outside, laughed and hollered at Harry's expense, bending and slapping her knees. "Ye've built the fire in the oven."

Embarrassed and angry with Alice for laughing at him, Harry scolded, "Don't laugh at your betters, Alice. Your impudence is inexcusable."

Alice laughed even harder, until she was wiping tears from her smoke-stained face.

Matthew handed Harry two buckets. "Go across the street to the pump and bring back water to put down the fire."

Harry was shocked. He stood tall and refused his father for the first time in his life. "No, Father, I will not do the work of a servant."

"Harry, the matter is urgent. The house is filling with smoke, and the fire brigade may soon arrive."

"Father, I have always done as you have asked, but this time it is too much." Harry's voice rose. "I shall not stoop to do a servant's work."

With a look of aggravation on his face, Matthew took the buckets and started for the pump, where a dozen servant girls stood in line.

Harry stood in shock, watching as his father pumped water for each giggling girl. When he had filled his own two buckets, he carried them back to the kitchen, where a still-chortling Alice tried to extinguish the flames.

"Now, my lad, you try it. Go and pump two buckets of water."

Harry felt somewhat ashamed watching his proud father lower himself to the task. He could no longer refuse. He hurried to the pump after the number of servant girls diminished and vigorously pumped, quickly filling the buckets. In his hurry to minimize his embarrassment, he ran back to the house, spilling half of the water.

Matthew stood at the kitchen door thinking, *If mortification were fatal, Harry would soon be dead.* He leaned against the doorframe watching, his arms crossed over his chest. *There is much Harry needs to learn in this land of America where Jack is as good as his master.*

That evening, Harry wrote a letter to Annie telling her about the long voyage and New York, but he didn't mention the fire in the oven.

***

The following Sunday morning, the family rode in a rented horse-drawn hack to Brooks Assembly Hall for Sabbath meeting. There, Matthew was asked by Elder John Taylor to address the congregation and tell of his missionary efforts and the growth of the Church in India and Burma.

At the conclusion of the meeting, Matthew and Elder Taylor chatted about the McCune family's plans to emigrate to the Salt Lake Valley. It took only a few minutes for Elder Taylor to explain what was on his mind.

"Elder McCune, would you be willing to lead the group that will be traveling from here to Iowa City by train? There are about twenty of them who attended the meeting today, and I would feel greatly relieved to know that they had an experienced leader at their head."

Matthew didn't hesitate. "Of course, Elder Taylor, if you feel I am qualified."

"There will be another group gathered in Delaware who will join the main company in Iowa City. I will need you to acquire wagons for them when you purchase your own as many of those folks are dependent upon the Perpetual Emigration Fund. When the full group is assembled there, the company will be led by Captain Jacob Hofheins. He's the only man in the group who has crossed the plains previously."

"I will have the wagons ready for the Delaware group and will make myself available to Captain Hofheins during the journey."

The two men shook hands and followed the members of the congregation outside, where a late snow was falling. An inch already lay on the ground, turning the city white. Many of the children squealed and raced about with their mouths open, catching the flakes on their tongues.

The McCune children had never previously seen snow. George, Alfred, and Edward scooped up handfuls and shouted, "*Dako cheyney hai*" in Hindustani, thinking the snow was sugar.

But they noted with disappointment that it swiftly melted, chilling their hands. Edward shook his cold hands and ran to Sarah. "What is it, Mother? It's cold. I don't like it."

"It's snow, Edward. Snow is always cold. You will see snow here in America often."

"I still don't like it."

***

Life at 75 Grand Street took on a comfortable regularity for the next three weeks, with Alice cooking and washing and Sarah directing the studies of the three younger boys. Though a little embarrassed that her guests had to use the trunks for seating, Sarah and Matthew looked forward to the occasional presence of Apostle John Taylor in their home, where he met with Matthew and several other men to discuss preparations for the looming trek west to the Salt Lake Valley.

***

April 25, 1857
New York City

Before long, the McCune family had bid farewell to Alice and vacated the three-story brownstone. The previous day, she'd willingly assisted Sarah in putting together a large basket of cheese, bread, cooked meats, boiled eggs, boiled rice, and oatmeal cookies, hopefully enough to feed the family for the two days it would take to reach Chicago by train.

Matthew shepherded the group of twenty members, all recent converts to the Church, in addition to his own family, onto the Chicago-bound train. The children in the group kept themselves busy for much of the first day getting acquainted with each other and watching the passing scenes from the windows of the train car. Soon the cities were replaced by small towns, and eventually the vast prairie spread before them for several hours before darkness enveloped the landscape.

Finally, Edward climbed onto the bench where Sarah sat. "Mother, when will we get there? I'm tired of riding, and these benches are hard."

"Why don't you lie down by me and go to sleep. When you wake up, we will be that much closer to Chicago."

The adult passengers and older children slept as best they could sitting up or leaning against one another, with the younger children asleep in their laps or on the floor at their feet. When morning came, the journey was half over.

***

While in Chicago awaiting the train that would take them to Iowa City, Matthew led the men to purchase wagons from a large blacksmith firm near the cattle pens about a half mile from the train station. He purchased two for his family plus six more, per instructions, for the families from Delaware. The pieces of the wagons were loaded into one of the freight cars. Harry watched closely, counting the number of wheels and wagon beds to make sure each wagon would have all the necessary parts.

***

When the train was three miles from Iowa City, it came to a halt, and as the conductor walked through the train cars, he announced, "Passengers with property in the freight car must collect it at this point. The train will remain here only one hour while all shipped freight is unloaded and the train takes on water."

Matthew rose and, in a voice loud enough for all in the car to hear, authoritatively stated, "All of you making your way west with the Saints must collect your goods and leave the train here. Iowa City is the end of the line." He turned to his sons. "Lads, get your bags. We've got work to do. George, take your mother's bag."

"I can do that, Father," Harry responded.

"Harry, I have a bigger task for you. Stay close to me."

As they climbed down from the train, Matthew looked around at the prairie and asked the conductor, "Why are we forced to get off here? It appears we are in the middle of nowhere."

"Take a look at the railroad water tower over there. It's the last water supply from here to Iowa City, and you folks are goin' to need it. In Iowa City we'll pick up eastbound passengers, and if you folks were still on the train, it would cost us a lot of time we don't have. Since most of you folks will be here for a time while you put your wagons together, I recommend that you tell everyone to put their buckets under the spout when they need water and watch that they don't pull it down too far and drown themselves."

The darkness had come by the time all wagon parts and additional bags and trunks had been unloaded, identified, and sorted. By nine, with the assistance of one another and the light from the fires they'd built, each family had the tent they had purchased for the journey raised against the cool night air. The following morning brought the task of assembling the wagons.

Through his experience in Burma, Matthew understood the construction of supply wagons, cannon mounts, and carriages, so once the parts of his two wagons had been located, he called out to the men in the group, "Come and watch while we put our wagons together. If you will watch and assist me and my lads, we will return the favor."

As Matthew, Harry, and four young men in their twenties heaved the fully constructed McCune wagons onto their wheels, the entire group cheered.

Matthew then walked from family group to family group giving instructions, and, whenever needed, he and Harry offered to help complete each wagon. The wagons were nearly assembled by noon, with the exception of those waiting for the Delaware families to claim them. The owners congratulated themselves at having completed the task. While they were slapping each other on the back, a man and three young boys in their early teens arrived, driving forty-eight head of unbroken oxen to the camp.

"Who's in charge here?" the man hollered as he and the boys slowed the plodding animals to a halt.

Several of the men turned to Matthew as if he had been formally elected camp captain. He stepped forward. "You can talk with me," he responded.

"Here's your ox teams, paid for by the Perpetual Emigration Fund. You'll need to put four to a wagon." He leaned tiredly on his saddle horn and looked directly at Matthew. "Look, Brother . . ."

"McCune, Matthew McCune."

"Well, Brother McCune, I'm really sorry to tell ya that these oxen ain't broken to the yoke. Yer pretty lucky we could even find this many right now as there's been such a passel of companies headed west. You'll need to train 'em yerselves." He straightened in his saddle and called out, "Anybody here ever handled oxen or trained them to the yoke?"

Matthew raised his hand. One other man raised his, though a little tentatively.

"Two of ya. Well, I wish you luck training these animals. They ain't been exactly co-ah-per-a-tive." He pronounced each syllable as if it were unfamiliar. "My name is Barton, and I'm the agent for the Church here in Iowa City. I been told that there's some extra wagons for the folks from Delaware who arrived by train two days ago. Most of 'em are . . . er . . . well . . . they'll need you men to put them wagons together and train them there oxen that'll pull 'em. Sorry to add to your burdens, but that's the way it's got to be. When ya get them animals trained, you can drive the wagons into camp, 'bout three miles west of here, just this side of the town. Report to the company captain, a German named Hofheins. He's the only one who's ever been over and back to the valley before." He wheeled his horse and started back, the boys with him following his example.

Matthew looked at his sons and nodded his head toward the herd. "Let's pick our animals, lads." Matthew and the other men walked among the animals, who had begun to graze. Ignoring everything except size and muscle strength, he selected two. He put ropes through the rings mounted in the nose of each animal and handed both to Harry. He nodded toward the wagons, where Sarah stood with Edward. "Take them over there, lad."

He continued moving through the animals and called out to men still standing around and watching, "Come over here, men, and select your teams."

Matthew selected two more animals for his family, then walked them to the edge of the herd and handed the ropes to ten-year-old George, who looked like he was trying to put on a brave front. "Lead them over to the wagon, lad. Go ahead. If you act like you're the boss, they will believe you." The boy leaned into the ropes, and the big animals slowly lumbered after him.

Another of the large animals was selected and led to Alfred. Matthew handed the rope to the eight-year-old boy. "Lead it over to the wagon like George did. Just pull on the rope and make it follow you." Alfred looked skeptical and a bit frightened but did as he was told. "Tell your mother to send Edward over," Matthew called after him.

When Matthew had selected three more animals, he called out to Sarah, who would not let go of Edward's shoulder. "Sarah, send the lad over. He needs to get accustomed to working with the animals."

She called out, "But, Matthew, he's only a small lad." Her voice was full of alarm.

"The animals don't know that. He can learn to handle the animals at his age just like the young lads in India do." She hesitantly let go of Edward's shoulder, and he ran to his father excitedly, but as he neared the animals and their size grew more apparent, he slowed, his confidence ebbing.

"Edward, just take this rope and lean into it. The ox will follow you."

Trusting his father, he quietly said, "All right, Father, if you think it knows what it's supposed to do."

"Yes, son, it will follow you."

Matthew pulled the last two over to his wagons and tied each of the animals to a wagon wheel.

The balance of that day and the next two were spent with Matthew instructing the wagon owners in the training of the oxen. Matthew had handled ox teams in Burma when weapons and supplies had been hauled from camp to camp, so all he had to do was learn the commands in English to replace his useless Hindustani.

When basic instructions had been given, the other men began the challenging task of determining which animals would work as a team while yoked together. Some of those looking on laughed until they were exhausted as many of the yoked oxen dragged their new owners and wagons all over the prairie surrounding the camp.

Finally, with Matthew driving one team and Harry learning to drive the second, the column of wagons started for the camp in Iowa City, with substitute drivers handling the wagons for the Delaware families.

CHAPTER SIXTEEN

April 30, 1857
Iowa City, Iowa

THE HOFHEINS COMPANY, AS IT was called, was combined with the Delaware group. Captains of ten were assigned, and Matthew was appointed captain of the guard and head of the hunting group. All were to follow Hofheins's orders. When supplies were checked, those who had not followed instructions and made sure they had brought everything required were sent back into town to obtain what they lacked.

Harry wrote another letter to Annie.

Dear Annie,

It has been stressful and at times very tiring to this point in our journey. Though I think of you every day, there has been no opportunity to send another letter. I hope your family is well, especially your mother. I cannot offer you an address to reply to this letter, but hopefully in a few months or even weeks, I will be able to do so. I go to sleep each evening thinking about you and praying that your father has determined to leave the army so he can bring his family to Zion.

Sincerely,
Your Friend, Harry McCune

As they traveled, Sarah labored at learning to cook with the limited supplies she had. Noting the delicious aromas floating in the air near the Andrews wagon and the fact that the Andrews were British like the McCunes but from Northern Ireland, she sought out the advice of Isabella Andrews.

A bit self-conscious, she approached Isabella and quietly explained, "I am struggling to learn to cook for my family. I haven't done it for many years. I am at my wit's end over the task. Please tell me how to prepare a good meal over an open fire with my barrels of flour, cornmeal, beans, dried peas, salted pork, and small amount of rice. It seems that every meal I fix is the same—beans, salt pork, and corn bread. What am I to do?" She was thoroughly frustrated.

Isabella handed her infant son to her daughter, Elizabeth. "Here, Issy, take the bairn." She put her arm around Sarah. "Your meals will be no better and no worse than any of those prepared by the rest of us. I expect our menfolk will bring us game and we will add that to our meals, and I'm sure we will all be glad to eat whatever can be fixed after the long and tiring days of this great journey. As we continue on, I'll share a few ideas to make some of the meals a bit easier to eat, but I'll need some fresh game—venison or buffalo."

The two women sat together on a log as Isabella shared her wisdom and a few recipes. Sarah thanked her, and as she returned to her wagons, she whispered to herself, "Oh, where are you when I need you, Leela?" That night the McCunes ate cornbread and beans, as did every other family.

The next day, Matthew brought her three rabbits he had shot. He was pleased with himself, but her heart sank as he extended them toward her. "Here's supper. Rabbit stew will be a welcome change from beans and salt pork."

Indeed it would, if she understood how to skin and clean the furry carcasses. She took them hesitantly, and Matthew was quickly off to attend to another matter.

Harry had been watching the exchange. He noted the desperate look on his mother's face. "Mother, give them to me. I'll find someone to show me how to clean them."

"Ask John Andrews to show you. Perhaps he knows how."

Harry watched Brother Andrews process the first. The man then handed him the knife and watched as he cleaned and skinned the last two. As thanks for the instruction, Harry offered one to him. The look of relief on his mother's face when he brought two of them back ready to cook was reward enough for Harry.

"Sister Andrews told me to tell you that you should boil them in a pot of water until the meat falls off the bones. Then remove the bones and add some flour to make a gravy, then add a cup of dried peas and a handful of rice."

During supper, Matthew stated as he cleaned his tin plate, "This rabbit stew is wonderful. What a cook you are, Sarah. You may serve it as often as you like." Sarah looked at Harry, and they shared a knowing smile.

"I'm so glad it pleased you, Matthew, but to serve it again will require additional rabbits."

***

At the end of the camp devotional that evening, Hofheins stood and announced, "The rain not so bad now, and Elder Taylor says ve can start anytime. The mud on the trail isn't so bad as it vas. Be packed and ready to line up by six tomorrow morning. Ve start for Vinter Qvarters." He turned away from the group and then turned back. "They call it Florence, Nebraska. Ve'll meet up with a group from St. Louis there. Everybody's been told vhat supplies are needed. If you don't have all the supplies you vere told to bring, then that vill be your problem. Nobody owes you help. You have been varned."

The harshness of his words made Sarah wonder about his suitability as a leader.

***

May 3, 1857
Iowa City

To have the wagons packed properly and breakfast out of the way, the McCune family rose at four. By six, the company began its move westward. With the blessing of Elder John Taylor, the Delaware captains of ten hung back, promising to start the next day.

Over the following days, the oxen gradually became tractable in their yokes. Each time they camped, families would claim the land they camped on by laying various items used in their travels around their sites. A fellow camper could find a seat on an ox yoke or a log or a stool and feel as if they were a visitor in that family's sitting room.

When the company passed through the settlement of Newton a few miles east of Fort Des Moines, crowds of locals came to offer employment in an attempt to entice the men of the company to settle there and work for them. Though they were refused, some of the locals stayed for the evening devotional to see what the Mormons believed. They could find no fault with Brother Joseph Foreman's sermon.

Matthew was able to purchase a horse in Newton, and as he rode beside the second wagon, giving instructions, George gradually became nearly as adept a teamster as his older brother. Though Sarah said nothing, she had to fight the tears as she rubbed bacon grease on her young son's hands each evening to treat the blisters. *Matthew expects so much of our lads*, she thought.

***

A short way beyond Fort Des Moines, some of the children came upon a large flock of prairie chickens, and many of the birds were added to the evening meal. When Matthew handed three of the dead birds to Sarah, she looked at Harry with a plea in her eyes.

He responded by telling his younger brothers, "Lads, let me show you how to pluck these birds. You will find them the best meal we've had on this journey yet."

George frowned with distaste but set about the task. Alfred wrinkled his nose, and Harry had to motivate him by saying, "If you don't do your part of the plucking, A. W., you won't get any of the bird for supper."

After the meal had been cleaned away, Sarah sat on the log near the fire for a quiet moment. It had been a long and tiring day.

Matthew had gathered with many of the other men to discuss the road ahead, and some of the younger boys of the camp had found enough energy to play a game of tag before the night set in. As she sat dozing, exhausted from the journey, she felt a small body snuggle up against her. She put her arm out and pulled Edward closer, neither of them speaking for a few minutes.

"Mother, can we go back to Calcutta? I don't like it here." His voice was little more than a whisper.

"Why do you want to go back to Calcutta, Edward?"

"I'm tired of walking every day, and I miss my bed and . . . and I like the way Leela cooked. I'm tired of beans and . . . and I want to play with Tommy Meik. But mostly I'm tired, and I want to go home."

"I understand. I'm tired too. Everybody's tired."

"Then why can't we go back to Calcutta?"

Sarah was quiet while she tried to think of a way to explain the matter to the child. She understood his feelings. "The Lord wants all of us to go to Zion where we can live our religion without anyone trying to burn down our houses or cut the ropes on the tents when your father preaches or try to stop us from worshipping the way we want."

"Will we have a big house in Zion like our house in Calcutta?" His voice was hopeful.

"Not for a while, Edward. Maybe someday." The two of them sat together in silence until Matthew and Harry returned to the campsite. Matthew lifted a sleeping Edward from his mother's side and carried him into the tent, where he tucked him into his bedroll.

***

On May 23, the wagons reached Council Bluffs on the great Missouri River, where they camped for two days. When the Delaware company caught up with them, Elder John Taylor instructed the combined companies to cross the river the next morning and camp upstream in Florence. "The St. Louis company will be here in a few days. They're coming by steamboat and will join us there."

That evening he shared supper with the McCunes. Sarah was relieved that he seemed fine with the plain meal she'd set out. It was no different than what the other families were eating.

In the morning, when the company lined up at the Missouri River, it was learned that the ferry could handle the wagons but not the animals.

Harry swung down from the wagon seat. He stood looking at the river with his hands on his hips and muttered, "The third great challenge of the journey."

His mother had been walking next to the wagon and heard him. "What do you mean, Harry? What makes this the third great challenge?"

He laughed ruefully and kicked at a clod of dirt. "Mother, I consider crossing the Atlantic Ocean the first and assembling the wagons and breaking the oxen to the yoke the second."

Hofheins stood in the back of his wagon and called out, "The ferry can take the wagons, but the cattle will have to swim the river. Line up for the ferry."

The cattle numbered well over two hundred and would have to be driven into the river with ropes against their rumps and gunfire. Harry was among the six young men Hofheins selected to oversee the task. At seventeen, he was considered both old enough, mature enough, and good enough on a horse to be among those assigned the task.

When Harry and the other young men started to drive the animals into the river, Sarah grabbed Matthew's arm and whispered, "Matthew, stop him. He may drown."

"Harry is as fine a horseman as any man in the company. He will be safe," Matthew responded with confidence.

She said no more but held her breath until the animals started to climb out on the far side of the river at a low point on the bank. The oxen were hitched to the wagons again, and the riders drove the other animals to the campsite."

Florence proved to be a well-established settlement comprised of several hundred log cabins and sod houses, numerous dugouts, and at least twenty permanent buildings used by its various merchants. A good number of settlers had been there for more than two years, and many much longer. They had planted crops to help feed both themselves and the wagon companies passing through.

Sarah was grateful when Matthew rented a two-room log cabin for a dollar. "We do not know how long we will be here," he said, "and having a roof over our head will make it a little easier on us all."

After resting for a day, many of the wagon company members celebrated their successful arrival by taking out their treasured instruments, and a warm and hopeful harmony rose from the camp into the night air. At Matthew's insistence, Harry and George took out their flutes and joined the impromptu concert on the more familiar tunes.

Harry watched several couples as they danced the Virginia reel in the firelight and thought of Annie Meik, feeling guilty that she hadn't crossed his mind for many days. *So much to do and so much think about that has pushed her from my mind. I'll try to think of her more often.*

Sarah and Isabella sat on a log and watched the dancers. Isabella hummed to the music while she rocked her five-month-old infant son, Michael John. When John approached his wife and asked if she would like to dance, she quietly answered, "It's best if I sit. I'm feelin' poorly."

"Bella, you look tired. Has the little lad been ill?" Sarah whispered as she looked down at the wide-eyed baby.

"No, no, he always sleeps the sleep of the just. Let me have Issy put him in his cradle, and we can talk awhile."

Eleven-year-old Elizabeth heard her mother and gently took the infant from Sarah to put him to bed in the wagon.

"Was the journey from Iowa City hard on you? You look worn out," Sarah stated. "It was hard. Some days ago, the cattle were stampeded and Nephi fell out of the wagon. The wheel passed over his foot, and he's been ridin' ever since. See," she pointed as the boy carefully and slowly approached the log and sat near his mother, "he's limpin' yet."

"I could ask Matthew to look at the lad's foot. Maybe he can do something."

"Oh, 'tis nearly better. Don't bother Matthew."

"Surely if we help one another, we'll all joyfully see the end of this journey—hopefully hale and hearty," Sarah said encouragingly.

"I dearly hope so." Isabella's voice was so low Sarah almost missed the words, but the tone was clear. It was full of anxiety.

"You speak as if you fear that might not be so? If you're doing poorly, maybe Matthew has an herbal tea that might help. He has many herbs he brought all the way from India."

"I thank ye for yer kind thoughts, Sarah." Her voice was flat, as if she were speaking of events far removed from the time and place. "I never really got my strength back since the birth of the last bairn. I feel like it's spinning out of me as steady as a spider's web. I fear that some other woman will raise my family."

Sarah put her hand over Isabella's where they were folded together in the woman's lap.

"Bella, you mustn't talk like that. You will see the end of this journey. I promise." Sarah spoke forcefully, trying to give the weary younger woman—and herself—courage. She continued conversing, trying to distract the woman from her dark thoughts. "Tell me about your family. They are fine children."

"Aye, my Issy is a bonnie lass and a good one too. She is my great help. Her brothers are strong and willing lads. No mother could ask more of those the Lord has let me keep."

"How many have you lost?"

"I expect ye've noticed that Issy be four years older than Nephi. We buried two 'tween the two of them. The other three lads be blessed with good, strong bodies. Even little Michael John born in January be thriving, no matter that I am still weak. T'was a hard birth." She grew silent for a few seconds before she added, "But I be talkin' too much about meself."

"No, no, I understand what you're telling me. We lost four in India. Our firstborn, Alexander, died of rabies after he was bitten by a dog." Sarah shuddered at the memory and whispered, "It was a terrible way to die."

Isabella waited for her to regain her composure. Finally, she asked, "How did ye lose the other bairns?"

Sarah took a deep breath. "My daughter, Grace, died not long after Alexander, and two years later we lost our little Alfred and his brother William within an hour of each other. All three died of Asiatic cholera. I do believe I would not have survived if the Lord had not spared Harry. Thank goodness George was born a few months later."

Both women were quiet while the memory of their losses filled their hearts with pain. The music had stopped, and now the sound of the men's voices floated over to them on the night air.

"The men are returning," Sarah quietly said as she stood. "Bella, thank you for sharing your feelings this evening. We have much in common, much we can share."

Isabella stood and smiled weakly. "And I thank ye for yer patient, listen' ear. Should ye need a recipe for venison, I'll be glad to share mine."

As Matthew neared and saw the two women standing together, he lifted his hat to Sister Andrews in respect. Then he extended his elbow toward Sarah, and she put her hand through the crook in his arm.

"Good night, Bella," Sarah offered.

"Good night, Sarah." Her words were quiet and resigned.

As they reached their own wagon, Sarah shared her concerns about Isabella Andrews. "Matthew, is there anything you can do for her? She has never recovered from the birth of her baby in January. She is weak and doesn't feel she will survive the journey to the valley."

"I don't know. I will look through the herbs and see if I have anything that might be helpful. I do have some chamomile, which might help her sleep. Rest is a wonderful healer."

He took the powdered chamomile to Isabella and urged her to steep it in hot water and drink it before she retired.

"Yes, I'll do that. I thank ye for yer kindness."

In the morning, Sarah and Matthew were both pleased to see that Isabella seemed better rested.

While Sarah prepared supper the next day, Alfred entered the cabin covered in mud to his knees. He held a bouquet of flowers with lavender petals and large central cones. He pulled at his mother's apron. "Mother, look what I found for you. They're pretty, aren't they?"

She wiped her hands and took the bouquet. "Yes, Alfred, they are beautiful." She bent and gave the boy a hug. "Thank you for thinking of me." She turned and spoke to her husband, who was studying a map spread out on the trunk that served as a table. "Look, Matthew, see the flowers Alfred has brought me."

Matthew paused and, with heightened interest, reached out for the bouquet. "May I see those, Sarah?" He patted the chair next to him. "Come over here, my lad. I think you have discovered something wonderful. Will you take me to see where you found these?"

"Yes, Father." The boy beamed. "We can go right now."

As Matthew was pulled toward the door by the child, he handed the flowers to Sarah. "Take care of them, Sarah. They may be of great use."

An hour later, Matthew and Alfred returned, each with an armful of the blooms. Additionally, Matthew had both pockets filled with what looked like peppermint leaves.

He pulled one of his homeopathic medical books from the large trunk used for sitting. Then he sat down on the trunk and opened the book to the chapter on medicinal plants. After a few minutes, he examined the heaping bouquet on the lid of the smaller trunk.

"These are echinacea blooms, just as I suspected—and these leaves that look a bit like mint are actually thyme. They were growing in a great cluster on the sunny side of the hill by the stream."

He rose and pushed the small trunk over to the only window in the cabin and began to spread them out in the sun. "We must dry them carefully. They will be a blessing as we travel."

"How will you use them?" Sarah asked.

"Echinacea leaves can be used as a tea for a cough or when one is feeling poorly and can be pounded into a paste for wounds, burns, and insect bites."

"Oh, do take some to Isabella when they are dried."

"I will do that." He examined each stem and bloom as he spoke. "The thyme leaves can be made into a tea for coughs, congestion, and stomach upset. In the morning the lads and I will return to the area along the creek where we found these. It seems that someone in the past may have established a small herb garden filled with plants with possible health benefits. They grow wildly on the hillside now." He turned to his young son and smiled broadly. "Alf, my lad, you have found plants that can be used for medicinal purposes." The child again beamed at his father's praise, even though he surely didn't understand what *medicinal* meant.

As soon as the sun rose the next day, Matthew grabbed an empty flour sack, and since Harry was on morning guard duty to keep the cattle from straying, he called George and Alfred to accompany him. They hiked more than a mile up the little creek to the spot where numerous plants grew in wild profusion. There, Matthew was pleased to find St. John's Wort, its bright yellow blooms clustered on the hillside above the stream. Leaning over the water that flowed quietly at its base was a cluster of white willow trees. He cut branch after branch and handed them to George. "The leaves and bark of this tree are very useful for stomach upset."

He handed the flour sack filled with the St. John's Wort to his second son. "Take the willow branches and the flour sack back to the cabin. Get another bag and hurry back." George sped away with his arms full.

By the time he had returned, Matthew had located a cluster of broadleaf plantain he could use as a poultice or for a tea for diarrhea. He had put Alfred to work carefully pulling dandelion plants. "Try to get the root of the plant," Matthew urged him. "That is the most important part. Don't worry about the yellow blooms."

When a perspiring George arrived and held out the second flour sack, Matthew pointed at a cluster of white flowers a hundred feet farther up the stream. "Collect as many of those plants as you can. I think they are yarrow. I won't know for sure until we get back and I can look in my book."

"Is this one a hollyhock, Father? Is that one some kind of a thistle?" Alfred asked excitedly as he pointed.

"No, my lad, this is the marsh mallow plant. Admittedly, it looks a bit like a hollyhock. It is useful for many ailments. And that one is the great burdock. Both are common in England and may prove very useful to us."

"What are they good for?" George asked as he carried his sack of yarrow plants back to his father.

"The leaves and seeds of the great burdock plant can be pounded into a paste and used as a poultice to treat boils, burns, bruises, even rashes and open sores. And the marsh mallow plant—the one that looks somewhat like a hollyhock—its root can be made into a tea for digestive problems and even to help breathing for ague or a bad cough. If it is made into a paste, it can also be used on bruises, aching muscles, and even insect bites."

"I've got a few of them." George scratched at a mosquito bite.

The flour sack was soon full, and the three returned to the cabin smiling broadly. Matthew spent the balance of the day hanging the plants to dry on a cord stretched across the cabin.

While their father dried the plants they had gathered, the younger boys went about roaming the nearby prairie in search of treasures of all kinds.

In the morning as Sarah began breakfast preparations, she admonished George to watch his younger brothers. "You must keep a close eye on Alfred and Edward. Watch out for rattlesnakes. Remember, they give little warning and strike much more quickly than a cobra." The boys respected the cobras native to India, but familiarity had bred contempt, and they did not particularly fear them. Sarah wanted them to understand that the snakes of the territory they were crossing were of a more untrustworthy nature.

She was grateful George could watch over his brothers since, during the days that followed, Matthew and Harry were both extremely busy. Each day, Matthew had to assign guards for the nearly 260 head of cattle that grazed on the prairie near the settlement. Despite the guards, nearly every evening, many of the animals would bolt, and the young men would be called on to chase them down and round them up. That included Harry.

When not busy with that, Matthew and Harry mended the wagon covers, replaced an axle on the wagon Harry drove, bought a butchered hog, and bartered for grain, vegetables, and seeds. Sarah washed, mended, and ironed until she was stiff from the effort.

It wasn't until after days of exhausting labor that, one evening after supper, Matthew opened one of the trunks and took out the four flutes. "Lads, we finally have some time this evening. It's time to improve your music."

He ignored the scowl on Alfred's face and after a few minutes stated, "Harry and George, you are both noticeably improving in your skill. Alf, you and Edward would improve if you spent more time playing the instruments rather than trying to kill flies and mosquitoes with them."

But Edward had no intention of improving his skills with his instrument. His favorite possession quickly became the small, empty preserve jar his mother had given him, where he could keep the fireflies he and his brothers caught in the evenings.

***

At the end of the first week in the cabin at Florence, Sarah felt Alfred pulling at her skirts as she prepared dough for biscuits. "Mother, look what followed me home. Can I keep him? He's hungry."

Sarah looked at the dirty animal and recognized that there was a dog somewhere under the filthy, matted fur coat.

"No, no, Alfred. He's very dirty, and we have nothing to feed him." The thought of all the vermin buried in the animal's fur left her horrified.

"He can have some of what I eat." The boy's face was full of pleading.

"No, Alfred. He must belong to someone. Take him around the camp and ask if he belongs to anyone."

"But, Mother, I'll wash him and make him obey."

She shook her head and stated firmly, "Your father would not approve."

Harry had been listening to the discussion from where he sat mending the traces for one of the ox teams. "A. W., I'll go with you, and we will find a home for him."

The boy's head drooped in disappointment, but he followed his older brother, bringing up the rear behind the filthy dog.

They returned a little more than an hour later, as Sarah was stirring the beans. Alfred's countenance had changed to one of cheerfulness.

"Brother Mousley said he would give him a bath and a haircut and teach him to help guard the cattle at night. He's going to call him Wolf. And he said I can come and visit him anytime."

Sarah breathed a sigh of relief.

The next evening as supper was being readied, Alfred arrived at the cabin dustier and more tired than usual.

"Alfred, why are you so dirty?" Sarah asked, her hands on her hips.

The boy looked at his dirty shoes and clothing and shrugged his shoulders.

George arrived behind his little brother. He grinned and answered for him. "A. W. decided that if he couldn't have a dog for a pet that he would catch and tame a prairie dog instead. He didn't have much luck."

"They sure can run fast—and they hide in the ground." Alfred's tone conveyed aggravation and disappointment.

Sarah shook her head and muttered under her breath, "Thank goodness."

The next evening as Sarah was completing supper preparations, a dog began to bark not far from the McCune cabin. Ignoring the noise, Sarah asked Harry, "Where's Alfred? The meal is ready."

"He went to play with Wolf at the Mousley's cabin," George stated.

Harry motioned for George to follow him. "Let's go find him so we can eat supper."

They located the barking dog about a quarter mile from the settlement. The animal was stiff-legged and barking frantically, its hackles raised, reflecting an unusual fierceness. Alfred was kneeling next to the dog.

"A. W., what's going on? What's the matter with Wolf?" Harry called out as he approached.

Alfred stood as he answered. "I don't know, Harry. He won't calm down."

As Harry approached, he saw what had upset the animal. A rattler lay coiled on a warm, flat rock a few feet from the boy and the dog. It had raised its head and was shaking its tail in warning. Alfred had not noticed the snake nor heard it above the barking of the dog.

"A. W., don't move," Harry ordered. He turned to George. "Go get my rifle right now!" George turned and ran.

"A. W., stand still!" Panic filled Harry's words. "There's a snake not far from you. Stand still and maybe it'll leave you alone."

Alfred turned to look for the snake, then looked at his brother, his eyes filled with fear.

"A. W., don't move!"

Harry suddenly realized that he needed to rein in his panic in order to help Alfred, who was surely more afraid of Harry's reaction than he was of the snake. He forced himself to speak more calmly while trying to be heard above the barking of the dog. "Just stand really still, A. W. George has gone to get my rifle. I'll kill the snake when he gets back, but it's important that you stand very still."

George could be seen coming toward them, with his mother and father behind, running as fast as they could. Panting, George handed Harry his Enfield rifle. Harry quickly took aim and shot the snake. Once it lay still, Wolf grew quiet and approached to examine it with his nose. Sure that it was no longer a threat, the dog trotted up to Harry for a pat on the head, his tongue lolling out of his mouth.

Alfred had not moved, his eyes still pinned on his big brother. Sarah ran to him and dropped to her knees to put her arms around him. "Are you all right? The snake didn't bite you, did it?"

"No, Mother. Harry shot it. I didn't see it when Wolf started barking. I couldn't tell why he was barking until Harry got here and saw the snake."

Matthew picked up the boy. and asked, "You're sure you are not injured, my lad?"

"No, Father, the snake didn't get me."

"You must thank your brother for that."

"I will, Father. I will. Can you put me down now? I'm too big to be carried. I want to thank Wolf too." The boy put his arms around the dog's neck and patted his head.

***

That evening Sarah lay awake, reliving the rattlesnake encounter and listening to Matthew snoring soundly. The wind that always seemed to blow on that vast prairie intensified and began to whip the rough-hewn shutters at the single window against the house. The plank door moved back and forth, bumping the doorframe; the only thing keeping it somewhat closed was the leather latchstring. *How like our lives*, she thought, *blown from one side of the world to the other on a wind of faith—a faith as unseen and unseeable as the wind. Thank heaven that I have not lost any more of my children.*

In the morning, several of the women approached Sarah as she finished cleaning up after breakfast and suggested they organize an informal school. "What a wonderful idea. I wholeheartedly support it," she exclaimed. Against their objections, Sarah insisted that the three younger boys attend. She couldn't know how long the school would last, but she was pleased to have less cause to worry about what the boys were up to during the day—especially Alfred. And even though Sarah found that the time passed more quickly while she and the boys were engaged in school, she continually wondered how long it would be before they left for the valley.

On June 10, a handcart company of sixty-eight elders going east to preach the gospel reached Florence boasting that they had made it from Salt Lake City in only forty-eight days. Three days later, the first handcart company of the season prepared to head west, in a hurry to get ahead of the wagon companies. The following day, the William Walker company of twenty-seven wagons departed, leaving many in the Hofheins company wondering why they were still in Florence.

"We wait for the St. Louis company," Hofheins explained abruptly. "We do not move without them."

Finally, the steamboat *Silver Heels* arrived on the nineteenth, and the weary members of the St. Louis company disembarked. The combined company was now comprised of the group from New York that had traveled under Matthew's leadership, the Delaware company led by John Taylor, and the St. Louis company under Captain James Hart. The unified company now consisted of 60 wagons, 129 souls, 240 oxen, 150 cows, 20 calves, and a handful of horses.

***

July 1, 1957

With the Stars and Stripes on a tall staff mounted in the first wagon, the company started west. A sense of relief permeated the air as they began the longest and last leg of their westward journey. The next evening, Elder John Taylor spoke at the end of the devotional meeting. "I recommend that as long as the grass for the livestock is adequate, the company remain united for safety. Some of the tribes you may run into are not necessarily friendly. When you get to Fort Laramie, the grass for the livestock will be thinner there. You may need to break into smaller groups from that point on." After a few more words of advice, he added, "I leave you my blessing and the blessing of the God of Israel and bid you all farewell as my son George and I will be leaving in the morning for Salt Lake City."

The next morning the two men mounted their mules and, with a wave, struck out west ahead of the company, knowing they would move faster than the wagons. They were in a hurry to get to Salt Lake City to notify Church leaders of the size of the companies on the trail behind them.

***

When the company reached the Elkhorn River, they stopped to celebrate the Fourth of July. The morning devotional was filled with speeches from the captains of ten and company chaplains. Rules for traveling were voted upon and friendships established and deepened. The youth and children spent the day becoming better acquainted with the members of the St. Louis company. Harry became fast friends with Will Robinson and Tom Featherstone.

At midday Edward ran into the cabin and called out, "Mum—" but he paused and looked at Harry, then corrected himself. "Mother, we get to have a party today. How come?"

"Today is the celebration of America's independence. About eighty years ago, they fought to gain their freedom from England." His mother was ironing one of Matthew's shirts.

"Why did they do that? We're English, aren't we? Isn't it good to be Englishmen?"

Sarah set the iron down and pushed a strand of hair out of her face. Her youngest son was always so full of questions. How could she explain when she herself didn't really understand the history of this young nation?

"It happened a very long time ago. We don't really understand why," she offered. "Just have a good time today as the company won't be moving." The little boy hurried out of the cabin to find a friend to play with, and Sarah returned to her ironing, relieved that he hadn't pressed her for more information.

That evening a dance was held amid much excited laughter and singing. They were finally on their way to Zion! After playing a few songs with the others in the little band, Harry put down his flute and danced with nearly every girl between the ages of twelve and twenty. Annie was forgotten for the evening until he returned to the tent. As he lay down on his bedroll, he suddenly realized that he had not thought of her for some time. The guilt he felt was much less intense than the previous time he remembered her after having forgotten her for many days.

The company remained camped for another day while the women continued to wash, bake, mend, and iron. Once on their way, the first major obstacle they faced was the Loup Fork, a branch of the Platte River. There the water was swift and wide and the river bottom full of quicksand.

CHAPTER SEVENTEEN

AT THE MEETING THAT EVENING, Captain Hofheins talked about the danger facing the wagon company. "This stream is a bad one, with much quicksand. In the morning I need some men to ride upstream and find a place to ford it where the quicksand isn't so bad."

Harry volunteered to join the group, using his father's mount. In the morning, along with Tom Featherstone and Will Robinson, he searched both riverbanks. It took two hours to locate a place that appeared to be firm enough to support the animals and wagons. Matthew, Harry, and every other able-bodied man helped to hitch twelve oxen to each wagon. Then the animals were driven with sticks to move as fast as they could through the wide, sandy, soft river bottom to prevent the wagons from becoming mired and tipping over.

About midday, when fifteen of the wagons had made it across, some of the men began to complain that there had to be a better place to ford. Hofheins snapped at them as he oversaw the process. "Just keep the animals moving and save your breath."

The exhausted men were too weak to cheer as the last wagons neared the riverbank as the light was fading in the sky.

Hofheins was not too weary to yell, "You! You there at the end—Tom Terry, you get those last two wagons moving faster."

That night everyone pitied the men and older boys who, in their exhausted state, still had guard duty.

***

The next day, Edward ran to Harry as he climbed into the wagon seat and asked quietly, "Will you let me ride with you, Harry? I've got a big blister on my foot."

"I guess a blister will make it all right, Edward." Harry lifted the five-and-a-half-year-old onto the seat, and they both looked around to make sure Hofheins wasn't within view. It was against the rules to ride unless ill.

The company reached the little settlement of Genoa, which had been established by members of the Church who had stopped there a couple of years earlier. The wagons paused for two hours to buy supplies before Hofheins demanded that they move on. They hadn't yet made the twenty miles he'd expected.

Both the animals and humans were beginning to feel the stress of the journey. Tempers flared and the oxen were slowing, but Hofheins was unwilling to ease up. The entire camp listened as he began to shout at Brother Sabry, the man who served as his teamster.

"I tell you when we keep going. You do not tell me what to do. I am the captain of this company."

"The oxen are at the end of their strength, Captain Hofheins. Some are bleeding at the nose. They need to rest. We need to make camp." Sabry's voice was not as loud as Hofheins's but still carried in the evening air.

Several men halted their wagons and approached the Hofheins wagon. As the argument continued, Hofheins raised his hand and struck Sabry across the face with his whipstock. "When I tell you to, you will make the animals move. It is not for you to tell me they are too tired."

Several men hurried to intervene, but Hofheins ordered them to stand back. "This man will do what I say or he will leave the company. If you interfere, you will also leave the company." The veins on his forehead stood out, and his face was scarlet with rage. "He tries to tell me what to do." In one last surge of anger, he tore the shirt off the man's back before jumping down from the wagon. Then he stormed around to the back, where he pulled the man's trunk and bundle of clothes out and dropped them on the ground.

He pointed at Sabry with a shaking hand. "He will not travel with us anymore. And no one will take him in their wagon. Is that understood?"

When several men stepped forward again, Hofheins shouted, "If you do not follow my orders, you will stay behind. Now get in your wagons and get moving. We will go two more hours tonight."

Sarah knew she would remember the scene—Brother Sabry in his tattered shirt kneeling in prayer as the wagons moved on—for the rest of her life.

That night as they lay down to sleep, Sarah quietly asked, "Matthew, why didn't the men stop Hofheins from abusing that poor man? Why didn't you step in?"

"Sarah, this company is not so different than an army unit. Authority must be respected, even when it is misused. Hofheins is tired, like all of us, and has grown impatient. In a day or two, when he is calmer, I will try to have a long talk with him. You needn't be too worried about Brother Sabry. We are only a few miles from Genoa."

***

In the morning, Sarah was surprised when Brother Sabry appeared at the camp with two elders from the Genoa settlement to confront the wagon master. Hofheins was forced to meet with the men for an hour, and surprisingly, he came out of the meeting agreeing to be less harsh in the future. In the presence of the men from Genoa and many of the men of the company, Hofheins and Sabry shook hands.

The next day the wagons spread out in rows twelve wide across the long prairie grass so as to avoid the dust the wagons often faced when traveling single file. The row of wagons that included the McCunes' was nearly at the top of a gentle rise when Edward pointed at those in front of them. "Look, Harry, those wagons have stopped. Maybe you should stop the oxen so we can find out why."

Harry directed the oxen into an opening between two other wagons at the crest of the hill, and his breath caught. Before them a herd of buffalo fanned out like a living brown blanket all the way to the horizon, moving like the slow waves of the sea.

Edward cried out and grabbed his brother's arm. "Harry, what are they?"

"You don't have to be afraid, Edward." He tousled the boy's hair. "Those are buffalo. You remember eating buffalo meat before we got to Florence. Their skins make wonderful robes to sleep under on cold nights."

"But I never saw so many. They're so big." His voice was almost a whisper.

By that time, half the wagons had reached the crest, and many of the men, including his father, had grabbed their rifles and were stealthily making their way toward the large animals. Harry quickly followed their example and picked up his rifle. "Stay here, Edward. Don't leave the wagon."

He dropped to the ground, and as he moved toward the herd, Edward called out, "Be careful, Harry."

Within five minutes, three of the great wooly-headed animals had dropped in a hail of gunfire that startled the rest of the herd into a massive ripple that quickly turned into a stampede toward the horizon. Some of the oxen and cows grew panicked and started to run as if drawn by the buffalo. The scene quickly turned into chaos. Men called, "Stay in the wagons! Stay in the wagons!" to their families, but many were too fearful to listen or obey and ran about in a frenzy.

By late afternoon, the only sign of the herd was the massive amount of dust hanging in the air. Two wagons had been badly damaged and fifteen head of cattle lost. Three company members were injured as they fell from the wagons or from having a wagon pass over their legs or feet. The remaining daylight hours were spent assessing the damage and attending to injuries while several volunteers engaged in skinning and dressing the carcasses. Supper that night included buffalo meat.

The next morning, three of the families who had lost livestock turned back for Genoa, where they hoped to replace the animals. If they could, they would catch up with the company in a few days.

As the company traveled the next day, the strips of buffalo meat hung from the wagons like fringe on a buckskin suit to dry in the sun.

When Matthew and Sarah entered the tent that evening, the three younger boys were still dressed but asleep on top of their blankets, too tired to undress. Sarah took a minute to remove their shoes before she tucked the blankets under their chins and stroked their hair.

She turned and noted that Matthew, also fully dressed, was already asleep on his blanket. *How very unlike him*, she thought.

***

When the camp halted for the midday meal the following day, a massive storm struck. The thunder cracked and rolled through the heavens like cannon shot. Matthew spurred his horse and rode from wagon to wagon, calling out, "Put your animals in hobbles if you have them. Try to keep the cattle from bolting. The storm will frighten them." As he spoke, the agitated animals began to low in nervous distress, and the herd began to churn as the lightning hit a hillside a few hundred feet away.

"Sarah, where are you? Where are the boys?" Matthew's distressed voice reached her as she stood in the back of the wagon measuring out cornmeal from a barrel.

"Here, Matthew, in the wagon." It was unlikely that he could hear her above the thunder and sounds of the frightened cattle.

From where she was standing, she saw him leap off his horse and tie it to the log near the cooking fire. Seeing her in the rear of the wagon, he grabbed George and lifted him so he could climb into the wagon. "Get in and stay with your mother," he ordered loudly. "Harry, put Edward into your wagon and try to keep the oxen calm."

Harry grabbed Edward and half lifted, half tossed him onto the wagon seat before immediately stepping on the wheel hub and springing into the wagon. "Edward, get inside the wagon and hold on to something. We may be in for a scary ride."

The boy's face was white, but he did as he was told.

Matthew took one fast look around the camp and yelled, "Where's Alfred?"

George called out, "He went to play with Nephi Andrews."

Seeing the agitation of the cattle increasing and realizing that there was no time to search for the boy, he shook his head and pulled himself up and onto the wagon seat of the second wagon. Even though both Harry and his father had the reins for the teams tightly in hand, the frightened animals began to move forward.

Matthew called out, "Sarah, George, sit down and hold on to something."

By this time, a dozen wagons were being dragged over the prairie, and with the next clap of thunder and bolt of lightning that seared through the heavens, another five began to move against the wishes of their masters. Wagon wheels jounced in and out of prairie-dog holes. Chairs, baskets, buckets, and washtubs fell from the sides of the wagons, adding to the noise and confusion. The oxen lowered their heads and pulled as if they could separate themselves from the storm by sheer determination. Another ten wagons began to move.

Matthew and several other men yelled as their wagons lumbered across the rutted prairie. "Stay in the wagons! Stay in the wagons!"

Terrified, a number of men, women, and children disregarded the warnings and jumped out, some being stepped on by oxen or run over by the wagons behind them. The screams of the injured added to the chaos, which continued for nearly half an hour.

As the storm weakened, the exhausted oxen slowed and finally stopped. Matthew, Hofheins, and other able-bodied men climbed down off their wagon seats to assess the damage. Many injured lay moaning while others lay silent and unmoving.

Matthew hurried through the carnage and then back to the wagon calling out, "Sarah, we need bandages and clean water—and see if I have any dried basil for the open wounds."

Sarah opened one of the trunks and pulled out two petticoats. George looked perplexed and asked, "What are those for, Mother?"

"They will make good bandages." She located her sewing kit in the trunk and pulled her scissors from it, then steadily cut long strips from the petticoats. "George, wrap them in little bundles."

As he wrapped the long strips of fabric into little balls, she climbed from the wagon and located a pail for water. "George, get your father's herbal bag. See if there is any dried basil in it." He offered her a small fabric pouch marked "Basil."

"You are to stay in the wagon, George. Hold the reins and keep the teams quiet."

Without waiting for the boy's answer, she went in search of Matthew. She found him kneeling beside sixteen-year-old Wilhelmina Mousely, whose face was streaming blood from a great gash made by the hoof of an ox or cow.

Harry looked white as he tried to hold the sobbing young woman still so his father could examine the wound.

"Here are some bandages, Matthew." Sarah set the pail of water next to him, and he carefully began to wash the wound.

"Did you find the dried basil?" he asked.

"Yes, here it is."

He pressed the dried leaves into the wound and then wrapped a long strip of Sarah's best petticoat several times around the young woman's head. Looking at Sarah Mousely, the young woman's sister, he instructed, "Keep the wound covered. The basil will help stave off infection. Keep her quiet but have her sit up in the wagon. Don't let her lie down for several hours or the bleeding will start again."

Matthew then moved from one injured person to another, cleaning and wrapping wounds long after the dried basil was gone and the bandages were getting low.

Tom Terry approached him. "I don't know much about fixing broken bones or cuts, Brother McCune, but John Dutson and I think we ought to give the injured folks a blessing, if that seems right to you."

"Yes, Brother Terry, that is an excellent idea."

Matthew next located James Hart, who was sitting against a wagon wheel holding his foot. His wife, Emily, was trying to pull his boot off with one hand. In her other arm, she held her crying infant son.

Matthew hurried to stop her. "No, Sister Hart. Leave the boot on. If you remove it, his ankle will swell and it will be difficult to splint if it is broken. He might not be able to get a boot or shoe on for weeks. Do you have a dish towel or rag I can use to bind it?"

She handed her infant son to Sarah, who had followed Matthew, and climbed into the wagon. Within moments she climbed back down and handed Matthew two large white dish towels. He tied them together and wrapped them tightly around the ankle and under the arch of Brother Hart's foot. "Try to keep off your foot, Brother Hart, until it begins to heal."

Matthew, Sarah, and several of the uninjured men and women worked throughout the day and well into the night, washing and bandaging injuries. Many more petticoats belonging to the women of the company were sacrificed.

Hofheins rode through the camp, noting the number of injured, and informed anyone who was listening, "We stay in camp tomorrow and maybe the next day."

After the injured were treated, more than a dozen men, including Matthew, rode out to locate the cattle that had strayed for several miles in every direction and then drove those they found back to camp. They returned well after dark.

As Matthew dropped onto his bedroll, Sarah offered him a drink of water. He downed it swiftly. "It has been a long day," he commented before he laid down and slipped into an exhausted sleep.

***

Three days later, while some of the injured were still recovering, a hunting party of Sioux Indians crept unobserved near the camp in the middle of the night and, rising in unison, whooped until a good number of frightened cattle stampeded into the darkness. When daylight came, the men were better able to assess the seriousness of the loss. Matthew and Harry realized that two of their eight oxen were missing. In total, forty head of cattle were gone.

"Father, how can we travel without one yoke of oxen?" Harry's jaw was set in frustration.

"Surely Hofheins will send out a group of riders to see if the animals can be located."

Harry was one of sixteen volunteers, and with his saddlebags stuffed full of buffalo jerky and biscuits, he joined three young men who had decided to ride in a westerly direction. The others separated into small groups and went in other directions.

The four young men quickly located the tracks of some of the cattle and pressed their horses into a steady trot while trying to avoid the prairie dog holes that littered the ground.

Three hours into the ride, they were disappointed to see the tracks mixed with those of a herd of deer, obliterating them. They rode for another seven hours until they came across a small stream, where they paused. Harry called out, "Let's give the horses a rest. They need a drink, and so do we."

"We need to separate so we can cover more ground," Tom Featherstone said after they had climbed off the horses and had time to eat some buffalo jerky and get a drink upstream from the horses.

Will Robinson agreed. "Yeah, let's separate into two teams. The moon is full, and we can cover a lot more ground. See that spire on the ridge? Let's meet up there by morning unless either team locates the cattle." He was pointing toward a high point on a ridge that ran east and west well north of the Platte until it was almost out of sight on the western horizon. "If either team locates any of the cattle, they should be driven back to camp."

"If we find the cattle, why don't we fire a rifle to let the others know?" Charles Sharp asked.

"You don't want to take a chance on stampeding them and losing them again. If either of us doesn't show up at the meeting place, we'll figure you've located some of the cattle and headed back to camp."

They all agreed. "Come on, Will," Harry called. "You and I will check out any canyons along that part of the ridge. There's going to be a full moon tonight." The young men climbed back onto their horses and urged them into a trot.

Tom called out to Charles, "We'll see if there's any way through that ridgeline. Perhaps there's a canyon or a large gully where the cattle are hidden." He and Sharp set off to the northwest.

***

The camp waited, and wives and mothers worried. Sarah stood, hardly moving, watching the horizon for much of the day. That evening, three exhausted men who had run out of supplies returned without any success, but not Harry or his friends.

"Matthew, what if the Indians have captured them?" she asked as she served supper.

"The Sioux in this area haven't proven to be hostile, Sarah. My concern is that the lads may have ridden so far from camp they'll have a very long ride to get back. Have faith."

***

August 1, 1857
American Prairie

The camp waited two long nights. Around midafternoon on the third day, several more of the searchers returned. They had located seven head of cattle. That evening, Harry, Will, Tom, and Charles returned, having slept little, and that was in the saddle. The horses were as exhausted as the men. When asked if they'd had any luck, they dejectedly shook their heads. Hofheins disgustedly returned to his wagon without speaking to them.

When Sarah embraced her son in relief, Harry looked at Matthew and apologized. "I'm sorry, Father, but we didn't find them. The Indians must know the area much better than we do. Perhaps they have a box canyon or a gully where they hid them. The tracks were mixed with those of a herd of deer that had passed earlier, and we never located them again. What will we do with only three teams?"

"In the morning before we leave, we'll move a large part of the supplies in the second wagon to the first so the load on the single team is lighter. Somehow we'll make it work. Don't condemn yourself." Matthew patted Harry's shoulder. "You need to get some rest."

As Harry sat down on the ground to eat some of the beans and venison his mother had prepared for supper, Hofheins approached.

"Harry McCune, it's your turn to stand watch. You relieve Joe Dutson at two." His voice was harder than usual. "You know the rules. Don't think you'll be getting out of it."

Sarah could not stop the words that came out of her mouth. "Captain Hofheins, Harry is exhausted. He has been without sleep for three days. Surely someone can take his place."

Matthew stepped forward. "I will."

"No, you won't. You know the rules. No substitutions for guard duty." He turned and walked away.

Harry stood unsteadily and put down the empty tin plate. "It's all right, Mother. If you or Father will wake me a few minutes before two, I'll fulfill my assignment."

"But, Harry, you're exhausted." Sarah was white-faced with worry.

Matthew put his hand on his wife's arm. "This matter has been decided by Captain Hofheins." He turned to Harry. "Harry, I'll set my pocket watch and wake you in time."

"Thank you, Father." Harry moved to his bedroll under the wagon and dropped immediately into an exhausted sleep. He didn't stir until Matthew shook him awake.

"It's time, Harry."

Harry smiled wearily, then picked up his gun and a blanket to put over his shoulders to keep away the night chill, saying nothing as he moved out to take a position near the last wagon in the camp.

***

As the sun rose, before the members of the camp had begun to prepare breakfast, a man's voice was heard raised in anger. "Harry McCune, you fell asleep on guard duty!" It was Hofheins's, easily recognizable by the heavy German accent. "You should be shot," the man yelled. The more he yelled, the more his anger grew, and as his anger grew, his language became coarser and his voice louder.

Matthew rushed out to see what the uproar was all about. He found Hofheins standing over Harry, who sat on the ground, leaning against a wagon wheel where he had fallen asleep. The young man struggled to rise, leaning on his rifle for support.

Hofheins sputtered with rage. He pointed at Harry and said, "You—you we will deal with at the morning meeting!" He stormed away.

At the daily eight o'clock morning gathering of the camp, Hofheins stood to call the group to attention. He dispensed with announcements and prayer and stated in a loud, harsh voice, "This morning we will make an example of anyone who falls asleep on guard duty. We will tie Harry McCune to the wagon wheel he found so comfortable last night and whip him until he learns his lesson!"

Tom Featherstone caught Will Robinson's eye, and they both stepped forward, Tom addressing Hofheins. "You knew Harry had been out searching for the cattle for three days without sleep, and you still insisted he stand guard duty. Of course he was too exhausted to stay awake."

Charles Sharp stepped forward and angrily added, "You could have asked someone to take Harry's place." He was growing red in the face.

John Stevenson joined in. "Why would you whip a man for being exhausted? There wasn't a man in camp who could have stayed awake under those circumstances, and any of the men who hadn't been searching for the animals would have willingly taken his place."

Hofheins raised the whip above his head and, undeterred by the comments of the other young men, stepped toward Harry, who stood unsteadily in front of him. "I am captain of this company, and I say he should be whipped."

As he raised the whip to signify his intentions, the three young men who had ridden with Harry on the search surrounded the agitated man and yanked the whip out of his hand.

Charles Sharp growled out, "Maybe Hofheins needs a taste of his own medicine. He's always demanding work from others he isn't willing to do himself. Maybe we should use the whip on him."

Many had chaffed under Hofheins's heavy hand, and their voices now joined in assent.

Matthew moved to Harry's side and, facing the crowd, raised his hand and called out, "Let's not have any vigilante justice. What say you, Harry?"

"My father is right. Let's not turn the situation into violence."

Another voice called out, "Then let's send Hofheins out to look for the cattle and see if he is so quick to whip a man for being exhausted when he gets back. Get your horse, Hofheins, and go spend three days looking for the cattle."

Other voices echoed the sentiment, and Hofheins was literally lifted onto his horse and handed some jerky and a canteen. Someone slapped the horse's rump, and Hofheins was forced out of camp.

The angry and disrespectful manner in which some of the men referred to Hofheins troubled both Matthew and Harry. "The man has upset many members of the company in the past few weeks with his arbitrary, harsh manner, but I'm worried that some of the men want to deal with him the same way he wanted to deal with me," Harry commented at supper the second day of Hofheins's absence.

Sarah was deeply troubled over the incident. "I think the man has made many members of the company angry with his unreasonable ways and some will demand an apology on his part before he is allowed to return."

The evening of the third day, Hofheins returned to the camp, out of food and contrite. When he and his horse neared his wagon, he was surprised to find Will Robinson and Charles Sharp camped there, anticipating his return, their arms folded across their chests.

As soon as he saw them, he stopped and slowly dismounted. No one said anything for a full minute. Finally, Hofheins cleared his throat and spoke. "I was wrong. The young man was too tired to stand guard duty. I should have asked someone else."

"If you want to rejoin the company, you'll have to tell the McCune family, especially Harry, what you've just told us."

The man nodded stiffly, and with both young men watching, he slowly walked to the McCune wagons. As he passed each family's camp, conversation stopped, and all turned to watch him.

Sarah was washing the tin plates the family had used for supper when she saw Hofheins. She stood motionless as Matthew and Harry stepped forward and waited for him to speak.

"I've come to tell you that I was wrong. I should have asked somebody else to take the guard duty." Neither Matthew, Sarah, nor Harry spoke, so Hofheins added, "Vill you allow me to come back?"

Harry stepped forward and put out his hand. "Of course, you are welcome as far as I'm concerned."

Matthew also offered his hand as many company members quietly watched. As Matthew and Hofheins shook hands, several others approached the McCune camp and shook the man's hand, welcoming him back.

At the meeting the following morning, Tom Featherstone rose to speak to the group while Hofheins stood aside. "I've been taking a survey of the men in the company, and it has been generally agreed by all that we vote on a new captain. I am putting the name of Matthew McCune before the group. What say you?"

A unanimous, affirmative voice vote rang across the prairie, and Matthew McCune was elected captain.

As they lay down in the tent that evening, Sarah whispered to her husband, "I'm proud of you, Matthew. You will do a fine job leading the company, but more importantly, you have treated Brother Hofheins with a kindness many others would not have extended."

"We don't know what kind of life Brother Hofheins has led. His life has probably been very difficult. Perhaps he is beginning to realize that consideration of others is not a sign of weakness. He is very angry, and I will need to consult with him about landmarks on the trail. I hope he will be cooperative."

She was quiet for a few minutes while she waited for the three smallest children to drift off to sleep, her thoughts tumbling through her mind. The events of the day were pushed away by her continuing concern for her friend, Mary Anne Meik, before she spoke again. "Matthew, do you suppose Patrick and Mary Anne have decided to come to America?"

"We must hope so, my dear."

CHAPTER EIGHTEEN

July 1857
Calcutta

MARY ANNE STOOD ON THE second-floor balcony of the house that had once been the residence of her dear friend. She leaned against the spindled balustrade, watching for the arrival of her husband, much as Sarah had done a few years earlier. Her forehead was creased with worry. *Why is Patrick so late?* When he had not appeared at five o'clock as usual, nor by six or even seven, the worry began to creep into her mind like the rising river waters of the monsoon season. He was a punctual man, so much so that some of the native merchants depended upon the passing of his tanga to determine the time of day.

Annie, who at sixteen stood taller than her mother, insisted on waiting with her. Madhuri, the children's Hindu nanny, had collected the younger children an hour earlier to bathe and ready them for bed.

Mother and daughter watched the road, silently sharing their worry. Both could hear Madhuri singing in her high, wailing voice. It rose and fell as she sang songs in Hindustani to three-year-old Joseph. Each night he insisted that she sing the folk legend of Lord Rama and his love, Lila. He was charmed by the lilt of the words and melody.

"What do you suppose is keeping father tonight?" Annie finally had to ask.

"Perhaps Lord Campbell has come for an unannounced inspection." Mary Anne tried to fill her voice with a confidence she wasn't feeling. "Would you please check on the younger children and make sure they are ready for bed?"

Annie smiled. "Yes, of course," she said as she pulled her flowing skirts around her and headed into the children's quarters.

Annie returned in a few minutes. "The three little ones are in bed waiting for you to come give them a kiss good night. The other two will be soon."

"Thank you, dear." Mary Anne continued to study the road where it ran past the outside of the fort's protective wall. As she did, her fingers played a nervous, silent melody on the banister. Even if her husband was hidden in the darkness beneath the carriage awning, she would recognize Jamal and his familiar yellow turban as he sat straight as a tent pole in the driver's seat.

She finally turned away in disappointment and went to plant a kiss on each child's forehead and arrange the mosquito netting around each bed. After the children were settled, she returned to the balcony to take up her watch again.

"I know you're as worried as I am, but I'm sure the delay will prove to be something as mundane as a lame horse," she whispered to her daughter, trying to reassure herself as much as Annie.

"I'm sure you're right, Mother." She tried to echo her mother's confident tone. "If it had been anything serious, surely he would have sent a messenger to tell us what has delayed him."

Twenty minutes more passed before the sound of horse hooves and carriage wheels were heard. By the time Jamal had reined in the horses so Sergeant Patrick Meik could step down from the carriage, Mary Anne and her daughter had descended the circular stairs and reached him.

"Dear, we've been so worried. What has kept you?" Mary Anne was breathless with relief.

He spoke in a distracted fashion. "Jamal, please give the horses an extra helping of feed and plenty of water before you rub them down. They stood in the rain for a long time today."

"Yes, sahib," Jamal responded in his deep voice before he urged the horses toward the carriage house.

As the sound of wheels on gravel faded, Mary Anne took her husband's arm as they moved toward the spiral staircase and repeated her earlier question. "Patrick, what kept you? We've been so worried."

As they reached the top of the stairs, he quietly responded, "A great deal has happened today, my dear. I couldn't help the delay."

At the top of the stairs, she pushed open the louvered door to the large drawing room, passing into the light that spilled from the filigree oil lamps hanging from the ceiling.

"Leela has kept dinner warm. Please take off your jacket and sit down at the table. You must be famished."

Mary Anne smiled at Leela, and the woman quietly bowed and disappeared behind another louvered door.

Patrick sat without moving for several seconds. In the lamplight, his normally tan face appeared ashen.

"Patrick, what is it? You look distressed. Has the uprising spread? Surely the news can't be so very bad . . . can it?" his wife added hesitantly. Patrick was normally a man of good cheer and an excellent appetite, but he appeared totally distracted this evening.

He took a deep breath, as if he were planning to dive into a deep, cold lake. "Along with the other officers at Fort William, I've spent the day discussing the reports brought by three men who escaped the siege of Lucknow."

Mary Anne's face blanched, and her fork clattered to her plate. "Lucknow is under attack? What about Martiniére College?"

He reached out and protectively laid his hand over hers. "My dear, don't panic. The boys are all well. All fifty of them and the masters were brought to the commissioner's residency. The loyal sepoys have joined the British officers there for protection now that the rest of the city has fallen."

Mary Anne's hand went to her throat as if to control her panic and prevent its overwhelming her. "The city has fallen? When did this happen?" Her voice was tight.

"About the middle of June. The telegraph lines from Lucknow and Cawnpore were cut a week or two earlier, so what information we have received has come from these brave and exhausted men. It's a miracle they were able to make their way to Calcutta. According to their reports, grain and other supplies were gathered and brought into the residency, so there's no likelihood that those taking shelter there will starve."

His daughter's questions came quickly. "When you say the boys of the college are all well, you mean as of the middle of June? Do we know anything of Alexander? Is he well—and safe?"

"The reports stated that the boys were safe and well."

Reproach filled his wife's eyes. "Patrick, we should never have sent Alexander so far from home. We should have used tutors to complete his education, as with James and George." Her voice rose with emotion. "Why did you insist he attend a school so far from home? You insisted that we send him hundreds of miles away to Martiniére despite my opposition."

His eyes were suddenly filled with so much pain that Annie glimpsed the depth of his distress. Her proud, often unbending father suddenly looked broken. "I was wrong. I was wrong, but how could I have known?" He put his elbows on the table and laid his head in his hands with his fingers in his hair. Silence hung in the air like an unfamiliar fragrance. His wife's normally loving face seemed carved in stone.

A new fear occurred to Annie. "Is help on the way to Lucknow?"

He raised his head and tried to answer soothingly. "I'm sure it is."

Mary Anne pulled the handkerchief from her pocket and bowed her head as she wiped her eyes. Though her words were quiet, they were filled with a recrimination almost as wounding as blows. "We should have gone to America with the McCunes. Matthew and Sarah urged us to leave India and go with them. President Jones warned that the wrath of God was going to be poured out on this pagan country."

Fear for her son had forced the words from her. She couldn't have stopped them had she tried. "Why wouldn't you agree to go with them, Patrick? Why?" Her voice was rising. "You never explained why you were so set against it." The look in her eyes wounded him further. "Was that next promotion so terribly important?" She rose from the table so fast the chair she had been sitting in clattered to the floor. She hurried from the room.

Annie rose to follow her mother. "Excuse me, Father. I think I should be with Mother. She shouldn't be alone right now." He nodded.

The food was hardly touched that evening.

***

The large grandfather clock in the drawing room struck midnight before Annie rejoined her father, who was still in the drawing room pacing with his hands behind his back.

"I've given Mother one of her sleeping draughts. She's resting now. Father, what else do you know that you have not told us?" Her voice was low, but each word was insistent.

He had always found it difficult not to answer his oldest daughter's probing questions. She was mature beyond her years, and she had eyes that could look straight into his soul. He halted his pacing and sat down at the end of the long table. Running his hands through his thick brown hair, he looked at her with eyes that pleaded for a withholding of judgment.

"Annie, I haven't told you even half the news. I couldn't tell your mother all I have learned. I'm afraid of what it might do to her. Of the three men who managed to escape the siege at Lucknow, one carried letters from officers and some of the boys of the college. One was from Alexander. I didn't tell her about it as it holds nothing but horror for a mother. You must not let her know how trying the situation is there. She would be frantic." He waited until she nodded her assent before pulling the folded letter from his shirt pocket and beginning to read.

Dear Father,

I think it would be wise if you did not share this letter with Mother. The news is not good. The rebel troops attacked the city on May 30, and for the following two weeks, the British officers and the loyal sepoys were able to withstand the attack. The school was not harmed, but that may have been an oversight on the part of the rebels. Sometime in mid-June, General Sir Harry Lawrence determined that it would be safer to prepare the area of the commissioner's residency for defense. It is walled, and there are some outbuildings on the grounds that offer some protection from the elements. It was at that time that we boys and the teachers from the college and Mr. Schilling, the headmaster, were brought in from our somewhat isolated location. All available supplies had been gathered and brought in, but the area is not large, and by the time all the civilians, British officers, loyal native troops, and the boys from the school were inside the residency walls, there were nearly 2,100 persons seeking shelter there, over five hundred of whom are women and children. I do not count the boys of the school as children as those of us fourteen years of age and older have been armed with rifles and are posted as if we were regular troops.

He took a deep breath before he continued.

You must understand, Father, the residency is by no means a fortress, despite the wall. Native houses have been built up against it on three sides, and snipers using the roofs of those houses have accounted for as many as twenty casualties a day. The conditions are appalling. The women and children and the sick suffer greatly from heat, rain, and nonexistent sanitary conditions. Disease is beginning to take its toll—cholera, smallpox, dysentery. The children and the wounded are sickening and dying in increasing numbers.

When not at our assigned post, we boys of the college are assigned to sit in the overcrowded hospital, which was previously an outbuilding used for storage. We fan the flies off the sick and wounded and offer them water when they thirst. It is a dismal place filled with pitiable moans and cries of pain, foul smells, and darkness as all the windows are barricaded and light comes only from the doors at each end of the building. We also assist with the burials, including the heavy task of burying the bullocks and horses that are killed almost daily by shot and shell. Food is sufficient, though of poor quality. If help comes soon, we will not starve, but our numbers will be fewer. Please, Father, do all in your power to send us relief.

Your loving son,
Alexander

The last words were whispered. The letter floated to the ground as his grip on it faltered.

"Father, I am so sorry. Alexander was right. You must not let Mother know how bad the conditions are." Annie moved to the back of his chair and put her hands on his shoulders. There was little comfort she could offer.

As he dropped his head into his hands once more, he spoke above the sound of the increasing wind and monsoon rain. "Your mother is right. We should have gone to America with the McCunes." He remained silent for a full minute. "But some of the children were so young and your mother's health so fragile. I feared I might lose some of you if we made that long voyage, but now I may lose . . ." He didn't finish the sentence. He didn't need to.

CHAPTER NINETEEN

Early August, 1857
The American Prairie

FOR WEEKS THE WOMEN HAD been rubbing animal fat on their lips, faces, and hands to ease the sun- and windburn they dealt with daily. The buffalo flies followed the company as if they knew the way to the valley. The company continued along the North Platte River, excitedly noting they were near the midpoint of their journey.

As camp was made for the midday meal, Alfred asked his father, "What is that big rock pointing at the sky?"

"My lad, that is Chimney Rock. It means we are halfway to the valley."

"Is that all?" the disappointed boy asked. "I'm tired of walking."

"This afternoon you may ride with me on my horse. Will that make it easier?"

The boy nodded enthusiastically. "Yes, sir."

Just beyond Chimney Rock, the members of the company could see Scott's Bluff to the west, where the great sandstone formation towered 750 feet above the prairie. For several days the trail ran between the great rock fortress and the North Platte, where the river was cleaner. Without seeking parental permission, some of the children, including the three youngest McCunes, located a spot where they could easily get into the water. They jumped in to splash and play and have the first bath any had had in many days.

Matthew decided to add something new to his family's meal. He had watched some of the men cut the great pads from the prickly pear cactus plants they had passed on the trail. They'd removed the plants' long needles before their wives fried or boiled them. He followed their example and presented a half dozen of the large pads to Sarah as she prepared their food.

She looked at him in amazement. "Matthew, what am I to do with these?"

"We will eat them. I think we should try frying some and boiling the rest. The Indians do. Let's see how they taste. They will offer us a change in our diet."

Sarah took them and tried to smile. "Well, they certainly will be a change from beans." And they were.

"The slightly wild flavor is not something that will rank high on future menus, but it is a change," Matthew commented as he chewed.

While the sun was still high in the sky, the children teased each other into climbing the steeply sloping rock hillsides of the bluffs. When they could go no higher, they carved their names in the sandstone with sharp rocks. Most were ordered back into the river to wash the mud from their clothing before supper.

When Alfred and Edward did not appear, George and Harry went to look for them. They found them searching among several large anthills with at least a dozen other children. When Alfred looked up and saw his big brother in the dusk, he ran to him and held out his hands.

"Look, Harry. Look what I found on the anthills. These are beads the Indians lost. The ants think they're pretty. I'm going to make a necklace for Mother with mine." The child held a small handful of beads similar to those on the buckskins worn by the Indians they traded with.

"A. W., I hope your efforts are worth the ant stings you're getting."

"Father will make a poultice for them," he stated with confidence.

After supper, with his tongue between his teeth, Alfred worked at threading the beads onto the needle and thread his mother had given him until she insisted that he go to bed.

"But, Mother, I'm making a necklace for you."

"There will be more anthills and more beads tomorrow and the next day. Tonight it is time for sleep."

***

As the wagons moved steadily northwest along the North Platte, the company talked excitedly about reaching Fort Laramie.

Matthew asked Hofheins, "How much farther to the fort?"

"When you see the snow on Laramie Peak, then a few days more."

It was nearly mid-August when the company arrived at the adobe fort, with its fifteen-foot walls. It sat on the banks of the Laramie River about a mile and a half from the confluence with the North Platte. The nights grew steadily colder, and those families with buffalo robes were glad for their warmth despite the odor that clung to them.

The man in charge of the fort was named Bordeaux. "Welcome, welcome to my fort. The American Fur Company and I are pleased to have visitors." He greeted the company in an expansive manner and encouraged the men to shake hands with several of the French trappers who used it as a meeting and trading place between trapping seasons.

After camp was made, the members of the company celebrated. Prayers were offered, and Matthew delivered a discourse on the importance of faith in meeting challenges. Violins and a guitar were unpacked, and Matthew insisted, as usual, that his two oldest sons unpack their flutes and join the little band. The able-bodied men and women of the camp danced until nearly dawn. Harry and George eventually put down their instruments and joined in the fun. Harry was kept busy square dancing and learning the Virginia reel. Every young woman over thirteen or under twenty wanted to dance with him. As he sat to catch his breath, he thought of Annie. Would she have enjoyed the dancing? Would he even ever see her again? It was the first time that thought crossed his mind, and it saddened him.

The atmosphere of celebration was dampened the next day when the men of the company were invited to look over a large herd of oxen the trappers proudly offered for sale.

"Captain McCune, I recognize my own team of oxen. They're trying to sell me my own animals," John Dutson complained.

Even John Andrews said in his quiet manner, "My cow is standing right over there, the one that disappeared the night the Indians frightened off the animals."

Several other men recognized their oxen and cows.

When the men approached Matthew about the matter, his answer was direct. "We can't accuse these men of being in league with the Indians. They would have no way of knowing these oxen were stolen from our company. Even if you must buy your own oxen back, do so without making trouble as we will need to purchase other supplies before we leave this place. We would not want them to refuse to trade with us."

Matthew set the example for the other men and purchased the two oxen the Indians had stolen. After he and Harry hitched them to the second wagon, they repacked the load between the two wagons more evenly.

For the next two days, wagon repairs were made and deer hides and foodstuffs purchased or bartered before the wagon company headed out to be led across the North Platte by the McCune wagons. On the south side of the river, they joined the Oregon Trail.

James Hart approached Matthew after the evening devotional. His limp was still evident. "Captain McCune, this trail is heavily traveled and overgrazed. I think it's time to follow Elder Taylor's advice and separate our wagons."

When Matthew didn't immediately respond, Hart added, "The Saint Louis wagons could hold back a couple of days and give you folks a head start. Do you agree?"

"We will miss your company, Brother Hart, but you are right."

With the addition of the fresh teams acquired at Fort Laramie pulling several of the wagons, the company moved steadily northwest until the trail angled sharply downward.

"Harry, I want you to wait here and, as each wagon reaches you, instruct the men to lock their wheels. Tell them they will need to use chains or a log as a drag to make it safely down the steep trail ahead."

Those who followed his instructions held their breath as the oxen stumbled down Mexican Hill. Tin cups, plates, and other loose belongings went flying out of the wagons, hitting the rumps of the oxen before tumbling down the hill ahead of their owners, but the wagons reached the bottom safely.

Those who didn't follow instructions, believing it would be easy for the oxen to handle the wagons as they moved down the steep slope, were soon seeing their belongings scattered across the ground as their wagons toppled.

The Andrews wagon tipped precariously when the left front wheel slipped over a two-foot drop created by the crumbling of the trail. Eleven-year-old Elizabeth Andrews had sprained her ankle the previous day and had been sitting on the wagon seat by her father, holding her baby brother. The three were thrown from the wagon, which then rolled on top of the young girl.

Isabella Andrews ran to her, screaming, "Issy, Issy, are you hurt?" Looking around desperately, she begged the men for help. "Please! Lift the wagon off her!"

The baby was crying but appeared unhurt as he was handed to his mother. Eight men quickly gathered and lifted the wagon back onto its wheels.

John Andrews had had the breath knocked out of him, but as soon as he could speak, he frantically asked, "How's the lass? How's my little lad? How's my Issy?"

"The baby is fine. His mother has him," he was told as he rose unsteadily and limped to where his daughter lay unmoving.

Someone yelled, "Get Captain McCune. The girl's hurt."

After Matthew made his way up the sleep slope, he knelt beside the girl, who still wasn't moving. "Get the wagon down to the bottom of the hill." He stood. "I need five strong men and a blanket to carry the lass. When the wagon reaches the bottom, I want ropes tied to the inside of the staves of the wagon cover so we can hang the blanket like a hammock for her to lay in."

When the blanket was brought, Elizabeth was gently lifted onto the blanket by her father while her mother stood by weeping as she held the baby against her. "How bad is my lass hurt? Can ye tell me?" she pleaded of Matthew.

Matthew shook his head as he and the five other men picked Elizabeth up and started down the steep hill, trying not to jostle her as she moaned in pain.

When they reached the bottom of the hill, she was laid down, and Matthew knelt beside her. "Elizabeth, where are you hurt? Are you in pain?" She didn't respond.

Matthew's voice grew more insistent. "Issy, your father and mother need to know how badly you are hurt. Can you tell us?"

She opened her eyes, and seeing Matthew's face above her on the right and her father's on her left, she whimpered, "My back hurts somethin' terrible. Oh, please make it stop."

Matthew looked at her father. "John, we need to give her a blessing."

Those gathered around quieted as the two men placed their hands on the girl's head and gave her a blessing, promising her that the pain would be removed from her.

As they lifted their hands from her head, she smiled up at them weakly. "The pain in my back is not so bad now. Thank you, Papa. Thank you, Captain McCune."

The blanket was lifted into the wagon with the girl in it, and while the men held it, the corners were tied to the ropes that had been attached to the wagon staves. As the company began to move again, it swayed gently as the wagon rattled over the rough places in the trail. Not wanting to leave her daughter's side, Isabella put the baby in the cradle and sat by Elizabeth as they traveled, keeping a cold cloth on her forehead. As the hammock gently rocked the young girl, her mother wept and prayed.

When camp was made that evening, Matthew came to the Andrews' wagon to speak to John. "How is the lass feeling, John?"

She says she doesn't hurt anymore but complains that she can't feel her legs and feet. I asked her to move one of her feet, but she couldn't. When I touched her ankles, she couldn't feel it." The man was struggling to maintain his composure. "Captain McCune, what will happen to my lass if she can never walk again?"

Isabella had climbed out of the wagon and pulled at Matthew's shirtsleeve. "How bad is she hurt? Why can't she move her feet?"

"John, Bella, I think your daughter's back is broken. She may heal and be whole again, but she may not."

Isabella crumpled to the ground and sobbed. John tried to pull her to her feet. "Bella, get up. You must be strong. Issy musn't see you this way—she'll give up hope and die." His voice was firm.

Matthew helped John lift his wife to her feet. "Bella, you must put a smile on your face. Have courage, and your daughter will feel it. If you show her your fear, she will see it. Go to her and tell her not to worry but to rest." He paused when she didn't respond. "Will you do that?"

She wiped her forehead with her sleeve and nodded. "I will."

As she turned toward the wagon, Matthew took her arm. "When you are not with her, have one of your lads sit with her. Your boy Nephi is old enough to watch after her."

She nodded and climbed into the wagon. That night, Sarah fixed supper for both families.

***

The next day the company made ten miles and reached Register Cliffs. While the women made supper, the men tended the animals and the children hurried to carve their names into the soft sandstone above the camp, the younger McCune boys taking part.

Alfred hurried back to his mother. "I carved your name in the mountain by my name, Mother. Harry is helping Edward put his name on the mountain. Now everyone who comes here will see our names." He smiled with satisfaction at having achieved what was true immortality in the mind of a six-year-old boy.

"Thank you, dear. That was a thoughtful thing to do." She was infinitely grateful for a thoughtful, loving son, but as she watched him walk toward the wagon that night, an overwhelming concern for Elizabeth Andrews pervaded Sarah's thoughts. She walked over to the fire where John and Matthew talked quietly.

"She sleeps most of the time," John said. "I think that be a blessing. She says there is no pain." Despite his trying to be positive, his haggard face betrayed his worry.

Matthew tried to offer some comfort. "Be grateful for that, my friend."

***

The following day the trail took the company away from the North Platte River, and for the midday rest period, the company stopped at Warm Springs Canyon, where the women hurried to take their laundry to the spring. The water was so much warmer and cleaner here than the Platte. As the nearby streams were full of trout and salmon, the men unpacked their fishing rods and what few nets they had. In some cases, shawls were used as nets.

"Mum, look what I caught. I got a big fish," Alfred excitedly called out as he ran back to the wagon, forgetting the admonition to address his mother more respectfully. Every family ate fish that evening, and again, Sarah prepared supper for both her family and the Andrews family.

CHAPTER TWENTY

August 20, 1857
The Mormon Trail

CAMP WAS MADE AT THE confluence where Deer Creek drained into the North Platte. There, the company met a group of men traveling east from the Salt Lake Valley. Matthew was startled when he heard a familiar voice calling his name.

"Matthew McCune, is that you?"

Matthew halted his wagon and climbed down, trying to discover the source of the voice. He saw no one he recognized until a man in buckskins and a beard approached him and called out again, "Elder Matthew McCune, is that really you?"

The voice belonged to Elder Nathan Jones, but the man approaching him looked nothing like the former president of the East India Mission.

As the men vigorously shook hands, Matthew let out a full-bodied laugh. "Imagine finding such a friend here in the American wilderness halfway around the world from Burma." The men stepped back and thoroughly looked each other over. "Elder Jones, I and my family are here at your urging. Your advice has been honored and followed."

"Matthew, my good friend, I can tell you that you made a wise decision. Obedience is always best. Is the Meik family here as well?"

"No, Patrick was determined to complete his enlistment before considering emigration." Matthew shook his head regretfully.

The smile on Nathan's face faded. "The word from India is not good. According to the newspapers from California that have been brought to the valley, there is a widespread and very bloody revolt in some areas. The sepoys have arisen against the East India Company and all things British. Soldiers and company and civil officials have been slaughtered, as well as women and children."

He ran his hand through his uncut hair. "There has been much bloodshed, especially in the central cities. I have few details, but when you reach the valley, I'm sure you will find additional information in the *Deseret News*."

As Harry listened to the two men, the thought of the danger that surrounded Annie Meik and her family suddenly made him feel ashamed of the celebrating he had been part of on the trail.

Sarah remained quiet as she served a simple supper to her family and Elder Jones and the men traveling with him, but she listened to every word exchanged among them.

When she lay down next to Matthew in the tent that evening, she whispered, "Oh, Matthew, there is so much to worry about. How is Issy doing?"

"No better, no worse. Still unable to move her legs. I fear she will never walk again."

"There seems nothing I can do to ease Bella's and John's grief."

"It is in the Lord's hands."

She was quiet for a minute before she added, "What do you suppose has become of Patrick and Mary Anne and the children?"

"We may never know. All we can do is keep them in our prayers."

***

The next morning as the company prepared to leave the Deer Creek camp, Matthew shook hands with Jones. "Best of luck, my friend. May our paths cross again."

"Matthew, your company faces the hardest part of the trail between here and the valley. I am offering you a good, strong pair of oxen to replace your weakest." When Matthew started to object, Jones raised his hand to stop him. "I can see that one of your teams is trail weary. Take mine, and you'll make it in good shape."

Matthew nodded his acquiescence and gave Jones a firm pat on the shoulder. "Thank you, my friend. Your kindness will always be remembered."

After Jones and his companions left the campsite, Hofheins approached Matthew. "You need to have every family fill every barrel and jar they have with water. There isn't good water for maybe as long as three days after we cross the Platte."

Matthew directed the members of the wagon company to follow Hofheins's advice and was glad he had done so when, after being ferried across the North Platte at the northernmost point in the trail, the company started southwest over a barren wasteland.

Grass was scant and wood nonexistent. Two springs rose from the ground, but the water was full of salt and sulfur and smelled so foul that even the thirsty cattle refused to drink. The ground was so soft and miry in places that the cattle sunk to their bellies. The carcasses of thirty head of cattle from earlier wagon companies littered the area, and the air was filled with insects that inflicted painful bites. That night, a heavy frost covered everything and left a layer of ice on the water in the pails.

The next day, the animals were pressed to cover as many miles as they could without drinkable water. As Sarah and the three younger children walked by the wagon Harry drove, Edward said what everyone in the company was thinking. "This place is bad. It smells, and there's no good water. It's a horrid, stinky place."

"Indeed it is, my lad," Sarah responded.

Alfred had been looking thoughtful all morning and finally voiced his thoughts. "It won't be like this in the valley, will it, Mother? If it is, I'm going back to Calcutta."

Edward added, "And I'll go with you."

"No, it won't be like this in the valley. It will be green and beautiful." *At least, I hope so.*

Another dry camp was required that evening, and as the weary travelers tried to sleep, the babies cried and the oxen and cattle lowed with thirst and weariness. Edward had curled up next to Sarah for comfort, and as he slept, he moaned. "I'm thirsty, Mother." Tears traced a path down Sarah's cheeks.

The water barrels were empty by the time the company saw the great pile of sandstone called Independence Rock, which rose nearly 250 feet above the prairie. Cheers rose from parched throats when everyone saw the Sweetwater River near it. The oxen and horses had to be held back as they tried to drag the wagons into the water.

"Oh, Matthew, this river is perfectly named." Sarah sighed as they stood side by side and watched the flowing water with a tin cup full of water in their hands. They had both drank so much of the cold, clear water that Sarah felt she might never be thirsty again.

The two youngest boys had been prevented from jumping into the swift-flowing river when Harry grabbed them by the collar. "That river is too swift to go swimming, lads. Why don't you go explore that big rock. See if you can find the names of anyone we know carved on it."

They raced to the great rock dome and spent two hours searching its 1,200-foot length, reading the names of the hundreds of travelers who had carved or painted their names on the rock in previous years.

Harry turned when Matthew called out, "Men, grab your rifles. We will get some meat for our supper tonight." A dozen men took him at his word, and while the children played on the great mound of sandstone, their fathers located a herd of deer and brought back venison for the evening meal.

After supper the entire camp, including some of the women and small children, climbed to the top of the great mound to watch the sun set. It was a breathtaking view, but the steep slopes required that many of the children and a few of the women be "rescued" to get back down. Matthew was called upon to bind several ankles that evening.

The following morning after fording the swift, seventy-foot-wide river, they moved along the south side of it until a wagon with a broken axle prompted Matthew to call a halt and an early camp. The sound of rushing water enticed the boys to go exploring. When they did not return in time for supper, their mothers grew worried.

Matthew commented to his wife and eldest son, "Hofheins says this is a dangerous place. He told me when we made camp that there's a spot nearby where the river flows swiftly through a pass in the mountain called Devil's Gate. Harry, please find the lads and bring them back to camp."

Harry dutifully set off at a lope toward the sound of the water. When he did not return within the hour, Matthew determined to locate him and the younger lads and scold them soundly. He set off in the same direction at a fast walk and was startled when he came upon a place where the river cut its way through solid rock. The right bank was formed of perpendicular granite. The bed of the river was so choked with massive fragments of rock so thick that a wagon would never make it through.

A sheer cliff of nearly a hundred feet rose from the opposite bank, and he could see several young boys and men climbing over it and some sitting on the edge throwing rocks into the fast-flowing current below.

He started to run, angrily shouting, "You lads come down here right this minute. Come down here!" The boys couldn't hear him over the sound of the roaring water. He finally reached the base of the cliff and shouted at them again.

Harry was making his way down the steep hillside holding Edward over his shoulder and Georgie by the hand. A. W. was following them looking regretful at leaving all the fun. As Harry reached his father, he set the six-year-old down. "The lads couldn't hear you, Father. I've tried shouting. I finally had to go up after them. Wait here, and I'll go up and send the other lads down. We need to leave this camp early in the morning if we're to keep the lads away from the cliff."

The three younger brothers received a father's scolding before supper that evening.

At the evening camp meeting, it was agreed that the Delaware wagons would separate from the rest and leave several hours later the next day.

Sarah deeply regretted the distance that would be put between her family and the Andrews family.

***

Harry couldn't believe how many times the company had to cross the Sweetwater River as they traveled. Just when they thought they had left it behind, another sweeping curve would bring the river's path across theirs again.

After the fifth crossing of the Sweetwater, the McCune company paused to rest the animals for two days before attempting to climb Rocky Ridge. The oxen were weary, the men, women, and children even wearier. It was a difficult climb but necessary to avoid an impassable section of the river.

It required eight teams to be hitched to each of the wagons, with many of the men pushing from the rear or turning the wheel spokes by hand to help the oxen as they labored up the slope. Before evening, the company was forced to travel another sixteen miles to find a decent campground with wood and water.

***

September 1, 1856
The Wilderness of Wyoming

By the time the company forded the Sweetwater for the sixth time, Edward and George were coughing and shivering in their wet clothing, like many of the others. Edward stood on the banks watching the company cross until his oldest brother was forced to return through the chill water to get him. When he reached the child, he stated firmly, "Edward, you can't hang back. You must cross with the other children."

"Harry, the water is so cold. Isn't there another way?"

Without saying more, Harry dropped to one knee and pointed at his back. The child grinned and climbed on, putting his arms around his brother's neck.

"Don't choke me, Edward, or both of us will drown."

The child laughed. "You wouldn't let me drown, Harry."

That night as they lay in the tent, Sarah listened for the even breathing of the younger boys, which was interrupted by intermittent coughing. She whispered to Matthew, "Are there any more rivers to cross? I'm especially worried about George. I fear his cough is getting serious."

"I will see if I have any remaining herbs that would be useful as a hot drink in the morning. That should help them both. Hofheins tells me we have several wide but shallow creeks left between here and the Green River. After we get across that, we will head for Fort Bridger. Beyond it is the Bear River and then Echo Canyon. All in all, we have about two weeks travel ahead of us."

Sarah didn't know whether she should be grateful that there were only two more weeks or more concerned that the company faced more river crossings.

The next day, the wagons of the McCune company received stares and returned them as they passed a government train of twenty-six wagons headed the same way. Matthew rode over to the wagon master and spoke with him.

After the evening devotional, Matthew was asked, "What did the men on that government wagon train have to say?"

"It seems the US government has sent a large part of the army to oversee the Mormons in the Salt Lake Valley. Evidently, the government does not feel we can govern ourselves. The wagon master didn't have any better explanation for their presence."

"Are they hostile?"

"That was not the feeling I received from them, and evidently, they are not in any hurry."

In the morning, the wagons under Matthew's direction left the government wagons far behind.

***

Exhaustion, dwindling supplies, cold nights, and cold rivers increased the sickness among the company. At the 250-foot-wide expanse of the Green River, the wagons lined up under the branches of the cottonwood trees to make camp.

"We will make camp here for two days to rest the animals," Matthew announced at the evening meeting. We have good water and plenty of grass."

Those who could stand the mosquitoes, which included Harry, went fishing, catching trout for their families.

On the second day, the Delaware group, which had dropped behind a day, reached the camp. Sarah hurried to offer Isabella a greeting and an embrace. "How is Issy doing?" she asked quietly so as not to be heard by the girl.

Isabella couldn't fight the tears that were so close. "She is no better," she whispered. "She can't walk, but I thank God she feels no pain."

Sarah had no words of comfort to offer. She knew the woman's grief ran deep. She gave Isabella another long embrace.

In the morning, for fifty cents each, the wagons were ferried across the wide river on large, well-used rafts by the men of the small but permanent settlement there, while the cattle were forced to swim.

***

Three days later, the sight of Fort Bridger was greeted with weary but cheerful hurrahs.

"We're nearly there. We're nearly there," Sarah whispered to herself.

When the company camped that evening, they were disappointed to find that only flour and cornmeal were available for purchase. There was little else, but at least they would rest for two days. On the second day, many cheered when they recognized the wagons of the St. Louis group approaching.

When the company gathered around the main fire that evening, Matthew climbed up on a large tree stump to address the group. The crowd quieted so they could hear him.

"You will be pleased to know that we will reach the Bear River in two days. It is the last major river we will cross." There was a sigh of weary gratitude from the group. "The rivers thereafter are shallower and less of a challenge. Take heart, my friends. The journey is nearly over." A weak cheer followed as he climbed down.

CHAPTER TWENTY-ONE

THE RED SANDSTONE WALLS OF Echo Canyon rose up around the company and formed a deep defile where the wagons were forced to move single file down the wide, shallow Weber River that flowed the length of the canyon. Progress was slow.

Between rain showers, the children collected pretty rocks in the creek and picked late-blooming wildflowers for their mothers. As the canyon closed in around them, the children quickly discovered that sound echoed from the canyon walls in some places, and a competition immediately began to see who could create the longest, most-pronounced echo. The ears of the adults were soon ringing.

This is more difficult to tolerate than the early flute lessons, Sarah thought as she walked beside the wagon Harry was driving, *but the children are having so much fun.* Matthew rode along the length of the company and requested that parents keep their children close and quiet—at least quieter—but his admonition didn't make much difference. The children couldn't be shushed.

As he was considering riding the length of the company with the same admonition again, this time to turn the request into an order, Sarah spoke to him. "Matthew, it's been a long and difficult journey. Perhaps we should allow the children to enjoy themselves."

He turned her suggestion over in his mind. "Perhaps you are right. We will be out of the canyon soon."

The river was not deep, but it was rocky, and the water flowed fast, making it difficult to use as a road. A broken trail had been established on the wider banks on either side, but that required the river be crossed repeatedly. After several miles of laboring near and through the river, Matthew was pleased to have Hofheins point out Dixie Hollow to him.

From there, the wagons labored through East Canyon and eventually faced the most difficult obstacle of the entire trail, Big Mountain, which rose above that portion of the Wasatch Range of the Rockies like a sentinel. The wagons were halted, and the members of the company stood facing the final barrier between them and their long-anticipated destination.

When the enormity of the challenge they faced swept over her, Sarah rushed to the rear of the wagon George had been driving. She leaned against the wagon box and cried, overwhelmed by the sight.

Matthew urged his horse from wagon to wagon. "We will make camp for the night here. Everyone needs to get some rest. Tomorrow will be another strenuous day."

When he came upon Sarah, she quickly tried to wipe away the tears with the back of her hand, ashamed at what Matthew might consider weakness.

"Sarah, have you been weeping?" She turned away from him. "Yes, yes, you have. What has you so upset?" he asked, perplexed.

She took a deep breath and then, with an intensity he had never witnessed in her, pointed and stomped her foot. "*That* has me upset, Matthew, that mountain the Lord has put in our way. Nothing we have come through compares to it. Will He never stop testing us?" Her words ended as a quiet wail.

For a few seconds, her husband was speechless. To that point, Sarah had borne the journey with such uncomplaining fortitude that her anger surprised him. He dismounted and put his hands on her shoulders, forcing her to look at him. "It won't stop us, my dear. Thousands of Saints before us have managed to get over it and into the valley." He added more firmly, "It won't stop us."

The stiffness in her body relented as she leaned against him and wept again. "Oh, Matthew, had I known . . . had I known what we would face, I would never have left Calcutta." The words tumbled out between her sobs.

That statement silenced him for a moment before he admonished her, saying, "But we did, and thank God we did. We will soon be home." He pronounced the words slowly and firmly, as if to a child who couldn't understand. "We are nearly there, Sarah. Take heart. We are nearly there."

She pulled away from him and straightened, ashamed by her lack of emotional control, then wiped her eyes with the cuff of her sleeve. As she looked around, it became apparent that several other women had reacted as she had. Many were trying to hide their tears of disappointment and weariness.

In a voice she struggled to control, she responded, "Of course we will make it, Matthew. As you said, we are nearly there."

As the fires from the individual camps lit the night and the smell of beans and cornbread filled the air, Edward looked at his father and stated with childlike simplicity, "There's a big mountain in front of us, Father. How will we get around it?"

Sarah turned her head to hide the tears that quickly pressed behind her eyes. Trying to maintain a cheerful countenance for the children, she took a deep breath and answered before Matthew spoke. "Edward, we will get over it an inch at a time. And when we have done that, we will be almost close enough to the valley to reach out and touch it." Her words were meant to offer encouragement as much to herself as to the child.

"I will be very glad when we're there, Father. I'm tired." The feelings of every person in the company were summed up in Edward's words.

"It's been a long journey, Father. I'm glad we're nearly there," George added wearily.

"Me too," Alfred whispered.

The five-mile trail up Big Mountain was well worn. The wagons were halted at regular intervals while they were quadruple-teamed to get them up and over the steeper places.

When the crest was finally reached, where the oxen could be rested, the view drove away all weariness from the viewers. Many of the men threw their hats into the air and called out, "Huzzah, huzzah, huzzah! We're nearly home!"

In the far distance beyond a silvery lake were the soft blue, snow-capped ridges that formed another mountain range, one they would not need to cross. Beyond the smaller hump called Little Mountain, portions of the city of Great Salt Lake could be glimpsed, stretching out before them in a neat grid of street blocks with farms scattered to the south.

It wasn't until they started down the west side of the mountain that the hardest part began. It was late afternoon and the animals and humans were extremely tired, but camping on the mountain was impossible.

Matthew rode from wagon to wagon and ordered, "Set your brakes. If you have none, you must attach drag shoes or lock the wheels with chains or the trunk of a small cottonwood tree. If that isn't enough, cut down a larger tree and tie it to your wagon as a drag."

One weary man remained on his wagon seat. Matthew paused and said in a firm voice, "It is vital that your wagon descent be slowed to spare the animals. Otherwise, the oxen will be driven to their knees."

The weary man nodded and then climbed down, taking an ax to a nearby sapling.

Despite the glorious view of the valley, dark thoughts filled the minds of a number of travelers who were forced to pull aside to allow other wagons to pass while they labored to repair an axle, rescue a neighbor, calm an agitated cow, hunt for a wandering child, attach another drag, or upright a toppled wagon.

As she slipped on a rock and caught her balance before she fell, Sarah muttered, "Matthew, once we are in this valley, we will never leave it again, I swear." He couldn't hear her words, but her feelings were clear in the resolute look on her face.

When camp was finally made that evening at the western base of Big Mountain, Matthew invited Hofheins to join the McCunes for supper. After they had eaten, the two men talked quietly as they sat on a log near the fire warming themselves in the chill night air.

"You are sure we will reach the city tomorrow?" Matthew asked.

"Ja, ja, tomorrow ve vill get there after ve make it out of Emigration Canyon. President Young vill send someone to meet us and lead us to a camping place."

Hofheins said no more for several minutes. He finally took a deep breath and stated, "Capitan McCune, you have done a fine job leading this company. I have learned much from you."

Matthew could see it was a difficult admission for the man to make, and he respectfully clapped him on the shoulder. "But your experience made it possible. You're a good man to share your wisdom and experience with me for the benefit of the entire company." Matthew offered his hand. "I'm glad to consider you my friend." When Hofheins did not respond, Matthew asked, "You are my friend, I hope?"

Hofheins finally took his hand, and as they shook, he admitted almost grudgingly, "I am your friend."

***

September 21, 1857
The Salt Lake Valley

The company was greeted by two men sent by Brigham Young as anticipated at the mouth of Emigration Canyon. The wagons were led down the sloping trail from the mouth of the canyon to the Eighth Ward Square, where the McCunes and the other families pitched their tents.

As Sarah prepared supper, she whispered to Matthew, "I'm going to ask the Andrews if they would like to join us this evening. I don't think Sister Andrews is feeling at all well."

Though Issy remained in the hammock, other members of the Andrews family sat around the fire with the McCunes. As the meal ended, Sarah looked at Brother Andrews and asked, "John, is Issy any better?"

"She is unchanged. She complains little and sleeps much. At least she isn't in pain, but she still can't use her legs and feet." He looked grim.

"I am so sorry. She is in our prayers."

"I thank ye for that."

Sarah couldn't help but notice how weak Isabella was. When they had bid each other good night, Sarah gave the woman a tender hug.

The subject of greatest interest to the new arrivals that evening as they ate supper was the news that the army wagons they had passed were only a portion of the troops President Buchanan had sent. Other army wagons had been seen by the wagon companies, and word circulated that the troops had been sent to put down a nonexistent rebellion in the valley.

The majority of army companies appeared to be camped at Ham's Fork. A smaller contingent of men and officers had established what they called Fort Scott, near the burned-out remnants of Fort Bridger.

"Matthew, how will it all turn out?"

"One can only guess."

No one knew how it was going to impact the Saints, but all had heard that Brother Brigham had promised he would see the city of Great Salt Lake burned to the ground before he would let the US government push the Saints out and let their enemies take over all they had built, as had been done in Missouri and Illinois.

"This is not Nauvoo," he had thundered from the pulpit.

***

As Sarah and Matthew lay down in the tent that night, she voiced another worry. "Matthew, Isabella is just skin and bones under her dress. I fear for her. She looks so white that I wonder if she will live much longer. I fear that John will lose both his wife and his daughter."

"I wish I had some herbs to help her and the lass. I've used everything I brought or gathered on the trail. All we can do is pray for the Lord's will to be done."

***

Having heard of their arrival, the next day, Matthew's old friend from Burma, Elam Ludington, arrived to greet them. "Matthew, we've been looking forward to your arrival for days. You will, of course, bring your family to stay with us until you decide where you want to settle."

The men slapped each other on the back, and Matthew laughed heartily. "Brother Ludington, you cannot know what a beautiful sight your face is." Matthew pulled at the man's beard. "We will be privileged to stay with you for a few days and talk of old times in Rangoon."

***

While staying with the Ludingtons, Sarah wept when she learned that her friend's fears had been fulfilled. Another woman would have to raise Isabella's children.

That night she quietly shared her thoughts with Matthew. "She never recovered from the birth of her youngest lad before they faced that voyage across the ocean and the journey across the plains. I believe she was so weakened that her grief over Issy's injury was too much to bear."

"But her journey is over now. She followed the urging of Church leaders and died in the faith. Her place in heaven is secure. You do not need to worry about her any longer."

"It isn't her I worry about now. It's John. He will need to remarry soon for the sake of the children, especially the littlest lad."

After giving so much . . . after offering continual obedience, it seems impossible to understand why Bella's journey couldn't end more happily, Sarah thought as she drifted off to sleep.

***

After three weeks of crowded days with the Ludingtons, Matthew followed the advice of an old friend, Truman Leonard, and the McCunes packed their wagons and made their way north a few miles to the young community of Farmington.

"Be sure to meet up with Daniel Miller and his wife, Hannah. He's one of the early settlers up there, and he'll see that you get some acreage and a place to live," Brother Ludington advised as they climbed into the wagons.

***

Brother Miller welcomed Matthew and the family with open arms. "Yes, yes, yes, we've got just the place for you and your family. You can use my old cabin. It's only two rooms, but you can make do until you can build something bigger."

He saddled a horse and led the two McCune wagons to the little cabin. "It will be crowded, but I can continue to sleep in the wagon," Harry reassured his mother.

"Now, you folks come back and join us for supper at seven," Dan called out as he mounted his horse.

"But, Brother Miller, there are so many of us to feed," Sarah called after him.

He turned in the saddle and laughed. "When you see the size of my family, you will realize that you folks hardly make a difference." With that, he trotted away.

That evening the Millers and the McCunes sat on blankets under a tree outside the large Miller cabin to eat. Hannah passed a large pot of potatoes and plates of fried chicken around. Sarah quietly counted nine children ranging from about two to more than twenty years in age.

When Hannah sat down near her, Sarah stated, "You have a wonderful, big family, Sister Miller. I envy you."

Hannah smiled. "Lovisa is married with a family of her own up in Cache County, and we lost a son shortly after birth some years ago, or there would have been two more here tonight. Of those still here at home, Jacob is the oldest. He's over there talking to your oldest son. How old is your boy?"

"Harry is seventeen."

"Jake is twenty-two and a great help to his father. As you can see, we only have two other sons. Joseph is ten, and David is just two. The Lord has blessed me with a household of daughters, and what a blessing they are to me."

***

Daniel offered Matthew a plot on the twenty-five acres surrounding the little cabin. "You can rent the cabin for one dollar a month, and I'll sell you the ten acres of cultivated land next to it for fifty cents an acre. Those acres were planted last season, and we've almost completed harvesting the potatoes and wheat. You'll find them fertile and easy to plant, with access to water from the stream that comes out of Farmington Canyon. The rest of the land is uncultivated, so you can have it for twenty-five cents an acre. You don't need to make a decision right now. Give it some thought. Just let me know by the time we have the existing crops harvested."

***

But before that decision was made, the bishop stood on Sunday and announced, "On September 15, a letter was sent throughout the Church, calling upon every man from fifteen to sixty to enlist in the Nauvoo Legion to prepare to defend the Saints should the US government attempt to force the army upon us and prohibit us from practicing our religion.

"Since only a portion of the male members responded to the letter, the call has been restated. I say again that all men and boys from fifteen to sixty are called to enlist. Those with families will not be called into action unless the situation becomes grave, but we must have their names and support to face the United States Army, which is threatening to enter Salt Lake City."

That evening, after climbing into the rope bed attached to a corner of the main room of the cabin, Sarah quietly said, "What have we gotten ourselves—and the lads—into, Matthew? Have we come halfway around the world to face a war with the United States government? We were supposed to find peace here in the valley with the Saints."

For the first time in all their years of marriage, Matthew seemed to have no answers. After a moment, all he could say was, "Have faith, Sarah. There's purpose in it somewhere."

***

After working all day harvesting potatoes in the acreage near the McCune cabin, Jake Miller, Daniel's oldest son, approached the McCune cabin as Sarah prepared supper.

Harry answered the door, and Jake asked, "Well, Harry, are you gonna join up?"

Harry stepped out and quickly closed the door behind them so they could talk without being overheard. He pointed at the rail fence, and both of them climbed up to find a place to sit.

"Well, what do you plan to do?" Jake asked.

"I guess I'll be joining up," Harry answered quietly, as if keeping his voice low would prevent his mother from learning of his decision. "Tell me what I'll be getting into."

"The militia is headed up by Colonel Daniel Wells. Captain Lot Smith is heading up the men who will spend the winter east of the city building defenses in East and Echo Canyons. We hear that their orders are to prevent the US troops from entering the Salt Lake Valley before spring so the Saints will have time enough to leave their homes and relocate farther south, to avoid a fight with the federal troops. President Young said there's to be no bloodshed, but Lot Smith and his men are charged with slowing or halting the troops using about any means necessary."

"Mother won't like it, but if that's what all the other single lads are doing, I'll do my part."

"Can you be ready day after tomorrow? We'll have the potatoes harvested by then." Jake's face was full of excitement. "I want to see what's goin' on in Salt Lake."

Harry took a deep breath. "I'll need my father to help convince my mother, but I'll be ready to go."

They shook hands, and after Jacob Miller had mounted his horse and ridden away, Harry stood without moving as he tried to figure out how to explain his decision without alarming Sarah.

After supper, he asked to speak to his father outside. "Father, Jake said there are several young men about my age from Farmington already training with the militia. I think it's only right that I join up too. Jake wants me to go with him day after tomorrow."

Matthew looked thoughtfully into the chill of the darkening evening for a few seconds before he spoke. "I realize your mother will not want you to go, but Brother Brigham has put out the call, and you're probably better prepared than some. You had a year of training as a naval cadet, which is more training than most have." He put his hand on his son's shoulder. "You have my support. Somewhere along the way, I expect to be called up as well."

"You think the older men with families will be called on?"

Matthew nodded and returned to the cabin. Harry followed him inside. Against her will, Sarah was convinced, so on Wednesday morning, Harry rode out of the settlement on a horse named Star, newly purchased from Daniel Miller. As she watched him ride away with Jake Miller, she stood with one hand over her mouth to prevent herself from calling him back.

After a few minutes, she stated, "Oh, Matthew, I hope he has everything he will need. I will worry about him every moment of every day."

"He will make us proud."

Remembering how painful it had been to let Harry enlist in the naval cadets, she added quietly, "I know these separations with Harry are necessary as he matures, but it never gets easier." She looked into her husband's face. "What if he doesn't have every thing he needs to get him through the winter?"

"He has always been an obedient lad, and as long as he does what his leaders instruct him to do, the Lord will protect him."

***

The two young men talked and speculated about the adventures ahead of them as they rode south toward Salt Lake City.

"What brought on this conflict with the United States government?" Harry asked.

"It's the same old story. Our enemies tell lies about us, and the folks in the government choose to believe them. When we became a territory, the government sent a bunch of carpetbaggers out here as federal judges, surveyors, and Indian agents. Some of them hated us before they even got here. President Fillmore had appointed Brigham Young as governor, and that worked fine—until President Buchanan was elected. He decided right after he took office that he needed to get tough with somebody to show how brave he was, so he chose us.

"Buchanan sent some federal judges out here who just couldn't stop bad-mouthing us. A judge named Drummond was one of the worst of them. He enjoyed sitting in judgment over us. He would lecture us at every turn from the bench or before the territorial legislature—he even spoke in the Tabernacle—and scolded us on our "uncivilized natures" and our sinful ways when all the time he was living with some other man's wife. He and another judge named Stiles started to ignore the power of our local probate courts. They turned everything into a federal matter and insisted they were the only judges in the territory with the power to make legal decisions.

"When the Utah Territory was created, Congress passed something called the Organic Act, which said that the territorial government positions would be filled by appointees chosen by the president with the advice and consent of the US Senate, but they didn't consider the feelings of the folks here. That's where the trouble started."

They rode in silence for a few minutes before he continued. "I guess, to be fair, I've got to admit that a few of the appointees were honest men, but most of them, especially more recent ones, are totally unqualified for the post they hold, and others are"—he broke the next word into three syllables—"gin-u-wine reprobates."

He began to laugh as if at a private joke. "Some of the folks here ran out of patience with Buchannan's appointees and took things into their own hands. A handful of lawyers in Salt Lake got so heated about some of the stupid decisions coming out of Judge Stiles's court that, one night, they broke into his law office and carried all his law books and written decisions out to the privy out back and threw them in."

He had to laugh for another minute. "A few prominent folks voiced the opinion that Drummond and his friends should be run out of town on a rail, and I guess they took it seriously. They packed up and beat it back to Washington, D.C., about a year ago to tell anyone who would listen that the Mormons were in rebellion. It gave Buchanan the excuse he was looking for. The word is that he has sent 2,500 troops to put down our so-called rebellion." He suddenly grew serious and quietly and thoughtfully added, "I wonder how it's all going to turn out."

"How did President Young find out about the army's intentions?" Harry wondered. "When my father talked with the leader of the army company we passed on the trail, he said he didn't sense any animosity on the part of the army officers."

"Back in July, Porter Rockwell and Abraham Smoot, who held the contract to carry the mail from Independence, Missouri, to Salt Lake City, were told that their contract had been canceled and that the army was gonna bring the mail when they came to Utah to put down the rebellion. Since then, every "over and back" man going east from here to escort wagon companies coming this direction has confirmed that the troops are coming and that they're escorting a man named Alfred Cumming, who's supposed to replace President Young as governor."

The two young men rode in silence, each in his own thoughts for a few minutes before Harry asked, "Has there been any real confrontation with the army at this point?"

"No, and President Young doesn't want one. He sent word to Lot Smith that somehow he was to convince the army that we have a militia big enough to discourage the US government."

"How could Smith do that?"

Jake grinned. "I have no idea, but I imagine he will come up with something."

CHAPTER TWENTY-TWO

CAMPING ON THE EIGHTH WARD Square that evening, the two young men ate the jerky and biscuits sent by their mothers. More than thirty other young men had gathered, all to enlist in the militia.

The word was that the militia had burned Fort Bridger a couple of weeks earlier under direction of Brigham Young in the hopes that the army would be hard-pressed to find shelter during the winter months. Harry began to wonder if he had missed the militia's best adventures.

When a lanky, redheaded, quick-tempered Lot Smith arrived late that evening, some of the men called out, "Hey, Captain Smith, what're your plans?"

He simply replied, "You've all been assigned to me, so get your rest tonight. Tomorrow will be a long ride. You'll be joining the others assigned to East and Echo Canyons."

Jake drew everyone's attention when he stood and spoke. "I heard Brother Brigham has promised that we'll never again be driven from our homes to see our enemies take possession of them. Is it true that he said we'll burn the city to the ground first?"

Lot was not a man quick to respond, so Jake added more questions. "Is it true that he's got a hundred men assigned to be the rear guard? That they're charged with burning every building if the army comes into town? Is it true that he said a blaze like that will be seen all the way back to Nauvoo?"

His words hung in the air for a while before Lot nodded and responded simply, "Yep." He said nothing more before he turned in for the night.

In the morning, the order to saddle up was given, and the group rode east until midday, when they paused to rest the horses and drink at a small stream in Emigration Canyon. After they had filled their canteens and eaten a piece or two of jerky, Smith ordered them to rest for an hour while the horses grazed.

Before the hour was up, he called for their attention. "I'm sure all of you are wonderin' just what the plan is. It's up to us to make sure the troops don't enter the valley before spring. President Young wants 'em delayed long enough to get cold and hungry, so they won't be so enthusiastic about makin' war with the Mormons. The task is up to us. Now mount up."

***

The young men reached East Canyon late that evening. There, Smith ordered ten of them to remain behind with the militia members assigned to build defensive stone breastworks and rifle pits, to dam streams in preparation for the confrontation with the army, and to cache supplies for the winter.

The other men continued eastward until they reached Echo Canyon. In the moonlight, Harry looked around at the familiar canyon walls his family had passed on their journey into the valley just a short time ago. "Well, I never thought I would see these red walls again so soon," he muttered to himself.

***

Sarah arose the Sunday after Harry had left to join the militia and quietly began preparations for breakfast. Matthew was sitting at the rough-hewn breakfast table deeply engrossed in his three-day-old copy of the *Deseret News*. He didn't note her presence until she spoke.

"Matthew, what is it in that newspaper that is making you oblivious to the world around you?"

He shook the paper and turned a page before he looked up. "I found an account of the mutiny in India Nathan Jones told us about. The account is more than three months old but is probably the most recent news available."

He began to read aloud. "*The British government is reacting with all speed to reports of occurrences of mutiny in India, which continue to this time. It has been reported that native troops of the Bengal army of the East India Company arose in an outbreak of violence and murdered loyal troops, as well as civilian men, women, and children in unprovoked viciousness in Meerut Cantonment. British authorities have been quick to respond forcefully. Troops posted to China for the conflict there have been diverted to India, while regiments returning to Bombay from the successful campaign in Persia were ordered to Calcutta. It is anticipated that the mutiny will be put down swiftly.*"

Sarah's legs gave out, and she sat down hard in the nearest chair. "Is there any more information?"

"The article is brief." His expression was grim.

"I had so hoped that Brother Jones had exaggerated the situation." Her voice was filled with alarm. "We must write to Patrick and Mary Anne again and urge them to come to America immediately. I dread to think what will happen to them if they stay in Calcutta."

Matthew laid the paper on the table. He closed his eyes in resignation and pinched the bridge of his nose as if it would ease the tension he felt. "I wonder what may have happened to them already." His voice grew stronger as he added, "But I do know that had I stayed to complete my enlistment rather than resigning, we would be caught in it."

When the meal was over, he began a lengthy letter to Patrick while Sarah wrote to Mary Ann. They both recognized that the letters would not arrive in Calcutta for several months and that much could happen in the meantime.

At meeting that afternoon, another letter from President Young was read over the pulpit. In it he ordered all men of good health under the age of fifty north of Salt Lake City to report to Eighth Ward Square by October 16, or as soon thereafter as possible, for military assignment.

The adults in the congregation trickled out of the little rock chapel where they stood about in little groups with many of the women trying to control their fears, including Sarah.

Without saying anything, Matthew assisted her into the wagon. As the boys climbed or were lifted in, he said quietly, "We will deal with this challenge as we have dealt with all others."

As the sun began to set that evening, Sarah rose and moved to stand in front of the little window of the cabin, where she tried to steady her nerves. This was not at all like Matthew's posting to Rangoon. At that time, she and the boys had his military income to support themselves and a comfortable home with servants. *What will we do now? How will we sustain ourselves with both Matthew and Harry gone?* Her heart pounded so loudly she could hear it in her ears.

***

With the experienced help of Dan Miller and the inexperienced help of his own three young sons, Matthew was able to get twenty acres planted in wheat before he and several of the other men from Farmington rode into Salt Lake City to report for duty. There, they were informed they would augment the forces already in the city serving as guards. Additionally, they were told that if they could find vacant housing, they were welcome to bring their families into the city but that they should be prepared to take their families and flee the city at an hour's notice.

After two days of searching, Matthew finally located an empty cabin on the north side of the city. Its previous occupants had already fled south. It had a small shed in the back for animals. Pleased with his luck, he rode back to Farmington, where he informed his wife that they were moving to Salt Lake City.

"What about the crop, Matthew?" she asked. What she really wanted to ask was why they had to relocate again, but she knew it was a rhetorical question and would draw a short, impatient answer.

"The crop will take care of itself."

The three younger boys helped load the family's possessions into the two wagons, and with George driving one and Matthew the other, they set out for Salt Lake City. The cow and the horse were tied to the back of the wagons.

They stopped to rest for an hour, and the animals and humans drank deeply from a stream that flowed down from the mountains on the east to the hot springs just north of the city.

Sarah found the little cabin to be much like the one they had left in Farmington. As they moved their possessions into it, she mused quietly, "Here we are in another home—one more time."

Matthew reported for duty the next morning and was assigned to ride a circuit throughout the northwest quadrant of the city as a guard, watching for anything that seemed amiss.

The weather turned cold the end of November. The older men who were serving as guards were called together one evening on the Eighth Ward Square, where Colonel Wells stood in a wagon bed to address the group.

"It's apparent that the army won't enter the valley until spring. Lot Smith and his men are making that impossible, so President Young has given me permission to excuse any of you men over forty who have families. You are urged to take your families south before the weather prohibits such a move. He recommends that you go at least as far south as Provo."

Matthew rode back toward the cabin so deeply immersed in thought that he almost ran into Dan Miller on his horse.

"Whoa, Matthew, where are you headed in such a state that you don't recognize a friend?"

Matthew abruptly reined in his horse. "Dan, I offer my apologies. Were you at the meeting where those of us over forty were excused from duty and told we can head south for the winter?"

"Yes, but I'm headed back to Farmington. I've got a good crop of winter wheat that I don't want to lose to the deer. Maybe we'll go south in the spring."

"Hope you will keep an eye on my crop."

"I can do that. Where you headin'?"

"South, as President Young has recommended. I have no idea how far south. I'll get back up to harvest the wheat somehow. Best of luck to you and yours."

The men waved their hats at one another as they parted.

CHAPTER TWENTY-THREE

LEAVING MAJOR JOHN WINDER TO direct the men in Echo Canyon, Lot selected thirty-five men, including Harry and Jake, and led that group eastward until they neared the Continental Divide. There they joined a group under Colonel Robert Burton, who was planning a coordinated strike against both the federal infantry and artillery units camped near Pacific Springs, about a day's march apart. Burton's group would ride into the artillery camp at about three the next morning and make enough noise to stampede the animals. Smith's group agreed to do the same to the infantry camp.

After passing the sleeping guards, the men commenced yelling and firing their pistols, but the hobbled oxen and mules couldn't stampede. By the time the startled soldiers stumbled out of their tents, the raiders were gone. Though the episode had not ended with the results they had hoped for, some of the scouts chortled with laughter as they talked about the experience on the ride back to camp.

Harry wasn't amused. "Jake, I don't think I'm going to write an account of this adventure for posterity. We should have realized that the animals might be hobbled. The troops must be having a hearty laugh at our expense."

Jake nodded. "You're right. I don't think any of us will be having much fun out here on the high plains, likely freezing nearly to death at night and eating poor grub, just so we can make fools of ourselves."

The next day the snow began to fall, and by night, the driving wind made for limited sight. Smith's group decided to offer what the younger men called a "serenading party" using pans, dried raw hide "musical instruments," and anything else that was noisy enough to ruin the soldiers' sleep and stampede any animals not hobbled.

After more than a week, the men began to grow bored with that activity. Smith led his group to the Big Sandy Fork of the Green River. The location offered a good lookout from the bluffs over the trail, where they could watch for troop movements and supply trains. While there, a scout was sent to observe any activity. He returned about an hour before dark.

He swung out of his saddle and reported, "Captain Smith, there's a supply train of twenty-six wagons camped about four miles east of here. The teamsters and guards were just sitting down to supper when I saw 'em. There was some heavy drinkin' goin' on."

A broad grin slowly spread across Lot Smith's face. He scooped the last spoonfuls of his beans and bacon into his mouth and rose from the log where he had been sitting. He wiped his hands on his pants and started walking among the men. He called out, "Mount up," and motioned with his thumb over his shoulder. "Get your horses saddled and meet me by my tent."

It was dark before Smith and his men spotted the fires of the camp from a rise in the road. Lot held up his hand in the moonlight to halt those behind him. He looked the scene over and concluded that there had to be two wagon trains. A second large fire could be seen about two miles farther east of the first. Not to be dissuaded from his plans, he waited for the first camp to grow quiet. It was nearly midnight before the teamsters and guards drank themselves into a stupor.

He turned and instructed, "We're goin' in quiet like so as not to set up a ruckus that will warn the second camp. Stay just out of the light from the fire so they can't tell how many of us there are. "Jake Miller, you'll join me, and we'll go from tent to tent and wake 'em. We'll get 'em out in the light of the fire so the rest of you can watch 'em."

By the time the startled and chagrined troops and teamsters had been roused and their weapons collected, there were sixty of them standing around in their long underwear. Smith distributed the firearms he and Jake had collected to the militiamen and ordered the wagons to be searched. Every one of Smith's men was hoping that wool overcoats might be found.

When the only ammunition found was for weapons the militia did not possess, the disappointment was palpable. To make sure the army would never use it, Smith had several of the men remove the ammunition from the wagons to take with them before he grabbed a firebrand from the campfire and rode from wagon to wagon, setting them on fire. He left the tents untouched so the men would not be without protection from the cold.

As Lot led the militiamen into the night toward the second camp, they could hear unhappy complaints from the soldiers in the first about the fact that there had been so few militiamen in the group that had humiliated them. Had the soldiers known, the outcome might have been different, but since Smith had taken their weapons and ammunition, they couldn't even set up an alarm for the other camp. The whole situation was highly mortifying for them.

The same pattern was followed when they arrived at the second encampment. After the drunken troops and teamsters had been awakened, they were made to stand near the fire while Smith had their weapons confiscated. Looking through the wagons, the militiamen discovered a large supply of sulfur and saltpeter.

The wagon master protested. "Hey, if you Mormons set fire to the wagons, you're gonna hurt a lot of men and animals."

"All right," Smith responded. "Have your men collect their personal property from the wagons and move far enough away so's not to get hurt."

While they were doing so, an army express rider arrived, carrying the tardy news that the supply trains should always keep a night guard because "Mormons were in the field."

The wagon master said bitterly, "Yeah, we noticed."

Lot Smith set fire to the wagons himself. When the saltpeter and sulfur exploded, the militia scouts sent up a shout and rode away cheering. They arrived back at their own camp ready to drop onto their blankets for a couple of hours of sleep before morning.

The next day the scouts spotted a third supply train. Without the advantage of darkness, Smith decided he would need to disguise his numbers. He sent his men in a loosely organized line around a large knoll in sight of the wagon train, with orders to ride down into a deep gully where they would be out of sight. Then they were to come back around the back side of the knoll and pass in front of it again. They did this several times, giving the troops and teamsters the impression of a force several times larger than it was. Harry and Jake exchanged a broad grin in respect of Smith's maneuvers.

They rode swiftly into the camp, disarmed the teamsters, and demanded to see the wagon master. Smith yelled, "The rest of my men have you in their sights. Don't make any quick moves."

"Captain Simpson ain't here. He's down at the river," someone yelled at him.

Smith ordered to several scouts, "Keep a watch on these men." Then signaled a dozen to follow him as he rode toward the river looking for the wagon master.

Despite the fact that Smith and his men had gotten the drop on him, Simpson refused to give up his pistols until Smith and his men had every man with Simpson at gunpoint. After the humiliated wagon master blustered about wanting a fair fight, Lot offered to give back the weapons they had taken from Simpson's men and have a shoot-out if that would satisfy the man.

Simpson's belligerence melted. "Nah, we were hired to whack bulls, not fight." At that, the confrontation ended. As Smith's men followed Simpson and his men back to their camp, the wagon master worried aloud about his reputation. He begged Smith to leave them enough supplies so they wouldn't starve.

Smith figured the man had been sufficiently humiliated and agreed. "I'll leave you two wagons full of supplies, and I'll leave half the cattle for you. We're gonna liberate the rest."

Being in difficult straights themselves, the militiamen searched the wagons and took some of the foodstuffs, blankets, weapons, and ammunition before setting all but two of them on fire.

When Lot Smith heard that the burning of Simpson's wagon train had earned him the honor of a $1,000 reward on his head, he roared with laughter. "I guess my worth has just gone up. Hey, any of you men think I'm worth that much?"

"Not hardly, Lot, not hardly," some of the men called to him, laughing as hard as he had.

That night as they ate around the fire, Lot stood and praised them. "I know that bein' out here in the winter is hard on you men, but our scorched earth policy is makin' it much harder on the army. They're not gonna bother anybody this winter."

***

December, 1857
The Salt Lake Valley

The weather had moderated slightly despite the fact that it was early December. A large number of the families of the men over forty were preparing to follow President Young's direction and move south in the spring.

As she set the table for breakfast, Sarah spoke. "Matthew, where will we go? Here, we will know when the militia lads return, and we should be able to locate Harry without difficulty, but if we go south, how will he find us?" She set a bowl of wheat mush before him and each of the three younger children.

"I don't like this mush, Mother," George said quietly. "I want some rice."

"I know you would rather have rice as we did in India, but we don't have rice here in the valley," she responded softly. She poured cream from the morning's milking into his bowl. "We must get accustomed to doing things differently here."

Having been deep in thought, Matthew was oblivious to his wife's concerns that Harry be able to locate them. He suddenly sat up straight and nodded as if he had made a decision. "Tomorrow we will pack up the wagons and join any group gathering on Eighth Ward Square who are headed south. There's no reason to wait any longer. Some of the men spoke of traveling as far as the Iron Mission or St. George down south. We may not go that far, but there is no reason to wait until spring."

Sarah blanched but was determined to trust her husband. "Should we pack the household goods this evening?" She did not let Matthew hear the resignation in her voice.

"I must have the axle replaced on the larger wagon before it can be packed. Unless I do, it won't hold up on a journey of any length. I'll take it to the wheelwright after breakfast. He can probably have it done by tomorrow." After he had finished his meal, Matthew tied the reins of his horse to the wagon and started down the road.

In the absence of their father and with their mother's approval, the three boys went outside to play, an activity seldom permitted. Sarah sat down and tried to focus on her mending, but she could hardly work for the knot of worry in her stomach. *How will Harry find us when he returns?*

***

By noon the flowing day, two McCune wagons were lined up with a dozen others. George drove one, and Matthew drove the other with his horse tied to the rear. Alfred and Edward walked, assigned to take charge of the cow.

The journey progressed at walking speed, slowed by the short steps of the children and the cattle accompanying the group, which would produce calves in the spring. After ten days of walking, pausing only on the Sabbath, Sarah heard six-year-old Edward crying himself to sleep with exhaustion.

As Matthew entered the tent, she said with unusual forcefulness, "Matthew, you said nothing, but it was evident that you felt the settlement at Provo was too crowded for us to settle there, but I must ask that we halt at the next settlement of any size. We cannot make the lads walk any farther."

Startled at the unusual forcefulness in her voice, he looked at her in surprise. With a sensitivity not normally part of his usual military bearing, he nodded. "I'm told that we will be nearing Salt Creek within the next few miles. We will look that place over, and if it suits us, we will halt there."

She had been expecting a reproof, if not in his words, then in his expression, and so his acquiescence startled her. She smiled gratefully. "Thank you, Matthew."

***

By midday, the wagons that had not stopped at Provo reached Salt Creek, a three-block square enclosed by a high mud wall as protection from the Indians. Wagons and riders entered both the north and south walls through a large gate. The settlement was only six years old, and the homes inside were rough-hewn cabins or adobes. A few of the families of more recent arrivals were still living in their wagons or tents while they built more permanent shelters.

While the animals were watered at the wide creek that ran through the settlement, Matthew walked through the community. Several children had come to stare at the arriving wagons, and within a few minutes, the three boys were playing with them like old friends.

Within an hour, Matthew had returned. "Sarah, I have had a good talk with a man by the name of George Bradley, one of the original settlers here. He says this is a good place to grow wheat and there is plenty of good land available for homesteading. He plans to build a gristmill so the community will have a good supply of flour and enough to sell to travelers. I think we could do well here. This is a very attractive little valley. Up there to the northeast is Mount Nebo—the one covered with snow. There, to the southeast, are the Red Cliffs. What do you think? Could you like it here?"

"Matthew, I will be happy anywhere we can settle and have peace." Her voice was full of relief until she paused and looked at him with sudden concern. "Are there any Indian troubles here?"

"Brother Bradley said there haven't been difficulties with the local tribes since the Walker Indian War in '52. That was when the men built the wall around the settlement. Every night there are four men stationed at each of the gates." He looked around and, turning back to her, stated, "This will be our new home. Come, lads. We're going to set up the tent."

That evening after the three boys were asleep, Sarah approached her husband with the question she had asked several times but never felt she had received an adequate answer to.

"Matthew, how will Harry ever find us?"

He gave the same response he had given her previously. "Harry is an intelligent lad. He'll ask around." The last word was hardly out of his mouth before he was asleep, his casual but confident answer offering her little comfort.

CHAPTER TWENTY-FOUR

March, 1858
Calcutta

PATRICK MEIK ARRIVED HOME AS the grandfather clock struck nine. Mary Anne hurried to greet him when she heard his tanga in the drive. After one of the servants assisted him in removing his jacket, she excitedly took his arm. His face was gray with exhaustion.

"Patrick, we have a letter from Matthew and Sarah. It was sent last October, but they have so much news for us. Please, sit down and eat your dinner while I read it to you."

When he was seated, Leela set a plate of curried chicken before him. His eyes were red and lined with exhaustion. "What do they say?" he asked before beginning to eat.

She smoothed the letter. "This one is from Matthew. Sarah also sent a letter for me." She began to read.

Dear Patrick and Mary Ann,

We arrived in the Salt Lake Valley a few weeks ago and have settled in the community of Farmington, a few miles north of Salt Lake City. The soil is rich, and we expect to eventually produce a fine crop of wheat. Though there is not the comfort of our home in Calcutta, or even Rangoon, we have sufficient for our needs. We are all well and made the long sea voyage and the journey across the American continent in fine shape. We met Elder Nathan Jones on the trail and were distressed when we heard from him that there is rebellion in India. That information was confirmed by a small article in the newspaper here. We are fearful for you and your family. Again, we urge you to make immediate preparations to come to America and join the Saints here. Please, act on my words as they may save your family both physically and spiritually.

Respectfully,
Your servant, Matthew McCune

"Here is the short letter from Sarah addressed to me."

Dear Mary Ann,
I grieve at the news that India is in rebellion, and I cannot sleep for worry about you and your family. Please urge Patrick to make plans to leave that place and join us here in the Salt Lake Valley. It is a long journey, but with the Lord's help, we made it safely. He will protect you and your family as well. Of this I am sure. The experience has helped our lads grow strong, tall, and more self-sufficient. They make me very proud. Please join us here.

With much affection,
Sarah McCune

Mary Anne pulled her handkerchief from her pocket and dabbed at tears. Patrick reached over and took Matthew's letter from her hand. He reread it silently. Thoughtfully, he laid it down beside his plate and picked up his fork again.

"What do you think, Patrick? Can we go soon?"

He did not answer for a long moment. When he finally did, his voice was subdued and filled with regret. "I wish I had taken my family away from this place when the McCunes left, but now it is too late, at least until the revolt is put down. To attempt to resign now would be viewed as cowardice."

Realizing he was right, Mary Anne smiled weakly. "Please, Patrick, do finish your dinner before it is cold. I will write a letter to Sarah this evening. Are you too weary to write to Matthew?"

"No, I will write before I retire. The letters will go out in tomorrow's post. You should tell her of the welfare of the children and how we finally got our Alexander back home with us. I will write to Matthew about the progress in putting down the revolt."

Patrick wrote late into the night.

Dear Matthew,
I suggest that you do not worry your wife and family with what I must write. It is important for you to know that the violence has not reached Calcutta but is focused mainly around the great cities of the central plains: Lucknow, Cawnpore, Delhi, Allahabad, Agra, and others. In these cities, anyone with a white or nearly white face, including Anglo-Indians, is vulnerable to violence. Even women and children are not spared. Company officers and medical men are hacked down. Any natives who have converted to Christianity fare as badly. Employees of the company or its armies—be they Hindu, Muslim, or Sikhs—are cut down just

as quickly. Word trickles back to Fort William—the telegraph wires are always the first thing to be destroyed—that the reprisals against the rebels and any who sympathize with them made by the troops are sometimes as brutal as the actions of the rebels. The city of Cawnpore was retaken in July of last year, and Delhi was finally freed from rebel hands in September. Any British leader—such as Lord Charles Canning, the governor general—who is willing to show any mercy meets with a great outcry from the British community here in Calcutta. There has been a growing demand that he be recalled by Parliament. He has said he will not govern in anger and has proven himself a principled man.

Alexander was caught in the siege of Lucknow in July when the lads and their teachers at the Martiniére School were brought into the governor's residency in that city for their protection. Conditions deteriorated as supplies and medicines ran low during the bombardment. Additional supplies finally reached them in September when General Havelock and Sir James Outram arrived with troops, but the captives were not freed until November when Sir Colin Campbell and his troops arrived. Only recently has Lucknow been fully recaptured. We feel that the rebellion will soon be put down throughout the country, but it may take some months yet. We were glad to receive your letter and learn of your well-being and successful journey. Matthew, your decision to resign and leave for America when you did has demonstrated the blessings of obedience. May God continue to bless you and your family.

Respectfully,
Your servant, Patrick Meik

Mary Anne's letter was more brief but heartfelt.

Dear Sarah,
Your letter was received today with joy. You cannot imagine how grateful I was to hear from you and Matthew. Much has happened in the many months since you departed Calcutta. Our Alexander is finally home with us. He was four months captive during the siege of Lucknow, from July of last year until November. He was restored to us before Christmas. He is thin as a stick. It must have been a terrible ordeal as he is so very quiet now. He refuses to speak with me about his experience, but surely being here with his loving family will restore his spirit. Annie has been such a blessing to us in these hard times. Her brother James is stationed on a ship that patrols the Gomati River, and George has recently enlisted as a naval cadet. He so wants to be like his older brother. The younger children are doing well. Patrick leads the Wanderer's Branch of the Church here, which is meeting again, though we have a small group with very few men in attendance. How I wish we had left India with your family. Patrick and I often speak of making the journey to the Salt Lake Valley, but until the conflict here is over, he cannot resign. So we

pray and wait for a time when we can make such a journey. I hope this letter finds you and your loved ones well. Please write to us again.

With affectionate respect,
Mary Anne Meik

Patrick and Mary Anne could only hope that those letters would find the McCune's in their new country.

***

March 1858
The High Plains of Wyoming

Lot Smith's men struggled to keep warm through the winter winds and snowstorms, but as they waited for a warming spring, they established a well-hidden camp about two miles from the army camp called Fort Scott. Each man took his turn as lookout, keeping an eye on camp from a bluff and reporting any unusual activity.

They took note of a group of six men arriving from the south who appeared to be escorting someone of importance into the camp. Curiosity suffused Smith's men.

Smith doubled the surveillance on the camp. When a dispatch rider saddled his horse the morning of the third day and headed back toward Salt Lake City at a gallop, Lot and two of his men rode hard to catch up with him.

The man carrying the dispatch case was unwilling to surrender it to Smith. "I gotta put in it the hands of President Young, but I'll tell you what it says as there ain't nothin' in it that won't be common knowledge in a couple of days. That man we escorted all the way from San Bernardino to Salt Lake City and from there up here to meet with the army is Colonel Thomas Kane. He was a friend to the Saints when they was back in Illinois"—he pronounced it *ill-in-noise*—"and he's come all the way from the east by ship to California so he could help out with the negotiations. He's talked this man, Albert Cumming, into going with him into Salt Lake City alone to talk directly with President Young so an agreement can be reached that will avoid bloodshed. President Young pledged us to make sure nothin' happens to Cumming."

"When will they leave for the valley?" Smith's words were clipped.

"Day after tomorrow. They'll have a militia escort and head down Echo Canyon, the most direct route. Now can I go? I gotta get on my way."

Lot waved him on his way and, with the two men accompanying him, rode hard back to camp. As he pulled his horse to a halt and dismounted, he called out, "Pack up. We're headed back to Echo Canyon now!"

Within twenty minutes, the men had extinguished the fire and packed the tents and gear. They moved out at a full gallop, and within less than two hours they were able to wave as they passed the dispatch rider.

They arrived in Echo Canyon as the dusk was fading, their horses nearly spent. Lot called the senior officers under Winder to a campfire meeting where he explained the plans that had taken shape in his mind as he had ridden that day.

"It seems that we're gonna get the chance to impress Alfred Cumming, the man Buchanan sent to replace Brigham Young as governor. Colonel Thomas Kane, who's been a good friend of the Saints, will be escorting Cumming to Salt Lake City from the army's winter camp near Fort Bridger in two days. Cumming has been offered safe passage so he and President Young can parlay and maybe avoid bloodshed. This is our chance to make it clear to Cumming that the US Army would be wise to avoid conflict with the militia. We're gonna make sure he believes we have a militia the US Army won't want to face." He paused and asked Winder, who stood near him, "How many men do you have here in the canyon?"

"Maybe a thousand by now, not many more."

"We've got to make it look like ten times that number. Here's what we're gonna do. In the morning, we assign the men to gather every piece of wood they can find. They're gonna carry it up to the tops of the canyon walls, where they're gonna build some mighty fine bonfires close to the edge where they can be seen from the trail. Then about three hundred of us will stay up there. When we get word from the lookouts that Cumming and his escort are near entering the canyon, I'll fire my pistol as a signal, and those men will light the fires and move around in front of them so they can be seen from the canyon floor."

"What do you want the others to do?"

"The rest of the men will form up standing at attention on either side of the river an arm's length between them with rifles at the ready. What Cumming won't know is that we don't have enough militia to line the whole length of the canyon, so when he and his escort have reached the halfway point, those in the first half of the line will peel off, mount their horses, and beat it to the end of the line, where they will form up again. We're pretty sure the sound of the supply wagon with them will cover the sound of the horses, but the men have got to do this in the dark and as quietly as possible so's not to give us away. Get the word to your men first thing in the morning."

***

The next day was spent in hurried preparation for the arrival of the men escorting Kane and Cumming the following evening. A sense of anticipation permeated the entire camp. When the lookouts sent word that Cumming's escort was about thirty minutes away, Smith fired his pistol, and the men on the tops of the canyon walls began to light the fires. The other militia members took their places along the river. They followed Smith's instructions to wait until the two men and the supply wagon were far enough ahead that they would not see the men at the beginning of the line ride their horses as fast as possible through the river and canyon underbrush in the darkness to relocate farther along the river, extending the line.

Smith smiled with satisfaction as the bonfires raged and the men moved around them between the flames and the edge of the canyon walls, throwing their long shadows deep into the canyon.

***

As the little party of six escorts accompanying Cumming and Kane moved through the canyon, they watched the militia members watching them. The six tried to hide their grins, but no one said anything until Kane spoke about halfway through the canyon.

"Governor Cumming, I know we planned to camp here in the canyon this evening to rest the horses, but from the looks of the numbers of the militia, I think we had better keep moving. I'd guess there are several thousand men here, and they don't look friendly."

Neither man spoke until they had made the long journey out of the canyon near morning. When the escort and supply wagon had finally passed out of the canyon, Harry and Jake threw their arms around each other and joined in the hooting and shouting of the other men.

"We've just beaten the devil himself," Jake exulted.

"We did it!" Harry raised his voice with dozens of others.

Lot called the officers together after breakfast and announced, "Cumming will let the army know that they hadn't better try entering the valley through Echo Canyon, so we need to send a small contingent to cover Yellow Creek Canyon on the Bear River. They might try it there. Major Winder, choose a dozen men and head out." Winder selected ten men, including Harry.

***

On May 29, a dispatch rider brought a letter notifying Winder that the leadership of the US Army had agreed to the demands set forth by Brigham Young. The militia's efforts at inflating their numbers had motivated Cumming to notify the leadership of the army that they would be wise not to instigate a confrontation with the Utah militia.

The bottom line of the agreement between Young and Cumming was that there would be no aggressive action taken on the part of the army and that the troops would not remain in Salt Lake City. They were to march west on South Temple and not even make a temporary camp until they had crossed the Jordan River.

To make sure that the provisions of the treaty were honored, the men under Winder and Smith were ordered back into Salt Lake City. They arrived on the evening of May 31, Harry's eighteenth birthday. As they rode two by two into the city, he spoke to the man riding next to him. "It's like a great ghost town. Almost every building is boarded up, and there's hardly a civilian to be seen. I suppose this is what Nauvoo looked like after the Saints were driven out."

Every militiaman was ordered to take his rifle and find a place on the roof of a building or house or inside where possible. Smith called out, "When they come into sight, make sure they see you with your rifles trained on them. If you see any sign that the troops plan to damage or steal property or in any way violate the agreement, you're to let them have it."

The militiamen existed on biscuits and jerky as they waited and watched. Wherever necessary, they added straw and wood to that already piled in the buildings in case the order to burn was given. Smith instructed, "If you hear the cannon on Temple Square, the torch is to be put to the town."

About midday on the third day, the sounds of horses and wagons and the muffled *tramp, tramp, tramp* of boots against the hard-packed earth echoed in the street. The militiamen watched, motionless, from their very visible positions.

Harry felt a sudden sense of pity for the men covered with dust and grime so thick it was difficult to tell if they were clean-shaven or not. *They don't know any more about why they are here than we do.* The ragged uniforms hung on their thin frames. They looked around with eyes that were dull from exhaustion or full of hate coupled with fear. But per the agreement with Brigham Young, they kept marching.

***

Within days, many members of the militia, including Harry, were permitted to end their enlistment. Harry found the empty cabin in Farmington and only a half dozen men left behind to tend the crops. No one had any idea where the McCune family had gone, so he returned to Salt Lake City and stopped to ask anyone who might know where they were.

After a long month, he saw a familiar face from where he was standing on Main Street. Tom Smith, an acquaintance from Farmington, and his daughter were sitting high on the seat of a large freight wagon moving south.

Henry waved at the man, catching his eye. "Brother Smith, it's Harry McCune. I'm looking for my family. Would you know where they might be?" he called.

The wagon stopped, and Smith, with his elbows on his knees, leaned toward Harry. "Well, if it isn't Harry McCune. What did you say?"

Harry rushed to the wagon. "I'm looking for my parents. They left Farmington while I was in the militia, and I can't find anyone who knows where they've gone."

"I heard they settled in Salt Creek, eight miles south of Willow Creek, where I'm hauling this load of supplies. Tie your horse to the wagon and jump in. You can ride with us all but the last few miles."

CHAPTER TWENTY-FIVE

Willow Creek came into view after five days of riding in the wagon during the day and camping every night. Smith was a man of few words and his daughter even fewer. Harry had soon given up on his attempts to maintain any kind of conversation.

He felt lucky that Tom's daughter, though young, was a good cook. On the second evening after camp was made, the young woman offered him flour muffins, a real treat with his tin plate of rabbit stew.

"Sister Smith, the man who marries you will be doubly blessed. You will bring to your marriage both cooking skills"—she blushed at this—"and beauty." She blushed even more. He suddenly wondered if Annie would have been such a good cook.

"You are too kind, Brother McCune." It was the only thing she had said since he had climbed into the wagon in Salt Lake City.

***

He was filled with anticipation at finding his parents and brothers. After he left Tom Smith's wagon, he rode Star the last eight miles. He paused to allow his horse to drink from a small stream when he reached the settlement of Salt Creek. He halted each man he met. "My name is Harry McCune, and I'm looking for someone who can give me information as to the whereabouts of my father, Matthew McCune, and my family."

The third man put out his hand, and they leaned out of their saddles and shook. "My name's Zim Baxter, and I think I can help you out. Your father and brothers are out in the east field with some of the other men and boys, cutting wild hay." He pointed. "Just follow that path about a mile and a half, and you'll see them working there in the meadow."

When the figures cutting hay came into view, he halted his horse and watched as they worked. It only took a few seconds to recognize the familiar figure of his father. As he rode toward him, he waved his hat and called, "Father! Lads! It's Harry! I've finally found you."

When he dismounted, he was nearly toppled by his brothers as they threw themselves at him. His father approached and, with a wide smile, put out his hand. As they shook hands, Matthew laughed heartily. "I told your mother you were a smart lad and you would find us. You're looking a bit thin, but you stand an inch taller than you did when we last saw you. Your mother will need to put some flesh on those bones."

"I will be glad for her to do that, Father."

"Lads," he called out, "you load the hay into the wagon while I introduce your brother to the other men."

The other men and boys in the field paused, glad for a few minutes of rest while Matthew introduced his son to each one of them. "This is my oldest son, Harry, just back from the militia. This is Abe Boswell, and this is Brother Thompson . . ." And so went the introductions to men who would become lifelong friends.

As his father and brothers rode back to the settlement in the wagon, his younger brothers badgered him to tell them of his adventures while in the militia. His father put a stop to the coaxing. "Harry will share his experiences with us at suppertime after the chores are done and the stock is watered. Now, we will give no sign that anything is different than usual when we reach your mother."

"Father, are we going to play a trick on her?" Edward asked with wide eyes.

"Not a trick, just a wonderful surprise."

When they arrived at the tent, which was situated against the east wall of the fort, Sarah was bent over the pot that hung above the open fire. She didn't notice Harry until he stood next to her.

"Mother, here I am again."

When he spoke, she whirled and dropped the spoon. "Harry, you found us," she cried as she threw her arms around his neck. "Thank heaven you found us. I have prayed for this moment for months."

He put his arm around her waist, picked her up, and twirled her around before putting her down again. After months of absence he was struck by how different his mother looked now than she had in India.

His formerly beautifully coifed mother was sunburned, and her hair was dry, with strands that escaped her hair comb and hung around her face. Her hands were chapped and work worn. He had never seen her look so weary. He was suddenly aware of how much she had given up and how physically demanding this new role as a pioneer woman had to be for her.

As they ate that evening, sitting on logs and chests between the tent and the wagons, Alfred demanded, "Now you need to tell us about what you did in the militia. Did you shoot anybody?"

"No, no, A. W. Nothing so exciting." Between recounting his adventures, he watched his mother as she cleaned up the remnants of the meal. *This woman who had a house of forty rooms and ten servants in Calcutta is growing old under the hardships and challenges of life in America.* He suddenly wondered for the first time if his father had made the right decision when he had determined that the family would leave Calcutta and journey to the Salt Lake Valley. *Did Father realize the potential cost?*

"Mother, you look tired. I wish there was something I could do for you now that I am here."

She sat next to him and couldn't stop a tear of gratitude from falling as she squeezed his hand. "Oh, Harry, there is nothing you can do. I . . . I could bear it better if the heat were not so troubling. The heat . . . the heat is so difficult to bear as the air is so arid and makes it difficult to breathe some days. It is a different heat than what we experienced in Calcutta and Rangoon." She suddenly recognized the concern in his face and tried to make the best of the situation with a smile. "I am sorry to complain. It is no different for me than for anyone else in the settlement."

That evening before retiring to his bedroll under one of the wagons, he gave her a tender kiss on the forehead and whispered, "It is good to be back again, Mother. I will do what I can to see that you have protection from the heat."

"You are a good lad to think of me."

In the morning, Matthew woke his sons at first light. Harry's exhaustion required his father to shake him by the shoulder to wake him.

"Harry, I need you to go to the home of Isaac Grace and ask him when we can turn the water from the creek onto our crops."

Sitting up and shaking his head to clear it, he responded, "Yes, sir, but how will I locate his home?"

"Ask anyone on the west side of town. They will point it out. It's a story-and-a-half adobe, a bit larger than those around it."

Harry nodded and, after breakfast, started to walk toward the west portion of the city. He marveled that no one was more than three blocks from anyone else within the walls of the little community. The house was pointed out to him, but one man admonished, "You may have missed him already. He's usually in the field by this time of the morning."

He knocked on the door of the adobe, wondering if anyone there could tell him how to locate the man of the house. It was opened by fifteen-year-old Elizabeth Grace. The sight of the slender girl with a spindle in her hand made

Harry's heart nearly stop. Her short dress exposed her ankles and small bare feet.

Though he'd never previously thought of anyone but Annie being by his side for the rest of his life, he now knew he wouldn't ever be likely to think of her as he had in the past. He suddenly realized this young woman, whose last name was so perfectly suitable, would fill his thoughts more completely than any other person he had ever known. From that moment on, he would never look back to India. A quote from Shakespeare's *Henry the VI* floated into his mind: *"She's beautiful, and therefore to be wooed."*

He cleared his throat, suddenly recognizing that he was dusty and wrinkled. He quickly tried to smooth his longish black hair into place, embarrassed by his unkempt appearance. Excuse me, miss, but I've been sent to speak with Brother Isaac Grace. Might he be at home?"

"Please come in . . . sir." She wasn't entirely sure how to address this dark-haired, dark-eyed stranger. "My father has left for the field, but Mother expects him at midday. You could return then, or you might locate him in the field. He said he would be cutting hay in the south community field about two miles south of the fort." She hesitantly smiled. "May I ask who is inquiring of him?"

Harry cleared his throat again. "My name is Harry—uh, actually, Henry McCune. My father, Matthew McCune, would like to know when we may turn the water onto the field." He paused and turned his old, battered hat in his hands.

"Oh, you're back from the fight with the US Army. Your father has spoken of you to my father. I'm sure your mother has been worried about you."

Harry smiled broadly. He had been hoping to find a good reason to extend the conversation with the young woman with the beautiful eyes, and she was certainly cooperating.

"Yes, I would have found my family sooner, but I couldn't find anyone who knew where they were. It was lucky that I saw Tom Smith in Salt Lake City. He knew my parents had moved down here, and since he was bringing a load of supplies to this area, he let me ride with him and his daughter."

"Did you have any exciting adventures? It is true that President Young was ready to order the burning of Salt Lake City?"

"Yes, if the army didn't keep their part of the agreement." As much as he hated to, he knew he had to tend to business. "I'd love to tell you about my adventures when I have the time, but right now I've got to get back to Father to help in the fields. Could you tell me what color shirt your father is wearing . . . and anything else that would help me recognize him?"

"He always wears a red shirt, but it's very faded. He wears an eagle feather in his hatband. I hope you can find him."

Harry put his hat on and nodded. "Thank you very much. I hope we get another opportunity to talk again . . . soon."

He hurried from the house as Elizabeth stood at the door and watched him mount his horse.

***

Harry rose the next morning as the darkness retreated from the coming sunrise, and marked out a large square in the dirt near the tent. By the time the younger boys were awakened by his father, he had dug a ten-foot square to a level of one foot in depth.

At breakfast, his father asked, "Harry, what are you doing so early this morning?"

"I'm going to dig a cellar for Mother where we can put a cot in the coolness of the earth so she can escape the heat of the day."

Thereafter, every day except Sundays for the next ten days, Harry spent at least an hour before everyone else was up, and another hour after all work for the day was finished, digging his mother's "cellar." George and his father offered their help, and by early August, it was completed. Taking Harry's hand, Sarah descended the ladder and lay on the cot Harry had put there. In the six-foot-deep dugout, the sun was blocked by willows and sod and effectively shut out the heat of the day.

"Oh, Harry, there is a heavenly coolness down here. Thank you, my dear lad, for your kindness. Surely you are an example of a son who understands the commandment to honor thy mother and father."

Within the next few weeks, Matthew decided that the "cellar" should be expanded into a dugout large enough for the entire family to move into when the heat or cold was excessive. After it was enlarged, Matthew insisted that the tent be extended over it to prevent any rain from soaking or crumbling the walls. He stood with hands on his hips and commented, "This arrangement will give us some protection from the heat of summer and the cold of the winter months until we can obtain a cabin."

On Sundays after meeting, Harry found himself seeking out Elizabeth Grace, if only to share a few words before the two families went their separate ways.

Matthew quietly quoted the writer James Howell to Sarah as he watched his son's feelings for the young woman blossom. "*One hair of a woman can draw more than a hundred pair of oxen*," he remarked. He was not smiling.

After supper on the evenings when exhaustion did not drive him to his bedroll early, Harry found a series of reasons to walk to Isaac Grace's adobe, where he would offer to help Isaac with repairing harnesses or shucking corn while he watched Elizabeth spin the wool from her father's little flock of sheep into yarn she then wove into fabric on the loom that sat in the corner.

She seldom entered the conversation, but her gaze dropped to her hands whenever it met Harry's, which was often. She listened to him recount his adventures in the militia with an increasing sense of pride and attachment.

***

In September, Harry was ordained an elder, and immediately thereafter, both he and his father were each ordained as Seventies, as was the custom. He was admonished, "Remember that as a Seventy it is your duty to spread the gospel."

Harry couldn't imagine how he could do much sharing of the gospel in a community made up totally of Church members. *Maybe the opportunity will come*, he thought.

In October, it was time for the crop of McCune wheat in Farmington to be harvested. Upon returning from a visit to the home of Isaac Grace, Matthew stated as Harry came in the door, "Harry, you and I will be leaving for Farmington in the morning. We have a crop of wheat waiting to be harvested there."

"Are you sure, Father? We haven't been there for nearly a year."

"Dan Miller promised to look after our fields."

Harry turned and started out the door. "Where are you going?" Matthew demanded.

"Over to the Grace home to tell Elizabeth . . . er, to tell them that I will be leaving for some time. I promised to help Brother Grace harvest his wheat this week."

"No, you are not. Your mother can tell the Grace family when she sees them at church Sunday. It is time to get to bed. We will be leaving before first light."

Harry stood in indecision for a moment, torn and confused by his father's rigid demands, but the need to obey his father won out, and he gave his mother a kiss on the cheek and disappointedly retired to his bedroll.

In the morning after he hitched the two teams of oxen to the wagon, he and his father climbed in. His disappointment had turned to anger during the night. He could see no justifiable reason for his father to prevent his explaining his absence to Isaac Grace and Elizabeth.

With a wave to Sarah, they started north. Sensing Harry's quiet anger, Matthew said nothing as they traveled for several miles, but at the first opportunity to pause and permit the animals to drink at a creek, Matthew broke the silence. "Harry, I've said nothing for the past several weeks whenever you found an excuse to visit Isaac Grace and his family after your chores were completed. I want you to understand that I realize how a young man can find himself infatuated with a pretty lass like Isaac's daughter Elizabeth, but you must focus on your responsibilities to your own family. You are a fine lad, and if you are not distracted from your duty, someday your name will ring down through the ages. 'We know what we are, but know not what we may be.'"

Harry recognized the quote from *Hamlet* but made no response. It went against his nature to show disrespect toward his father by arguing the point.

His father pressed the matter. "Don't let a pretty lass distract you from your future."

This time something forced him to speak. "But, Father . . . Isaac Grace and his wife have three daughters, and two of them are little more than babies. Their only son is an infant. It is very difficult to manage the work on the farm. He uses Elizabeth as though she were a boy, but she can't do the work he needs done. It is not work fit for a young lass. I'm willing to help him when I can as long as I have completed my responsibilities to you and Mother."

"Your infatuation with Elizabeth Grace will pass. Concentrate upon improving the conditions of your own family."

Harry made no response, but how he wanted to shout, "You don't understand!"

During the rest of the five-day journey, Harry said little as his father talked of his plans for his eldest son. "You'll be an outstanding missionary to India—and Burma. There is no reason you can't have a multitude of converts in Calcutta since you speak Hindustani fluently."

And so went the one-sided conversation until they reached Farmington, where they were spotted by Dan Miller.

"Matthew, Harry, good to see you," he called from horseback as he neared the wagon. "I've been holding a letter for you ever since it arrived about the middle of August. Would have sent it on to you but had no idea where you had settled."

He pulled the letter from his pants pocket along with a wrinkled and creased copy of the *Deseret News*. "And I have a copy of the *Deseret News* I thought you would like to see. Something in it about India." He offered them to Matthew, who took them, pleased to have both. Dan continued, "Can we count on the McCune family returning to our fair community?" He slowed his horse to a walk to match the speed of the oxen.

Matthew tucked the letter into the pocket of his worn jacket. "No, Dan, Sarah and I have decided to remain in Salt Creek. The ground is good for crops and cheaper than here. Harry and I have just returned to harvest the wheat we planted before we left."

"Well, we figured you'd be back sooner or later for the crop. I'll find some men and boys to give you a hand. Are you sure we can't talk you into coming back?"

Matthew shook his head.

"Give me a couple of hours, and I'll be back with some folks to help with your harvest." Dan turned his horse and rode away.

While Harry drove the wagon toward the wheat field, Matthew read aloud the two letters, which had been folded together and sealed with a dob of wax. By the time they reached the field, the troubling news from Patrick left them both silent.

Harry pulled the animals into the shade of a large tree, where Harry shook his head and quietly stated, "I'm glad to hear Alexander arrived home safely after his troubles at Lucknow." He was trying to find a bit of light in a very dark situation. "Father, do you think Calcutta will continue to be spared the violence?"

"We must pray that the Lord will watch over those we care about in that great city."

Dan and Jake arrived with a group of men and older boys an hour later. After the two young men had slapped each other on the back, the wheat harvesting was begun. It was completed by twilight. The bundling of the wheat and threshing would be done over the next few days.

As the men stood in the shade and wiped the perspiration from their foreheads with their bandanas, Dan invited Matthew and Harry to his home to share supper with his large family.

When the meal ended and Hannah and two of her older daughters began to remove the dirty dishes from the table, Dan asked, "Matthew, might I ask what was in that letter I gave you when you arrived—if it's not too personal? I've been wonderin' ever since it came."

Hannah added, "There's so little news here of what's going on in the world that we would like to hear what your friends have written."

Matthew nodded and pulled the letters from his pocket. Every eye in the room was on him. "There are two letters here, one to myself and one to my wife from our friends Patrick and Mary Anne Meik, members of the Church still in Calcutta. I will be glad to read them to you. There is nothing personal in either one that would prevent me from sharing them."

After reading both letters, he looked around the room. "Even though some of you may have read the article in the *Deseret News* that Dan wanted me to see, I will read it aloud if you so desire, as it relates to the news in the letters." Heads nodded.

He pulled the copy of the folded newspaper from his pocket and located the short article on the fourth and last page. He read aloud, *"Calcutta: The violence continues on the Indian subcontinent as has been reported previously in this publication. It was reported that, in June, a massacre of more than 130 Europeans by troops loyal to the Raja of Bitur took place at Cawnpore. These innocent victims had escaped from Fatehgarh only to meet their deaths where they believed they would find relief. Two weeks later in that same city, an additional massacre of Europeans took place after a false promise of safety from the same rebellious leader."* Matthew pulled out his kerchief and, despite the cool evening, wiped a bit of perspiration from his brow. He continued. *"In mid-July, a third massacre at Cawnpore claimed the lives of two hundred women and children previously spared. Again, the leader of the murderous troops was the same rebellious leader, the Raja of Bitur, often referred to as Nana Sahib."*

Harry could remain still no longer. "Father, Nana Sahib was an ally of the British for many years. How could this happen?"

"When Satan rages in the hearts of men, the innocent often pay a terrible price," Matthew responded quietly.

"Just as the Saints discovered in Missouri and in Nauvoo," Dan Miller added. "I'm sorry to hear of the horrors that surround your friends in India. Is there any chance they might leave that country and come to America as you did?"

"I urged them to join us when we were preparing to leave, but Patrick was determined to complete his enlistment. Sarah and I have written to urge them again to do so. I hope they listen this time."

Hannah broke into the dark conversation. "Well, everyone, I have a bread pudding for dessert. Let us turn our thoughts to happier times and places."

CHAPTER TWENTY-SIX

As the bags of grain were loaded into the McCune wagon, genuine thanks and hearty handshakes were shared all around.

"Matthew, just in case you receive any more letters from India, where should I send them?" Dan asked.

"Just send them on to Salt Creek. Anyone there can get them to us."

As the wagon started south, Matthew stated firmly, "I do not want you to speak of the news in Patrick's letter to your mother. It will make her ill with worry. The letter from Mary Anne has enough good news in it to occupy her mind."

"What should I tell her if she asks about the letter from Patrick?"

"Just tell her he's stressed that there has been no violence in Calcutta."

Harry knew his mother would not rest until she had read the letter from Patrick for herself, but he said nothing.

By the time they reached Salt Creek, Matthew had arrived at the same conclusion. "Harry, I realize now that I will have to share the news with your mother, but I do not see that it will be of any use to worry the lads."

Harry simply nodded.

Matthew quietly read the letter from Patrick to Sarah after the youngest three were in bed, omitting the most alarming parts. He handed Mary Anne's letter to her. After she read it, she couldn't stop herself from sharing her fears.

"Oh, Matthew, we must send them another letter and beg them to leave India as soon as possible. If I allow myself to think about their situation, I will never sleep again for worry."

"Yes, my dear, tomorrow we will write another letter urging them to come to America—and we will tell them where we are so their response will find us here."

***

Some of the wheat brought back from Farmington was sold, and Matthew was able to purchase a small log house by the time the snow came. With Harry's help, it was reroofed and the logs chinked again to help keep out the cold weather.

Harry continued to sleep in the wagon to ease the crowding in the little cabin. Though the winter weather kept Matthew and his sons from the fields, he insisted that Harry cease his weekly visits with the Grace family.

But at Sunday worship services, Elizabeth often caught Harry's eye. Her look of disappointment begged an explanation, but Matthew was quick to march his family to their bench before the meeting began and quick to hurry them from the meeting, thus preventing Harry from speaking with her. Harry respectfully did as he was told but remained quietly angry. He seldom spoke directly to his father, only responding to his questions.

***

Spring, 1859
Salt Creek, Utah Territory

When the frost eased in the early spring, several of the men of the community gathered to discuss the possibility of establishing a new settlement south of Salt Creek. As Matthew sat at the supper table, he enthusiastically explained, "It's been determined that after the wheat is planted here, we will send about a half dozen strong lads down there to plant a crop of wheat and put together a cabin. I volunteered Harry. Some want to call the area Moroni. I was told that it has good soil and that several good streams flow from the mountains year-round. From everything I was told, I wonder why that area wasn't selected initially, rather than Salt Creek. It lays about twenty miles to the south."

Harry couldn't help but think that if he spent most of the summer in the new settlement, he would never get to see Elizabeth.

"Morning will come early, so get your sleep, lads. We will prepare the ground for the wheat planting this week."

When the wheat had been sown on the acres at Salt Creek, Harry was joined by five other young, single men who loaded their wagons and headed for the area now called Moroni. They spent three weeks plowing the ground, and when the seed was planted, they headed to Mount Pleasant Canyon to cut logs, which they used to build a large one-room cabin for their use at night. It offered some protection from the cold and from the Indians in the area. When the wheat began to appear above ground, Harry and three of the young men returned to Salt Creek, leaving two to protect the crop until they were relieved.

The first thing Harry did upon returning to Salt Creek was hurry to the home of Isaac Grace. He tied up his horse and removed his dusty hat as he knocked on the door. When Mrs. Grace answered, he cleared his throat and asked, "Is Elizabeth at home, Sister Grace?"

She smiled broadly. "Come in, Harry. It's been much too long since we had an opportunity to visit. I'll get Elizabeth for you. She's shelling peas in the kitchen. Have a chair."

When Elizabeth stepped through the doorway, she stopped. The expression on her face was one of confusion. "Good day, Harry. It's been some time since you came for a visit. Is there any special reason you've come today?"

Harry looked at the floor. "I came to offer you an apology, Elizabeth. I didn't mean to leave last October for Farmington without telling you I was going, but Father insisted we leave right away, and he would give me no time to say good-bye."

"But that was many months ago, Harry, and I haven't seen you since, except across the room at Sabbath meetings." She dropped her gaze to her hands, which were clasped in front of her apron. "But you owe me no explanation." Her voice was cool.

"But I do. Father has kept me so busy that it has been impossible for me to visit you . . . and your family, of course, and I just wanted you to know that I . . . I regretted it very much." He stood and self-consciously turned his hat in his hands. "I want you to know that it wasn't anything you had done. I've been down in Moroni putting in wheat, and now that I'm back, I'm sure Father has many things waiting for me, but I do hope that I . . . that we can spend some time together."

"That would be very nice." Her voice had warmed.

"I'd better be getting home now. Maybe we can talk for a few minutes at meeting on Sunday." He let himself out the door.

"I hope so," she said as the door closed.

***

But Matthew was determined to keep his sons occupied constructively and their time so filled that there would be no time for "useless socializing." He decided that it was time for the boys to apply themselves more earnestly to playing the flutes they had neglected while establishing themselves in Salt Creek. Even eight-year-old Edward was old enough to begin seriously working to play the instrument. Matthew decided they would spend an hour every Sunday evening after supper perfecting their skills. Matthew could hardly stand the cacophony raised by their practicing and always found an excuse to leave the cabin.

"Harry, you are really getting very good with your flute," Sarah told him after a few days of practice.

Weather permitting, Matthew insisted they practice outdoors. After some weeks, Brother Hawkins, one of the few musicians in the little community, came to visit. "Harry, I hear you play a fine flute. Our mutual friends Charles Sperry and Gus Henroid play the fiddle, and Tom Midgley plays the glockenspiel. We're meeting next Sunday evening at seven. We hope you'll join us. We're establishing a band. You'd make a great addition."

Has Father put Hawkins up to this to keep me from visiting Elizabeth? He looked at his mother. Her face was glowing with happiness at the prospect of his participating in the band, so despite his suspicions, he agreed. "Yes, Brother Hawkins, I'll join you Sunday evening."

***

The Sunday evening band practices lasted about an hour but brought an unexpected benefit. On the way home from the first practice, Harry walked to the home of Isaac Grace. Elizabeth's mother greeted him warmly when he appeared at the door.

"Harry, do come in right this minute. We are so pleased to see you. Please sit down. I'll call Elizabeth."

When Elizabeth entered, Edmund Spenser's words filled his mind. *"Her angel's face as the great eye of heaven shined bright, and made a sunshine in a shady place."* He cleared his throat.

Brother Grace entered immediately after Elizabeth, his role as chaperone unmistakable.

Thus the pattern was set. Each Sunday evening, Harry would arrive at the Grace home after band practice, allowing his own family to believe that the practices lasted two hours. He hoped his father would not learn otherwise.

On a night in early October, after a conversation that covered everything from the progress of the band to the condition of the wheat crop, Brother Grace looked at Harry and stated, "I really need help this harvest season. I'm sometimes forced to use Elizabeth, but it's poor work for a young woman. Her mother needs her help at home with the baby as well." He paused. "Harry, is there any way you could give me a helping hand?"

Isaac's plea touched Harry in a way his father's authoritarian manner never had.

Harry hesitated only briefly. "Brother Grace, I offered to help you last year, but my father insisted that we travel up to Farmington, so I was unable to do so. I have regretted that. I must first assist my father with the harvest here and in Moroni. Then I give you my word that I will come and help you until your fields are done. Will that be sufficient?"

"Harry, that's all I can ask."

***

Harry threw himself into the harvesting of the wheat in Salt Creek. It was completed in less than a week. Everyone in the family anticipated a day of rest before the harvesting in Moroni was to be undertaken, but Matthew arose unusually early on the following morning and called to his sons, "Lads, it is time to harvest the fields in Moroni. Collect your gear and put it in the wagon. We leave at first light."

Sarah had been sleeping soundly, but her husband's voice prompted her sit up in bed. She pulled the quilt around her shoulders to keep herself warm.

"Matthew, surely you are going to give the lads some rest after cutting and threshing wheat for five days."

He called out, "Let's not waste the day. Harry, George, Alf, Edward!" Harry could hear him from his bedroll in the wagon.

"Matthew, surely you don't plan to take Edward with you. The lad is only eight. I know you had him help with the sowing of the wheat, but the cutting and threshing will be so much more demanding."

"The lad is big enough to be of use. It is vital that my lads know how to work. Can you have breakfast ready in a few minutes? I'll need you to pack supplies to last for four, no, five days." Sarah rose and dressed. She recognized that arguing with her husband would be futile.

Alfred and Edward rode in the back of the wagon on the twenty-mile ride to Moroni, and despite the rugged, jolting ride, both fell asleep. Harry rode on horseback, and George sat next to his father on the wagon seat, occasionally dozing where he sat.

Five other men and their older sons soon arrived to harvest their fields. For three nights, the group slept in the large cabin built that summer.

With the harvest done and the winter crop planted, the McCunes gathered around a fire to eat supper. "Harry, I've been thinking that it would be a good idea if you were to spend the winter here to make sure the crop isn't damaged by the deer or the Indians."

Dumbfounded, Harry paused as he lifted his fork from the tin plate to his mouth. Beans fell off his spoon. "You want me to stay for the winter, Father?"

"Yes, after we ride back to Salt Creek, you can load the wagon with supplies to keep you through the winter. Take your flute and scriptures with you, and the time won't be wasted."

"But, Father, I've promised Isaac Grace I will help him harvest his crops. He has no sons to help him."

"By what right have you promised your services to Isaac Grace? Your services belong to your own family." Matthew's voice had taken on an unusual hardness. "Does it have something to do with the fact that he has a pretty daughter with whom you are infatuated?"

"Father, I am nineteen and nearly a man. I gave Brother Grace my word. If I choose to offer my services to someone else on my own time once my family responsibilities are completed, surely you won't oppose me in the matter."

"I do oppose you in this matter. I forbid it. You must not let your heart distract you from your future."

"Father, how do you know what my future is? Perhaps the Grace family is meant to be part of it."

"Harry, I will not allow you—" He stopped when Harry stood and quietly put his tin plate down on the log where he had been sitting.

Harry realized that the time had arrived. He stated in a quiet voice, "I have given my word. I will not break it again. I will leave for Salt Creek as soon as I have saddled my horse. Good night, Father." He looked at his brothers. "Good night, lads."

He swiftly gathered his gear and rolled it into his bedroll while Matthew stood speechless. In less than five minutes, the horse was saddled and the bedroll tied on. Harry swung his leg over the horse and started down the weedy trail, making his way by the light of the three-quarter moon.

Matthew's pride forced him to remain silent rather than call angrily after Harry. He sat motionless while he tried to understand Harry's inexplicable behavior. *Infatuation has done this to an otherwise levelheaded young man.* His three younger sons sat silently watching, deeply worried.

***

It was just after midnight when Harry arrived at the cabin in Salt Creek. He pulled the saddle off his horse and turned him into the small corral by the shed where the other animals were kept. Entering the cabin as quietly as possible, he moved by the moonlight that streamed in through the little window in the main room. Pulling off his boots, he climbed the ladder to the loft where his three younger brothers normally slept. He slid under the quilt and slipped into an uneasy sleep within a couple of minutes.

The sound of his mother carrying water in from the creek woke him. He pulled on his boots and made his way down the ladder. As she came through the door with another bucket of water, he spoke. "Mother, let me get that for you."

Startled, Sarah almost dropped the bucket. She still wore her once-lovely silk dressing gown, and her hair hung loose around her shoulders. For the first time, Harry noticed the gray in it.

As he lifted the bucket and carried it to the kitchen table where he set it down, she asked, "When did you get in last night? I didn't hear you. Where are your brothers and your father?"

"They are still in Moroni. I expect they will come home sometime today."

"Why are you here without them? Is something the matter?" She couldn't help but note the firm set of his jaw.

He took a deep breath. "I don't want you to be unduly concerned, Mother, but I have come to collect my things. Father and I have had a disagreement, and I think it best that I no longer remain here at home." He opened one of the large chests they had brought from India and pulled out his extra pair of boots. He picked up a carpetbag and put the boots in it, then lifted his clothing from the chest and transferred all of it to the bag.

"Harry, tell me what this is all about. What has come between you and your father that would drive you from your home?"

"Mother, I've tried to be a dutiful, respectful son, but it is not right for Father to insist that I break my word to Isaac Grace again. He taught me all my life to consider my word as my bond."

"Harry, I find it hard to believe that your Father would ask you to violate your word. Please sit down and tell me what has happened." She sat in one of the straight-backed chairs at the table and patted the one next to her.

He sat. "Last year I told Isaac Grace I would help him harvest his wheat. He has no one to help except Elizabeth, and the work is too heavy for a young woman. But at that time, Father insisted I go with him to Farmington to harvest the wheat we had planted there, and he would not give me the opportunity to explain to Isaac or Elizabeth before we left."

Harry reached out and took his mother's hand. "I am grown now, and I must make my way in this world. I must make my own decisions, and I have decided that this year, I will keep my word to Isaac Grace. I will not spend the winter in Moroni watching the wheat grow just so Father can keep Elizabeth and me apart."

He rose and crossed the room, where he picked up his extra belt and his flute. He put them in the carpetbag and then closed it.

His mother stood with her arms folded across her breast as if to hold in the hurt she was experiencing. She couldn't speak.

Harry stepped close to her and kissed her gently on the forehead. "Don't be unduly alarmed, Mother. At some point, every mother is forced to let go of her sons."

When she finally spoke, her voice was just a whisper. "Harry, where are you going?"

"I'm going over to visit with Isaac Grace and explain my situation. I will help him with his harvest as I promised. I'm sure I will see you at Sabbath meetings."

She stood, unmoving, as he picked up the carpetbag and his rifle and closed the door behind him. Two tears made streaks down her cheeks. "Oh, Matthew, what have you done?" she forcefully whispered.

***

Harry dismounted and knocked on the door of the Grace home. "Sister Grace, is your husband at home?" he asked as she opened it.

"No, Harry, he's out in the south field. He felt he couldn't wait any longer to begin cutting the wheat."

"I'll go immediately and find him. May I leave my things here while I work with him today?"

"Of course." She watched as he returned to his horse and removed the carpetbag from where it hung on the saddle horn. "Just set it here, inside the door."

"Did Brother Grace take his tools with him this morning? Perhaps I'll need to take some with me."

"I'm sure he had everything he would need in the back of the wagon."

Harry tipped his hat. "Thank you, Sister Grace."

She looked down at his bag and put out her arm toward him. "Harry, I hope you will stay for dinner this evening."

"Thank you. I'd like that very much."

CHAPTER TWENTY-SEVEN

WHEN HE SAW ISAAC GRACE in the field, Harry spurred his horse faster. He dismounted and left his horse near Isaac's wagon in the shade of the only tree for a mile in any direction. Water ran through an irrigation ditch nearby and was within easy reach of the animals.

Isaac straightened his stiff and aching back and watched Harry approach. "I'm glad to see you, Harry. I have arranged for two young men nearly your age to come tomorrow and help with the harvest, but you are worth both of them and more. Thank you for coming. I was wondering if your father would allow it." He put out his calloused hand, and they firmly shook. "Is your father's harvest completed?"

"Yes, we finished the fields in Moroni yesterday. I rode back last night."

"Without time to rest?"

"I gave you my word that I would help you with your harvest this year, and I was not about to allow anything to interfere."

"You say that as if there were something that would interfere."

Harry pulled off his hat and wiped the perspiration from his forehead with his sleeve. "Father wanted me to spend the winter in Moroni protecting the wheat fields from the Indians and the deer, and I refused. Other men in the community will go down there a week at a time. There is no need to have me stay the entire winter."

"Has your refusal created hard feelings on the part of your father?" Isaac's face reflected his concern.

"You might say that. I have removed my belongings from the cabin and kissed my mother good-bye."

"Harry, I hate to see my request come between you and your father. I never meant it to pull you away from your family."

"I know that, Brother Grace, but this time was coming. At some point, my father must be made to understand that I am my own man." Unwilling to continue the discussion, Harry looked around. "Where are your extra tools? It's time I went to work."

Isaac pointed. "Over there in the wagon."

The two men worked until the sun was high in the sky. From across the field, Isaac called, "Harry, come and sit in the shade for a few minutes and get a drink of cold water."

It was a welcome invitation. As the two men sat next to one another, Isaac handed Harry a chunk of the bread he had brought, along with a canteen.

After they had rested for a few minutes, Isaac asked, "Harry, where are you going to sleep if you have left your father's home?"

"I can camp out at night until the snow comes. I will find a place before then."

"Why don't you stay with us? Our home isn't very large, but there is a loft above the main room that is unused at present."

Harry's heart jumped at the suggestion, but he responded modestly and with genuine concern. "That would be a great imposition, Brother Grace. I couldn't pay you for the room and board."

"You would more than earn your room and board if you were willing to work with me in the fields and in the barn. You would be the grown son I've needed all this time." When Harry hesitated, he added, "You'd be a great blessing to me, Harry . . . and you'd be able to see Elizabeth on a daily basis." He grinned as he added the last comment.

Harry nodded and smiled broadly. "Yes, Brother Grace, I'll be glad to work with you. Thank you for your kindness." Though he was still concerned that he and his father were at odds, this new situation was more ideal than he ever could have imagined.

***

At Sabbath meeting, Harry smiled across the room at his mother, who returned a strained, stiff smile. His father refused to meet his eye, and when the meeting was over, Matthew hurried Sarah and Harry's three younger brothers out of the meeting.

That evening at supper in the Grace house, Isaac said quietly to Harry as the others were sitting down, "I'm sorry your father wouldn't speak to you, Harry. I know his hard feelings trouble you."

Harry nodded. "Yes, Brother Grace, but perhaps we are all learning things about one another we need to know." That evening he played his flute for the family before he left for band practice.

***

When George sat at the supper table after Sabbath meeting, he asked, "Mother, when will Harry be coming back home?"

Matthew put his fork down and stated firmly, "We will not speak of him in this house. He has forfeited his right to be a member of this family. He has turned his back on us."

Sarah had been offering a bowl of mashed potatoes to her husband but instead set it down hard. "Matthew, surely you can't expect us to cease all reference to Harry. He has been . . ."

Matthew raised his hand, and her words hung in the air. "I've made my will clear in this matter. We will not discuss it further." He rose from the table and left the cabin, closing the door firmly as if to put an exclamation point at the end of the discussion.

Sarah became inordinately quiet during the weeks after Harry left. She spent her time preparing meals, making candles and soap from fat drippings, churning butter, and mending clothing by the light of the fireplace. While she said nothing to Matthew about the hard feelings between him and their eldest son, her silence was more eloquent than words ever could have been.

One Sunday evening when his father was outside checking on the animals, Edward asked his mother, "Why can't we talk about Harry?" His face was troubled.

Sarah made a decision. "Let's do it this way. When your father is home, we won't speak about Harry, but when he is not here, you may, if you choose." As the weeks passed, she was torn. She wanted—she needed—to talk about her treasured oldest son, but she had always been an obedient and respectful wife. *Am I teaching the lads to disobey their father?* she wondered. Yet she continued to permit the younger boys to speak of Harry when their father was not present. Her heart ached to see and reach out to her eldest, but she was determined not to let her husband see how his decision had wounded her.

On a snowy evening as the three boys read their lessons around the fireplace, Edward asked, "Mother, why does Father want us to study Shakespeare? Did Harry have to read Shakespeare?"

Matthew looked up from the book he was reading, and his mouth opened to reprimand Edward for asking about Harry, when Sarah responded, "Yes, Edward, Harry studied Shakespeare. There is wisdom in his writings."

Matthew rose and, throwing on his coat, left the cabin. When he returned, Sarah refused to act as if anything were amiss, but the temperature in the room was chilly, despite the fire in the fireplace.

That evening as they prepared for bed, Matthew said accusingly, "You know my feelings in regard to Harry. I've asked the family not to speak of him, but you did not correct Edward this evening."

"And I'm not going to correct him or the other lads when they speak of their older brother. I will no longer be forced to pretend he does not exist." She turned over and closed her eyes, making it clear she was not going to discuss the matter further.

***

May 1859
Nephi, formerly Salt Creek, Utah Territory

An hour after breakfast, while Matthew and the three boys were in the fields, Zim Baxter dropped by the McCune cabin with a letter for Matthew and Sarah. "I just picked up my mail at the general store and thought I'd bring over the letter that's been waiting for you for a few days. Hope it's not bad news."

Sarah took it and turned it over in her hands. "Thank you, Brother Baxter." She stepped inside and sat down at the table. She knew she couldn't wait to read it until Matthew got home. It was postmarked from Calcutta, India.

She broke the wax seal and spread it out. It read:

November 15, 1858

> *Dear Matthew and Sarah,*
>
> *I write to tell you that my dearest Mary Anne passed away of Asiatic cholera a few weeks ago. I have not been able to take up the pen to write before now, as my grief has been too heavy. James has enlisted in the Royal Navy, and my Annie married a year ago and removed to England with her husband. Her younger brother George has enlisted in the Royal Navy like his older brother, and Alexander is serving in the naval cadets. Without my dear wife, I have been forced to place the younger children in a boarding school. I still look toward the day when I can join you in Zion, but without my Mary Anne, I dare not face such a journey.*
>
> *I hope and pray that you are all well and that someday we will be reunited.*
>
> *Sincerely,*
> *Your servant, Patrick Meik*

Though Sarah and Matthew had not talked about the Meik family in many months, the news of Mary Anne's death added to the heavy weight that burdened Sarah's heart. She had lost her dear friend. It didn't matter that she had died on the other side of the world.

CHAPTER TWENTY-EIGHT

THE MONTHS PASSED, AND HARRY found life at the Grace home pleasant, especially the hours he spent with Elizabeth as she worked at the spinning wheel or the loom while he mended the harnesses for the animals or sharpened Isaac's tools.

The snow fell that winter until the adobe was almost hidden. Harry would rise before daylight to shovel a path to the shed where the animals were kept, or to the street so visitors wouldn't have to push their way through the deep drifts. On spring and summer evenings, he and Elizabeth walked hand in hand and talked of the future.

Another fall and winter passed. His father's cold refusal to speak to him at Sabbath meetings made the otherwise pleasant situation difficult to bear.

***

Spring 1861
Nephi, Utah Territory

One Sunday in early spring after the meeting had ended, Matthew stood to escort his family from the little chapel. He halted and reached out for his wife. "Sarah, do you see the two lads standing at the doorway with Brother Sperry?"

She turned and studied the two deeply tanned men, who looked to be about thirty. "Yes, Matthew. Are they new to our community? I don't think I've ever seen them before."

"Surely you recognize them. I believe that is Benjamin Richie and George Barber, the two young sailors who brought us the good news of the gospel while we were in Calcutta back in '49. They have changed somewhat, but, yes—that is the two of them. Come, lads, come Sarah. We must speak with them."

He took her arm and hurried her across the room, where he laid his hand on Benjamin Richie's shoulder. The young man turned, and recognition filled his eyes.

"I know you, sir, of that I am sure, but your name escapes me. I remember meeting you . . . in Calcutta, wasn't it?"

"Yes, my lad. It is you and your friend here that my family can look to for our conversion to the Church and our presence here among the Saints."

George Barber turned to follow the conversation. "Yes, sir, I remember meeting in your sitting room in Fort William." He reached out his hand to Matthew, who shook it vigorously.

"You lads could have had no way of knowing that those few meetings you attended with the Plymouth Brethren in Calcutta could result in the baptism of many souls there and in Burma. My family, the family of Patrick Meik, and Maurice White were the first of many."

While his father introduced the two young men to the others, Harry and Elizabeth and the Grace family quietly slipped out and headed for the Grace home. That evening at supper, Harry was asked who the two young men were.

"Do you remember them, Harry?" Elizabeth asked.

"Yes, somewhat. I was only about nine years of age when Father had the Plymouth Brethren meet in our home, and my memories of them are vague, but I remember the two young sailors who attended three or four times. I was not present for any of the discussion about religion that went on while they were there."

"Will we get to meet them, Harry?" Isaac Grace asked.

"If it is their intention to settle here, I'm sure we will."

The community was small enough that over the next twelve months, Ben and George became acquainted with everyone in Salt Creek.

Harry continued to be the son to Isaac Grace that he didn't yet have.

***

Sarah spoke quietly as she and Matthew prepared for bed. "At Sabbath meeting today, I overheard Sister Grace telling Sister Baxter that Elizabeth and Harry consider themselves betrothed. When they marry, will we attend the wedding, Matthew?" When he did not respond, she repeated quietly but more forcefully as she slipped her feet under the quilt, "Will we be attending, Matthew?"

He had been pulling off his boots. He sat up ramrod straight as he dropped the second boot. "I do not anticipate that we will." He sat unmoving.

Sarah inhaled deeply. "Matthew, I have been about as patient as any woman could possibly be under the circumstances, but I think it is time I speak my mind." Her voice was low, but he could hear the steel in it.

"Enough, Sarah, or you will wake the lads."

"No, Matthew, it is not enough, and I will speak my mind whether or not I wake the lads." She took a pillow and put it behind her back so she could sit against the wall at the head of the bed. With her arms crossed over her chest, she gave him a piercing look. "Harry is a fine young lad, and any father," she paused and repeated with emphasis, "any *natural* father would be proud of him. He works as hard, or harder, than anyone I know, including his own father." Her eyes were hard. "His desire to find a wife at his age is as natural as sunshine or rain, but you insist on treating the situation as if he has given you some kind of unforgivable personal offense—as though you would settle the matter in a duel if it were fifty years ago." She sat up to look more fully at him. She spoke each word slowly, as if to make sure he fully understood. "What is it that has hardened your heart so inexcusably?"

His shoulders slumped just a little, as if the ice inside of him had begun to melt ever so slightly. "Sarah, I raised that lad to become a leader, to influence history. I have always felt that there is no limit to what he might accomplish if he resists the temptation to simply marry, settle down, and become just another farmer. He's meant to do more than that."

She pressed her lips together and said nothing for several seconds as she gathered her thoughts.

In the meantime, he stood and pulled on his nightshirt and sat on the side of the bed. He seemed hesitant to slide in next to her, and he sat there and said nothing.

"Matthew, get into bed. You will catch your death of cold." She was determined to finish what she had started. "You know it is not in my nature to challenge your will. We've spent too many years together, but I must ask what makes you think you have the right to override Harry's free will in this matter." Her voice began to soften and took on a slightly pleading tone. "Did you expect that he would spend his entire life in docile obedience to you?" She waited for his answer.

After what seemed like an eternity, he spoke. "I always believed that his will and mine would be in agreement." He turned and looked at her. "He had never disobeyed me until . . . until this young woman entered his life. I curse the day I sent him over to Isaac Grace's house to ask about the irrigation water." His words suddenly softened in disappointment. "I never dreamed he would turn his back on me."

"Did you expect to eventually choose a wife for him?"

"Yes . . . but not for a few more years."

"Harry is now twenty-one years of age, an age when many lads have married and settled down. He is no different than his friends."

"But I wanted him to be different." Matthew's voice was low and intense as he felt his dreams for his son slipping away. "I wanted him to become governor or a member of the Quorum of the Twelve. He has that potential."

"Yes, and his marrying now will not interfere with any plans the Lord may have for him. I'm tired, Matthew. I'm going to sleep. Please put out the lamp and be prepared to tell me in the morning how you plan to repair this breach with our eldest son."

She lay down and closed her eyes while her heart pounded in her ears. She had never challenged her husband in such a manner in all the years they had been married. She pretended to sleep to give him time to think about what she had said.

Matthew lay down, but he stared into the darkness for a long time before drifting off into an uneasy sleep.

CHAPTER TWENTY-NINE

MATTHEW SAID NOTHING AT BREAKFAST as Sarah placed bowls of wheat mush before each family member. He had been silent since arising.

Well, she told herself, *he will speak when he is ready.* She tried to pretend that nothing was amiss. "As soon as you have eaten, lads, we will spend the morning on your lessons"—she looked directly at Matthew—"unless your father has chores for you to do."

After he had emptied his bowl, he looked at his three younger sons and, as if he hadn't heard her, said, "Lads, the shed needs to be cleaned. The animals cannot be expected to stand in their offal. Before you feed them, muck out the stalls."

Sarah hated to see the boys sent out into the unusually harsh cold that morning, but she felt she had chosen her battle and could not expend her forces on other skirmishes, so she kept silent.

She could sense that something was coming as the three boys put on their coats and hats and headed for the small stable. Matthew took a deep breath and exhaled slowly. The conversation began quietly.

"Sarah, I don't want to hear anyone speak Harry's name in this house again. He has dishonored and disobeyed me, and I won't have it. I have tolerated your disobedience for months, and I am tired of it. You've set a poor example for the lads."

Sarah had been gathering the dirty dishes and lowering them into the large dish pan that sat in the dry sink. Without responding, she walked to the bucket of water that had been heating as it hung above the fire in the fireplace. She carried it across the room and carefully poured it over the bowls. She turned and wiped her hands on her apron.

"Matthew, I have always tried to be a dutiful wife and a careful mother. I have given up a large and comfortable home with many servants and sailed halfway around the world, nearly losing our oldest son to typhoid on that

voyage. I left behind many of my treasured belongings and suffered a long
and arduous journey by rail, only to be forced to walk with my children across
1,300 miles of prairie and mountain, facing dangers, hardships, and hunger
I could not have imagined before this journey began. Every step of the way,
Harry—" Matthew put his hand up as if to stop her from speaking the name.
She spoke more forcefully. "Every step of the way, Harry was an obedient son.
Upon arriving in the valley, we were forced almost immediately to relocate
while Harry"—she said the name more firmly so as to keep him silent—
"dutifully went off to battle with the militia through a cold and miserable
winter. Harry has been our pride and joy, an obedient and uncomplaining
son in every way."

Matthew straightened in his chair and appeared ready to contradict her,
so she put up her hand as a barrier between them to make it plain that she
would have her say.

"This difficulty between the two of you is of your own making. Your
determination to keep him from following his heart has made you blind to
the fact that it is natural for a young man his age to seek a wife. The Lord
himself told us in scripture that a man shall leave his father and mother and
cleave unto his wife. The unnatural thing happening here is that you think
you can order him to cease to care for this young woman and that you have the
right to point his life in a different direction than he has chosen. Harry must
make these decisions for himself. You grew upset because of his friendship
with Annie Meik when we were in India, and I said nothing because he was
still young enough that such a bond at that time was not proper, but now—
Matthew, Harry is twenty-one." She spoke carefully, as if trying to make a
child understand a difficult arithmetic problem. "He is the master of his fate.
Be grateful he has embraced this gospel so completely. He is becoming a fine
man, one who will someday make you proud in every way."

There. She had said it. She stood unmoving, hands upon her hips, waiting
for his response. Matthew looked almost stunned. "But she is a child. How
can he expect such a child to become a wife?"

"Matthew, that child will be eighteen on her next birthday. Many young
women are married at her age."

"You and I were much older." He stated the fact as if it were the measuring
stick for all marriages.

"Circumstances in England at that time were entirely different." She
turned to wash the breakfast dishes but said with her back to him, "I will not
cease to speak of Harry in our home. He is my eldest son, and a son who has
honored me in every way. He honored you in every way with the exception
of this unreasonable insistence on your part that he disassociate himself from

the Grace family." She turned back to face him. "Matthew, the Grace family is a fine family. They are good people."

He was leaning forward on his elbows, looking at his hands folded between his knees. "I know they are good people, but our oldest son has turned his back on us to go to work for Isaac Grace."

She set the bowl down hard on the drain board as if to pound some sense into her husband. "But you drove him to Isaac." She turned toward him again. "Harry was willing to complete our harvest and his other chores before offering his help to Isaac, and you demanded he break his word to the man— for a second time. This is your doing, Matthew, all of it. If you want peace in your own house, I suggest you give the matter a great deal more thought."

Silence hung between them until the three younger boys returned, chilled and soiled from cleaning the stable. After she helped them clean up, Sarah had them sit at the kitchen table to practice their sums as if nothing were wrong between her and their father.

***

July 24, 1861
Nephi, Utah Territory

When the crops were well established and the fruit hung low on the branches of the many orchards in the area, a great celebration was planned to mark the fourteenth anniversary of the arrival of the first band of pioneers to reach the Salt Lake Valley.

A great feast of homemade breads, pies, candies, roasts, ham, and early fruit was laid out in the square in front of the meetinghouse on long, rough-hewn boards supported by sawhorses. Bobbing for apples, a tug-of-war, mumblypeg, hopscotch, footraces, the rolling of hoops surreptitiously removed from wagon wheels, and every other conceivable game was played by the children and young people.

Matthew and Harry did not formally speak to one another as they passed, though they did nod stiffly when their eyes met. *Well, that is more than I have seen in nearly two years*, Sarah thought as she returned to cutting the cherry pies made from the early fruit of the season.

As the day wore on into a very warm late afternoon, the women spread quilts on the ground under the trees and chatted. The men stood in the shade and discussed prices for wheat and hogs. As dusk approached, a great bonfire was lit and drew the crowd to the benches made of split logs surrounding it. A program of song and original poetry marking the occasion began.

Small children leaned against their mothers and were sleeping by the time the program ended. As families began to gather their littlest ones, Harry stood and clapped his hands for the attention of the group.

He cleared his throat. "If I may have your attention, I want to make an announcement." He reached his hand toward Elizabeth, who was standing near her mother. She stepped near him and took it.

"Many of you are aware that Elizabeth Grace and I have been keeping company." The crown laughed loudly, enjoying that a well-known fact was finally being admitted publicly.

"Elizabeth's eighteenth birthday is in three days, and as an early birthday present for each of us, I am announcing our intention to marry this winter—at Christmastime."

The crowd burst into applause in anticipation of a wedding, the most enjoyable of all celebrations in the little community. The men streamed to Harry to shake his hand and made jokes at his expense. The women hurried to give Elizabeth a multitude of hugs.

As Matthew and Sarah watched, she spoke. "If you want to mend this rift between you and your son, now is the time to do it. Do not make an enemy of your future daughter-in-law—or her parents. If you do, you will lose the affection of your future grandchildren."

Matthew thought about what she had said before he stood. He knew she was right but couldn't bring himself to admit it aloud.

When he didn't move, she turned and stared at him for a few seconds. "If not now, Matthew, when? Are you going to let this opportunity pass?"

He shook his head and whispered, "No, no, you are right." The words were painful, but he made his way toward his son. Several men stepped back, giving him an opening. Knowing of the alienation between father and son, they watched quietly.

Harry looked up just as his father reached him and offered his hand. Harry hesitated only a fraction of a second before he took it. As they shook hands, both men put their free arm around one another's shoulders.

As they separated, Matthew looked into Harry's face. "Congratulations, son. She is a fine young woman from a fine family."

Sarah offered a great hug to Elizabeth. "You are going to be my daughter—my only daughter—at least for many years. I hope we will come to love each other."

"Mother McCune, I know we will."

Sarah moved to her son and embraced the tall, slender young man with the sinewy muscles. As she laid her head on his chest, she murmured, "God bless you, Harry. There has never been a finer son. I wish you much happiness."

He looked down at her tenderly. "And there has never been a finer mother."

Matthew watched the two and knew that, as hard as it had been, he had done the right thing.

***

As the Sabbath meeting ended and folks gathered to talk before returning home, Matthew stood near the door where everyone was forced to pass him and waited to see if Harry and Elizabeth would approach him. When they did, he offered his hand, which Harry took.

"Harry, I think your mother"—he cleared his throat—"your mother and I would like to have you come home to live. You are missed very much."

"I think I must remain where I am presently, Father. As I have mentioned in the past, Brother Grace has no son who can help him with the heavy work of his farm. His only son is scarcely three years of age. You and Mother are blessed with three lads. I hope my decision in this matter will not cause renewed hard feelings between us."

Matthew inhaled and stood a little taller, answering stiffly, "No, of course not." But Harry could see that his father was offended despite his denial. It had taken a great deal of humility to prompt him to ask Harry to return home, and Harry's unwillingness to do so was salt in a wound.

Though Sarah could see that her husband was unhappy about Harry's decision not to return to living under Matthew's roof, she was determined to throw herself into assisting with wedding preparations in any way she could, to make the wedding all that it could be in the small pioneer community.

Upon reaching home that Sabbath evening, she opened the chest of fabric she'd brought from India. She carefully lifted out a folded piece of white silk she'd saved for a special occasion. Wrapping it in a clean dish towel, she carefully laid it aside.

That morning after breakfast, while Matthew and the three boys were working in the shed with the animals, she latched the door behind her and hurried to the Grace family's adobe. When Sister Grace opened the door, Sarah smiled and held out the gift. "I've brought a wedding gift for Elizabeth. Is she home?"

"Yes, she's in the kitchen. I'll get her for you. Please be seated."

When Elizabeth entered the room, she halted for a moment before rushing to her future mother-in-law. "Sister McCune, thank you for coming." She seated herself next to Sarah on the small settee. "It's wonderful to see you. What brings you here today?" Sister Grace took a seat in the rocking chair across from the two women.

"I have your first wedding gift. It is the fabric for your wedding dress. It has come all the way from India. I have saved it knowing I would eventually find the perfect purpose for it." She carefully removed the dish towel she had wrapped around the bundle and set the folded fabric in Elizabeth's lap.

"Oh, Mother McCune, it's cloth from heaven," she whispered as she lightly moved her hand over the fabric.

Sister Grace rose and hurried over to examine the white silk. She too touched it reverently. "Sarah, it's breathtaking. What a wonderful gift."

Sarah smiled with satisfaction at the responses of Elizabeth and her mother. "I believe there is enough for a full skirt and a lovely bustle."

"Sister McCune, I've never worked with such a fine fabric as this. I've only sewn with homespun. Can you help me with the dress?" Elizabeth asked.

"I've never made a wedding dress, but perhaps between the three of us"— she smiled at Elizabeth and her mother—"we can make something beautiful."

Nearly every day for the next two weeks while Matthew and the boys were busy with chores, Sarah would slip away to spend time at the Grace home as the three women designed and stitched the dress with careful and gentle hands.

Though Harry voiced his desire to see the dress on Elizabeth when it was finished, his mother and future mother-in-law were determined he would not until the wedding.

At supper in mid-November, as he buttered a thick slice of Sister Grace's excellent bread, Isaac said in a matter-of-fact manner, "Harry, I know you and Elizabeth have been worried about finding a place to call your own. I hope my actions will meet with your approval. I have arranged to purchase Brother Sperry's old cabin for the two of you—as a wedding gift." Before either Harry or Elizabeth could speak, he added, "It hasn't been used for more than a year, but with some effort on our part, we can make it usable. It has two rooms, one of logs and one of adobe brick, and a fine fireplace."

Elizabeth rose from the table and hurried to throw her arms around his neck. "Oh, thank you, thank you, thank you. We will be happy there, I just know it."

"Thank you, Brother Grace. We are deeply grateful," Harry added.

"Since we are soon to be a genuine family, please call me Isaac, Harry."

"Yes . . . Isaac," Harry said with a broad grin.

Within a few days, Harry had found two chairs for the little house but was disappointed when he wasn't able to find a table anywhere in the settlement.

Elizabeth soothed his feelings by stating cheerfully, "You have told me of the huge old trunk that carried your belongings from India and across the plains. Surely your mother and father will let us have it. It will make an excellent table. We don't need furniture to make us happy. We will have a fireplace for cooking, two chairs for sitting, and a rope bed for sleeping. Anything else we need will come in time."

As the plans for the wedding proceeded, friends and family members gathered around to furnish other household goods and two beautiful quilts. Only Matthew remained aloof.

CHAPTER THIRTY

In late November, Harry and Elizabeth sat quietly on the settee in the main room of the Grace home. The younger children were finally in bed, and Sister Grace was tidying up the kitchen. Brother Grace sat across from them.

"Harry," Elizabeth's voice was quiet, "I am troubled by this distance—this coolness that continues between you and your father. Perhaps we should postpone the wedding. I don't want it to come between the two of you."

He took her right hand between both of his and looked into her wide, soft eyes. "Elizabeth, I have chosen you for my wife. My father has not yet let go of the idea that he can continue to make the decisions in my life. He must accept that fact. He must recognize that I have chosen to marry you at this time, and he will come to see that there could be no finer daughter-in-law in the world."

Elizabeth turned and looked at her father. Her eyes glistened with unshed tears. "Father, how can we heal this rift between Harry and his father?"

Isaac looked at Harry. "Your father was a branch president in the Church in Calcutta, wasn't he?"

"Yes, and in Rangoon as well."

"Then, with permission from President Young, he can perform the marriage. Someday in the future, when the families from our ward are called, the two of you will be able to go to the Endowment House where you will be sealed for eternity, but if your father will write to President Young immediately, he will have time to get approval to perform the wedding ceremony. I think such a request would melt any father's heart."

Elizabeth and Harry looked at one another, nodded, and smiled. She asked, "Is that acceptable to you, Harry?"

"I think your father is a wise man. We will ask my father to perform the ceremony. We will go tomorrow after Sabbath meeting to ask him."

The next evening the two of them walked to the McCune cabin. When Harry knocked, Sarah opened the door and beamed at them. "Come in, come in. What brings you for a visit this evening?" She stepped aside and motioned for them to come in. "Edward, your father and brothers are feeding the cattle. Tell them we have company." The little boy closed his book and hurried out of the house.

When Matthew and his younger sons entered, Alfred yelled, "Harry, you're here!" and threw himself at his brother.

George grinned and then looked at his father for his reaction.

"Sit down, sit down, everyone," Sarah insisted. She took a cloth and dusted the tops of two steamer trunks. Please sit here, Harry, and you, Elizabeth. The trunks are comfortable. Now, tell us what brings you here."

Matthew had yet to say anything.

Harry cleared his throat. "Elizabeth and I have come to make a request." The words hung in the air. He cleared his throat again. "We have come to ask Father to perform our marriage ceremony. Would you consider doing it for us, Father?" He paused and then added, "It would mean a great deal to both of us."

Matthew looked at his hands where they were clasped between his knees. He was suddenly aware of the calloused fingers, the broken and grimy fingernails he would never have tolerated in India. Not even in the battlefields of Burma had his hands looked like those of a peasant farmer.

A sudden awareness swept over him, an awareness that he was just a pioneer farmer, no longer carrying the authority that had come with rank and uniform. His family was growing up and would eventually leave him, much as Harry had. He looked at Sarah and took note of the gray streaks in her hair, her calloused hands, frayed hem, and worn shoes. He knew his cabin was humble and the clothing he and his family wore tired and worn. He was startled by the realization that all he really had of value was his family.

He stood and extended one hand toward Harry and the other toward Elizabeth. He smiled, at first a bit hesitantly and then more broadly. In response, the two young adults each rose and took one hand. They happily returned his smile.

"I would feel it a privilege to perform the ceremony. I will send a letter to Church headquarters in the morning to seek permission. He pulled them toward him and held them at his sides, like bookends. "Sarah, we now have a daughter, the daughter you have always wanted." He looked at Elizabeth. "Welcome to our family."

Sarah rushed to embrace the young woman. She made no attempt to hide her tears of happiness. Her family was finally, truly healed.

Edward pulled at Harry's sleeve. "Harry, will there be a big party when you get married?"

Harry ruffled his littlest brother's hair. "Yes, Edward, we will have a big party with music and dancing and food."

"Harry's going to get married! Harry's going to get married, and we're going to have a party," he chanted as he clapped.

The coolness between father and son had melted, the rift gone. The two men spent the rest of the evening chatting like old friends while Elizabeth and Sarah sat together and discussed the details of the wedding.

***

December 24, 1861
Nephi, Utah Territory

The wedding took place in Matthew and Sarah's newer, larger cabin, with forty friends and neighbors in attendance. When Elizabeth entered the main room in her white silk wedding dress, Harry was speechless. Her long dark hair was gathered in a cascade of curls that flowed to the midpoint of her back. The train of the bustle flowed behind her.

Matthew had to blink several times to see the words as he read the wedding ceremony. When each had pledged their love, Harry took Elizabeth in his arms and planted a kiss that made those present clap and cheer in delight.

The music began immediately, and he whisked her around the floor to the applause of the crowd. When they stopped to catch their breath, someone in the crowd called out, "Harry, tell us about your wedding gifts."

Harry cleared his throat and started listing them. "My father gave me a pair of three-year-old steers and a heifer calf. In addition to our cabin, my new father-in-law has given my wife a heifer calf, a sheep, and three chairs. My parents have given my wife some beautiful jewelry from India and the fabric for her wedding dress." The crowd applauded.

Another friend called out, "Did you give your wife something special, Harry?" After all, what could a young man give his love in such humble circumstances?

Harry grinned proudly. "I gave Elizabeth a gold locket from New York on a gold chain brought all the way from India."

That same voice responded, "Then maybe you are worthy of her." A great laugh and more applause followed.

The crowd stayed until daylight the next morning, Charles Sperry and Gustave Henroid playing their fiddles until everyone had danced themselves into exhaustion.

An existing family had been mended and a new family unit established, and so the cycle of life was renewed.

EPILOGUE

MATTHEW BECAME KNOWN AS DR. McCune during his years in Nephi, where he practiced homeopathic herbal medicine and was often depended upon to set broken bones and deliver babies. He was called to the Nephi Stake high council, and between missions to England, he became a speaking companion of President Brigham Young throughout Southern Utah.

Matthew and Sarah's son George died of pneumonia as a young man of twenty-four, leaving a young widow with two small children. Adventurous Alfred William, better known as Alf or A. W., became an entrepreneur of remarkable ability in railroading, mining, and freighting. He returned to Salt Lake City as a millionaire and built the McCune Mansion at 200 North Main Street. As an adult, Edward became known as James and remained in Nephi, where he sheltered his widowed father's third wife in his home for several years.

Family tradition says that Matthew delivered a baby on a cold, rainy October night in 1889 at seventy-eight years of age and, upon returning home, developed pneumonia and passed away within a few days.

Harry and Elizabeth went on to live long and honorable lives. In December of 1865, they attended the Endowment House, along with other eligible couples in Nephi, to be sealed as a family for time and eternity.

In 1884, when their youngest child at that time, Margaret Leah, was only a year old, Harry, like his father, was called to leave his family and serve a mission on the other side of the world. Whereas Matthew was called to serve in 1864 and again in 1882 in Great Britain, Harry was called as one of four missionaries to the East India Mission in 1884. His oldest three sons and Elizabeth's younger brothers were willing to aid the family in the absence of husband and father.

In India, he was reunited with George Meik, the second of Patrick Meik's sons. He was saddened to learn that when Patrick belatedly determined to leave for America, only his youngest son accompanied him. The other sons and daughters had chosen to remain in India, and of that large family, few remained in the Church.

After a year in Calcutta and a few weeks in Burma, Harry and his companion were directed to New Zealand. There, he taught the gospel to the Maoris, returning home in January of 1886. In Nephi, he found his family in a recently completed home, well fed and well shod. Two more children were born to Harry and Elizabeth, making a total of thirteen.

Shortly after returning from his mission, his friends nominated and saw him elected as Juab County assessor and collector. He was called as a member of the Juab Stake high council and a member of the Church Board of Education not long thereafter. The crown of his life was to attend the dedication and opening of the Salt Lake Temple at the request of the First Presidency, comprised of Wilford Woodruff, George Q. Cannon, and Joseph F. Smith.

As Sarah had said, there was never a finer son who honored his parents more completely.

John Andrews married within a year of the death of Isabella, fulfilling her prophecy that another woman would raise her children. "Issy" Andrews learned to move about without the use of her legs, sitting on the ground or the floor of her cabin in Logan, Utah, and using her arms to hold her body upright as she moved. She eventually married John Smith, bore nine children, and raised them in that humble cabin.

The McCune, Meik, and Andrews families, as well as tens of thousands of other pioneers, faced physical, emotional, and spiritual hardships and challenges and sacrifices we who are descended of them can scarely imagine. Let us honor them by keeping their memories alive.

WORKS REFERENCED

Allen, James B. and Leonard, Glen M. *The Story of the Latter-day Saints*. Deseret Book, Salt Lake City, Utah. 1976.

Cannon, Sarah M. Mousely, Diary, 2–15. In possession of Church History Library.

Dutson, John William, "A short history and genealogy of John W. Dutson," 28–39. In possession of the Church History Library.

Kimball, Stanley B. and Violet T. Kimball. *Mormon Trail: Voyage of Discovery, The Story Behind the Scenery*. KC Publications, Inc. 1998.

Kipling, Rudyard. *From Sea to Sea: City of Dreadful Night; On the Banks of the Hughli*. Published by Telelib.com/authors. Retrieved 2013-06-27.

Knight, Hal and Stanley B. Kimball. *111 Days to Zion*. Deseret News Press, Salt Lake City, Utah. 1978.

Llewellyn-Jones, Rosie. *The Great Uprising in India, 1857–58*. Woodbridge, Suffolk, United Kingdom: The Boydell Press, 2007.

McCune, George M., ed. *Matthew McCune Family History*. Vol. 1AB.; Vol. 2AB. Salt Lake City, Utah. McCune Family Association, 1986.

Ramos, Donna G. Utah War: US Government Versus Mormon Saints. *Wild West Magazine*, June 12, 2006.

Terry, Tomas Searles, Diary, 1857 June–1859 Dec. In possession of Church History Library.

Verney, G. L. *The Devil's Wind: The Story of the Naval Brigade at Lucknow.* London, England: Hutchinson, 1956.

ABOUT THE AUTHOR

JEAN HOLBROOK MATHEWS WAS BORN in Ogden, Utah, but spent more than half her adult life in Missouri, where she was elected to the Missouri House of Representatives for ten years and then appointed to the Missouri State Medical Licensing Board for four years, where she was elected as the first non-physician president. During more than twenty years of public service in Missouri, she traveled to Washington, D.C., several times each year, and she became well acquainted with many members of the Senate and House, testified before Senate committees, and became familiar with the inner-workings of the federal government. She presently resides in Mesa, Arizona.